# SNOWBOUND WITH THE SECRET AGENT

**GERI KROTOW**

MILLS & BOON

First Published in Great Britain 2019
by Mills & Boon, an imprint of HarperCollins*Publishers*
1 London Bridge Street, London, SE1 9GF

*Snowbound with the Secret Agent* © 2018 Geri Krotow

ISBN: 978-0-263-27399-1

0119

MIX
Paper from
responsible sources
FSC™ C007454

This book is produced from independently certified FSC™ paper to ensure responsible forest management.

For more information visit: www.harpercollins.co.uk/green

Printed and bound in Spain
by CPI, Barcelona

To Michelle Mioff-Haring.
Thank you for your friendship and
your tireless support of Silver Valley.

# Chapter 1

Something was wrong in Silver Valley, Pennsylvania, but Portia DiNapoli couldn't put her finger on it. It wasn't the weather, which had been hellacious since Christmas. She couldn't remember such a cold, snowy winter since her childhood. And it wasn't the stress of putting together the town's largest charity event, the gala to raise funds for the library she ran and the homeless shelter where she volunteered many hours. If she thought about it deeply enough, the sense of doom had more to do with the story she'd read in the Harrisburg newspaper that proclaimed the area was under siege from Russian Organized Crime. Silver Valley had been named as the center of ROC's efforts to move everything from illicit drugs to weapons. It struck at her heart, because Silver Valley was where she'd lived her entire life.

Although right now, having to dress in several layers to go anywhere in town, it was hard to believe even ROC could run criminal operations from here. Silver Valley had turned into a frozen tundra from the relentless winter.

She'd arrived three hours before opening to work at the Silver Valley Library. She needed the time to work on the gala, which was now less than a month away. And she loved the quiet of the historical building, the way it always felt like a warm hug, even in the January predawn hours. Pennsylvania remained gripped by the tenacious hand of a polar vortex; arctic air had mercilessly swept the state and frozen everything in its wake. More surface area of the Susquehanna River was frozen than ever previously recorded.

It took her a full two minutes to unwrap from her layers of winter protection. She'd opted to walk the few blocks from her small apartment, even in the cold. Portia loved the four seasons and especially winter, but even she was relieved to be inside the warm building and not on the icy streets.

As she settled into her spot behind the main circulation desk, she tried to let the library's familiarity soothe her, but to no avail. What was different this Monday morning from all the others she'd spent in the facility? Her week had started out great with her usual walk to work, she'd had a great cup of coffee at the local shop in the building next to her apartment and there weren't any pesky emails from the central library staff demanding her attention. But she couldn't shake the sense of danger, the feeling that made her skin crawl and her stomach churn.

This had to stop.

Besides reading about ROC, she'd spent too much time learning about the fight Pennsylvania was waging against the heroin epidemic, finding out that Silver Valley had more than its share of opioid ODs and near-ODs. Since one of her closest friends from high school had become a victim of a lethal dose of heroin laced with fentanyl right before Christmas, Portia had questioned everything about her life and the community she held dear.

She resolved to get lost in the more positive aspects of her job and clicked open the gala files. Reviewing the guest list to date led to perusing the silent auction items, which always buoyed her spirits. The generosity of the average Silver Valley citizen touched her pragmatic heart.

"Portia."

Portia jumped in her seat, startled by the sudden appearance of Brindle, her assistant.

Brindle had joined the staff while still pursuing her undergraduate degree at Penn State, Harrisburg and now was on to postgraduate work.

"What are you doing here so early? And, ah, good morning."

Brindle's mouth twisted into an apologetic grimace. "It's not that early."

Portia looked at the clock. She'd been here for two hours already?

"Sorry to startle you, but I had to get out of my sister's house. Her baby was up all night, and I have two exams this week. I've been at the diner since four, and I was hoping you were in early today. I left my car in their lot and walked over." Brindle knew that Portia came in early many days, especially in January, during the weeks before the gala.

"No problem. As you can see, I came in for the quiet, too." Brindle was taking night and weekend classes to achieve a master's degree in library science, and she also knew from firsthand experience how stressful working full-time and pursuing a degree was.

"I'll use one of the study rooms if you prefer." Brindle seemed truly sorry to intrude upon Portia's space.

"No, that's not necessary. I just boiled water for tea, or rather, I did when I came in. It's in the insulated pitcher. Help yourself."

"Thanks."

They settled into their respective workspaces and Portia's mind wandered yet again. She'd been doing a lot of this lately. Drifting when she should be getting something done, like finalizing the list of items to be auctioned off for the gala. Instead she'd scared herself half to death.

Robert hadn't helped. She'd dated the local politician, helped him organize the personal details of his campaign. She was vehemently opposed to most of his platform, so no way would she help him with the actual campaign events. If she dug deep enough, she had to admit that she'd hoped to change him. Make him at least see her point of view on many issues. But it had never happened. When had trying to change someone else ever worked for her? A snort escaped her and she tried to cover it by sipping her tea. Brindle looked up at her and offered a smile.

"Sorry. Thinking out loud." She raised the ceramic mug as if she hadn't spent another sleepless night tossing and turning, wondering where ROC's next victim would show up.

Robert hadn't supported anything that helped drug addicts, including the fund-raiser she'd done for Silver Valley's homeless shelter, where she volunteered at least one evening or day per week. She was glad she'd dumped his sorry butt. Unfortunately she'd also found out he'd been messing around with one of his supporters, a local lawyer. Her logical side demanded that his cheating ways would make the breakup that much easier, but it hadn't. She'd talked it out with her best friend, Annie, and decided to take a break from men for the time being.

Shoving thoughts of her cheating ex aside, Portia skimmed the morning emails, all the while regularly checking the one monitor dedicated to library security. There were five security cameras in the building, one on each floor and one at each entrance. The back entrance was employees-only and in fact only used as an emergency exit. The screen was divided into quadrants and she'd so far been able to help a senior who'd fallen in the back corner of the cookbook section, break up several different teenaged couples who were clearly aroused by the smell of paper and last fall she'd ushered out a raccoon who'd smelled the tray of cider donuts intended for the toddler Halloween story time.

But she'd never seen a person completely dressed in dark clothing from head to toe, fully hooded, trying to pry open the back door of the building with some kind of instrument. In broad daylight. Well, if not complete daylight, dawn, as the sun was climbing over the Appalachian Mountains.

Portia shot out of her chair and made for the back.

"Do me a favor and keep an eye on the back exit's security screen, Brindle. If it looks like anything serious, call 9-1-1 for me."

Brindle's eyes widened and she got up from the worktable and walked over to the monitor. "Will do." Portia would have laughed at her obvious trepidation but she had to get to the back door and tell the person to knock it off. It wouldn't be the first time she'd had to chase interlopers away from the back door. It was an easy place for teens to hang out, next to the 24/7 diner and two buildings down from the pharmacy.

Even so, she couldn't remember ever having to stop someone from trying to pry the door open before. The images of the headlines about ROC flashed through her mind and she forced herself to take a deep breath. Yes, Silver Valley was under fire from an established crime ring, but what were the odds that ROC had any interest in the town library?

Ludmila Markova couldn't shake the feeling of being watched, but it was nothing she wasn't used to. Whether the police or FBI or one of her superiors, someone was always keeping tabs on her.

So be it. Right now she had to make sure she delivered the goods to the library so that the other worker would know where to find their delivery.

She'd gained many points with Ivanov, ROC's local leader, when she'd come up with the communications plan. Because their cellular phone calls were always in threat of being monitored, and the same with email or SMS, they'd needed a way to pass information back and forth. The transportation manifests were complicated, especially the ones involving shipping heroin.

Exact instructions were needed for each delivery; each pickup and every gram of product had to be accounted for.

Let the American law enforcement groups search her group's technological devices. They'd never find what they were looking for. She was the best, trained by the Federal Security Service, or FSB, in Russia. It had earned her a visa to the US under an assumed identity.

She hoisted her backpack up higher, walking quickly to the library's back entrance. At this hour, with the building still closed for another twenty minutes, she'd get in and out with no fanfare. The only problem was the security camera, which she couldn't risk disabling because she wasn't certain if it was tied to the local police or not.

No matter, this was why she wore a ski mask. The camera would never capture her face, not with enough detail for identification. Someone would have to be in her personal space to see her eyes and her mouth, and even that wasn't always enough. Besides, if anyone got that close, she'd eliminate them. She never left a witness alive. It could spell too much trouble down the road.

She had to keep this job with Ivanov, her current boss. For just one more operation. Anything was better than going back to Russia and having to be at her government's bidding again. A one-nighter with an oligarch led to the slick deal that got her here.

She planned to keep herself out of Russia for the rest of her days. Whether she found a quiet life under an assumed identity in the US or Canada didn't matter to her. She wanted freedom from the constant killing, always having to take orders from above without question. Whether she'd be able to give up the life that she was the best at in the world was a valid question she needed to address, but not now. For now, she had to remain the trained assassin that she was, the best that ROC could ever hope to have on its side.

Only one more mission and she'd disappear, go somewhere where no one would find her. Start the free life she'd always dreamed of. Before her own government had killed her family.

The lock on the door would be an easy pick, but she preferred the much quicker muscle method. She pulled a long knife from her backpack and wedged the thin end into the line that separated the steel door from its frame. Using her body weight as leverage, she began to break into the Silver Valley Public Library. In three more minutes, she'd deposit the laptop where the next operative would find it, where she'd told them to look. It would take them all of thirty seconds to download the information onto a USB stick. If library personnel caught them, they could play dumb and claim they'd forgotten to sign the computer out at the front desk.

Her plan was foolproof, as was everything she did. Two more shoves and the door would open. She was three minutes from completing this part of her mission.

Portia's breathing ramped up as she passed row upon row of books, DVDs and then periodicals, making her way to the stairs, where she sped down to the children's level. The exit door was at the base of the stairs and the stairwell reverberated with the sound of metal on metal. The unknown person was still at it, working on the door.

What the hell?

Portia pushed the long bar handle in, shoved the door open and squinted against the bright motion detector light. The sun had begun its rise behind the building, as well; it was a sharp contrast to the stairwell's dim interior.

"Excuse me, can I help you?"

The person straightened, and the first thing Portia noticed was the cold emotion in the glacial blue eyes under the winter facemask. The second thing was that the person—a woman, judging from the figure under her jacket, the makeup on her eyes and lipstick on her very red mouth—was holding one of the library's dozen laptops. Portia knew it was a Silver Valley Library computer from the identification stickers on its cover.

"Hey, our laptops are for in-house use only. Why are you—"

Before she finished, the woman shoved Portia in the chest, knocking her backward. The assaulter whirled around and ran toward the railroad tracks that divided the library property from the rest of downtown Silver Valley.

Portia scrambled to her feet, and against the voice in her brain that screamed for her to wait for the police, she took off after the laptop thief. Silver Valley Library had mysteriously lost ten laptops in the past six months. It ended with her, today. *Now.* Without hesitating, she took off after the assailant. She hadn't lettered in track and field at Silver Valley High for nothing.

Kyle King swore under his breath, the interior of the beat-up truck he was hunkered down in filling with the crystallized vapor. He couldn't run the engine and heater while he was trying to blend in. He had to make it look like the truck was empty, parked behind the Silver Valley Diner. Right next to the town library, where he'd patiently waited for ROC's thug to show up. He hoped to figure out how the hell they were passing information on illegal drug shipments.

As an undercover agent for the Trail Hikers, a secret government shadow agency, second to none and headquartered in Silver Valley, he knew how critical it was to stop ROC's trafficking of illegal cargo, especially heroin and other drugs, into Pennsylvania. Silver Valley was a short fifteen-minute drive from the state capitol, Harrisburg, and the epicenter of transportation logistics for the entire US Eastern Seaboard.

Typical of ROC's blatant disregard for law enforcement, they'd set up their distribution headquarters in the shadow of a nondescript, medium-sized, everyday American town. Of course ROC had no clue about Trail Hikers, but it was public knowledge that Silver Valley and the surrounding county had succeeded in defeating the most heinous criminals over the last few years. Including an ROC human trafficking ring. Which made the fact that ROC still wanted to stake a claim here stick more deeply in his craw. The latest intel from Trail Hikers and FBI indicated that the criminals were somehow using the local library as a way to pass critical information about their local ops.

Kyle had operated on countless global missions for Trail Hikers over the last several years, after a short stint in the Marine Corps. After two tours to Afghanistan, he knew he wanted to continue serving, but in a different capacity. The offer to become a Trail Hiker agent had been too good to pass up.

That was seven years ago. The ROC op had brought him to Silver Valley three months ago to provide much needed support. He'd welcomed the switch and enjoyed being in an American town for longer than the usual few days his other ops had given him.

Fact was, Kyle was tired of the global travel and wanted to find a place to call home in between Trail Hiker ops. He didn't think it would be Silver Valley, though, as he was born and bred in California and missed the West Coast. He'd purchased land in California while he was still a Marine, needing to know he had someplace to go if he ended up out of the Corps and without a job. But anyplace in the United States was a good place after the rough places he'd been. If he hadn't been so tied up in this op against ROC, he might have enjoyed Silver Valley a bit more.

Kyle wanted to be the agent to smash apart Ivanov's reign of terror so badly that he could taste it. The current gang ROC had sent to Silver Valley was responsible for dozens of heroin ODs in this part of the state, and upwards of thousands nationally. After he solved this case, Kyle was due for time off, a full month. He planned to use it to go back west, see if the property he'd been paying taxes on could become home. The director of Trail Hikers wanted him out there for a bit to set up a West Coast office for the agency, so it all dovetailed neatly. Kyle liked things neat.

It'd be sweet if he could crack open this case sooner than later. Pennsylvania winters were colder than he'd imagined. The last weeks since the polar vortex had dipped down had proved brutal. He'd broken down and bought himself foot and hand warmers for the long hours outside, staking out the library, where he'd confirmed the information drop point was. In classic ROC fashion, they used something that seemed so obvious. Most criminal organizations held meetings or passed information in more clandestine spots, places that were difficult to figure out. Not ROC. By somehow passing information in the library, they'd hidden their methods in plain sight. He just hadn't figured out exactly how yet. The computers were the most likely tools but the Trail Hikers systems forensics expert hadn't found anything unusual on the desktops. Kyle had done a lot of his own recon inside the library, too, hoping to determine a pattern of behavior or repeat patrons who might be up to no good. He'd used different disguises to avoid any kind of recognition. Not just from Markova or her worker bees, but from the library staff.

The librarian in particular. A woman he'd found himself fascinated with. Portia DiNapoli.

But the librarian he'd also happened to monitor the last several weeks wasn't going to make his goal of catching Markova in the act possible. Not today, anyway. As an undercover TH agent, he had to avoid any contact with civilians as much as possible while trailing a target. And Markova was a big one. As he watched, he saw that the librarian was engaging Markova. Portia DiNapoli didn't know Markova was an ROC operative, though.

"Damn it, Portia DiNapoli. Why are you so good at your job?" And why was the town librarian so damn hot? More importantly, why was his dick paying attention at all when he was supposed to be tracking the movements of potential ROC thugs in the library, not Portia's attractiveness?

*You're lonely.*

Damn it, he wasn't lonely. Okay, he'd appreciate the loving of a good woman right about now, but he was too entrenched in his work to add another concern to it.

Portia DiNapoli was the epitome of distraction. The fact that he was spending mental energy on her when dating her, or anyone else, wasn't in his best interest or the woman's, raised his internal alarm. He needed to get it through his thick skull that he had a job to do that a woman, Portia or whomever, would only complicate. He'd had his share of committed relationships over the years but none had stuck. It always came down to him having to put his career first, and there was the added danger of anyone he was involved with becoming a target of the bad people it was his job to take down. Portia DiNapoli's nearly constant presence in his current surveillance had stirred something in him, though. He probably ought to at least think about dating someone again.

The thing was, he hadn't been tempted by any of the women he'd had the opportunity to flirt with, dance with, talk to at the local bar scene in Harrisburg. And he'd been out so rarely, the case taking up all of his time.

His casual interest, and that was all it was, a fleeting second glance, in Portia, was complicated. It wasn't because she was beautiful, and she was. Big brown eyes with long lashes, a full mouth with lips he'd fantasized doing a lot more than smile at her patrons. She wasn't short, but at least a head shorter than him. The perfect size to pull her in close and lay a kiss on her rosy lips. She always wore rose lipstick, or maybe that was her natural color. Her eyes dazzled behind oversize glasses and her curvy figure was stunning in her sexily delicious pastel cardigans. Portia seemed to have a collection of those, from what he'd noticed. She was all woman, all sexy curves. It might be a record-breaking cold winter, but the sight of Portia each time he'd gone to the library had warmed him up quicker than any wood stove. Today she wore leggings under a body-conscious, curve-hugging dress. The binoculars in his hands were the best technology on the market, but he didn't need them to know the shape of her sweet ass under her clothes. Not that he'd meant to notice it. But when she'd bent over to shelve books the other day, well, he'd happened to catch a glimpse of her sexy rear.

*Let it go, man.*

She probably had a zillion dudes lining up to take her out. He didn't know, because his physical observation of her began and ended with the library. After he'd found out her apartment was in the one next to his, he'd taken extra care to avoid running into her, using his back entrance almost exclusively. She favored the front, and liked to get a cup of coffee at the shop his apartment was perched over. He knew she wasn't married. And not just from the confidential dossier he'd run on her at Trail Hikers. From her bare left hand to the hours she kept, coming in before the library opened and staying well past closing, Portia DiNapoli was a dedicated career woman. With no commitments outside the Silver Valley Library, except the local homeless shelter. He'd felt no guilt investigating her. He'd had to; when the center of an ROC op was taking place in her library, he'd had to rule her out as a suspect.

Not that his background check on her or anyone was ever considered conclusive. The best bad guys, and girls, were good. Really good. They wouldn't leave any clues that they were doing anything more than visiting a library.

Portia's stance shifted and he recognized the defensive posture—he'd seen her use it last week with a patron who was angry about overdue fines.

But now she wasn't confronting a disgruntled library patron, but an ROC operative, a fully trained, lethal agent. His gut tightened and a distinct discomfort filled his chest. The thought of Portia being hurt by ROC was unthinkable.

Now it looked like the dialogue between Portia and Markova was getting heated. At least, Portia's face was turning red and he'd bet it wasn't from the frigid January temperatures.

"Fuuuudge," he said to himself in the truck, where he'd had his binoculars trained on the library's back entrance since he'd followed Markova here two hours ago. She'd driven from the drab mobile home she kept on the outskirts of town, parked her car behind a restaurant two buildings down and then walked the rest of the way to the library. Kyle figured he was lucky she'd never even looked toward the banged up truck he huddled down in. She never seemed to care about her surroundings but Kyle knew it was all part of her training, to appear as if she were any other civilian— not a trained assassin who didn't miss details others never noticed.

It was freaking freezing and he couldn't risk alerting her to his presence by turning on his engine. Parked behind the 24/7 diner, his vehicle looked like many of the other patrons' wheels: nondescript and dirty from the overdose of salt on the icy roads.

He'd determined that ROC was using the library

somehow to pass information but he didn't know how. And he couldn't directly ask Ludmila Markova, the woman whose file he'd committed to photographic memory months ago. She had to be caught committing a crime before he could tip off SVPD to arrest her.

As he watched, Markova hadn't been successful in getting the back door open, which he found surprising, as well as amusing. The thugs Ivanov employed were top notch and knew their way around locks of all kinds. And they usually were smarter than to attempt to sneak into a public building in broad daylight. But nothing was usual for ROC. They did whatever had to be done to accomplish their jobs, whether that was moving kidnapped underage immigrant women into sex slavery and trafficking illegal drugs, or laundering money made from all of the above.

He watched Portia DiNapoli speak to Markova and a cold sense of dread blanketed him. Emotions weren't allowed during his missions, but he never ignored his intuition. This could go south so very quickly, so very badly. Markova had at least the long knife she'd used to try to pry the door open, and she was adept at using it according to the profile he had on her. Besides her current work for ROC, a number of assassinations were included at the top of the long list of grim accomplishments in her FSB history.

By comparison, Portia DiNapoli's record was as squeaky clean as they came, and reflected an average American who did her job well and contributed to the community with her entire heart. People like Portia were why the Trail Hikers' work was so important. She was not someone who deserved to bleed out in the library parking lot because she'd been in the wrong place at the wrong time with a trained ROC killer.

Kyle eased himself out of the truck's passenger side, using a car parked next to his to shield his movements. His breath steamed in the frozen air and he kept his movements slow and steady. If luck was on his side, Markova would turn and leave without harming Portia.

Kyle never relied on luck. He listened to their conversation, which was taking place no more than ten yards away.

"Excuse me, can I help you?" Portia's voice, normally gravelly and sexy, sounded angry as she shouted at Markova. Making like he was walking toward the diner's back entrance, he hoped to be able to shout and startle the criminal, forcing her to leave the library parking lot.

But the word *laptop* got his radar up.

"Hey, our laptops are for in-house use only. Why are you—" From Portia's tone, there'd be no working it out. He heard it and so did Markova, apparently, who turned and fled. But not before she shoved Portia, who disappeared into the open exit.

Okay, that made it easier, at least. Portia would be safe.

Except that she'd decided the library laptop wasn't going to disappear on her. To his surprise and consternation, Portia was back on her feet and out the door in a blink. He watched her long legs stretch out, her arms pumping, and did what any reputable, competent undercover agent would not do. Kyle ran after Portia.

Portia followed the woman up and onto the railroad tracks, her feet screaming that her simple leather oxfords were no replacement for sneakers or snow boots in the frigid temperatures. Snow crunched under foot and her lungs burned with no scarf to help warm the air.

What was so important on the laptop that the woman would rather risk being criminally charged for taking it than just simply turning it back in and then checking it out again the next day? And why was she running from Portia? Why had she shoved her?

Portia's mind raced with the possibilities, but right now she needed to get the woman, get the library's computer. She was gaining on the woman and gave it ten more strides. As she drew close enough to touch her, she reached for her hoodie and tugged. The woman turned and faced her, still holding the laptop in her arm. Shooting Portia an evil grin that was revealed by the curve of bright red lips in the mouth opening of the knitted mask, she brandished a knife with menacing intent, and the winter sun flashed off the blade.

Portia drew up short, barely stopping herself from falling on the woman—and her knife. She felt the wooden train ties under her thin-soled shoes, her legs trembling, no, *quaking.* But not from the cold. From the shock, the sheer terror of facing down her own mortality. Before Portia could pull back, run from the knife, she saw the woman's eyes glint, narrow, focused on something behind Portia. Her lips curled upward again, as if the laptop thief liked what she saw. Without further threats, the woman jumped off the tracks and ran into the woods on the other side of town. Too late, Portia realized the pounding of her feet on the railroad track wasn't what made the frozen wood ties shake. It was a train. The sound of its whistle blowing was the last thing she remembered before being hit sideways by an overpowering force.

# *Chapter 2*

Kyle chased after Portia as he watched the train bear down on the pair in his peripheral vision. He'd seen it pass through the commercial district several times. A lot of times it slowed to a crawl, and then a complete stop as the tracks were switched to allow the container shipments to go to the other part of town that housed many national distribution centers. But this train didn't slow down, the conductor showing no sign of seeing the women on the tracks as it kept going, way too fast for a local. Kyle figured he had thirty seconds, tops, to prevent Portia from catching up to Markova, or worse, before the train hit them both. Because if Portia caught Markova, the knife blade plunging into her body was the last thing she'd feel.

Kyle couldn't believe that neither Portia nor Markova had noticed the train as he ran toward them. Portia continued her pursuit of the woman she thought was a mere thief, clearly ignorant of how lethal an encounter with her would be. ROC didn't put up with interference of any kind and made it a trademark to never leave a witness alive. No matter how trivial the crime, it left no one living to tell their tales. It was what made them so powerful, enabling their insidious network of crime to reach into the most seemingly solid communities.

He ran in a perpendicular line to the tracks, knowing he risked Markova seeing him, wondering if he was law enforcement, but he didn't care. He had to save Portia. The op would still be there—as far as Markova knew, he was either a Good Samaritan or a friend of Portia's who'd witnessed their altercation. Or even an undercover cop. Let ROC come after him. He'd be damned if they would add an innocent Silver Valley librarian to their tally of victims.

By the time he was within a few feet of the tracks, the women faced one another, the knife in Markova's hands poised to do maximum harm. He ran toward them and opened his mouth to shout a warning, anything to distract the knife-wielding criminal. But it was futile against the roar of the train engine, the wheels of the old cargo car squealing in protest as the engineer applied the brakes. Too late, though, to save either woman if they didn't get off the tracks.

He'd practiced so many dangerous scenarios in both his Marine Corps and Trail Hiker training, and experienced countless more in his work as a Marine Scout and then as an undercover operative for the past seven years. There were no surprises as he measured the situation, decided on his course of action and followed through just in the nick of time. Markova jumped the tracks a second ahead of him. As he hit Portia sideways, tackling her off the tracks and holding her as they rolled down the embankment, the roar of the train drowning out all other noise, he had only one surprise.

He hadn't screamed "look out" or "stop" or even "train." The word, the name that had scraped past his throat, dry from the cold air, had been the name of someone he'd never met, not in the conventional way.

*Portia.*

Portia was aware of a very heavy weight on top of her, her face smooshed against a thick winter coat of some type, the scents of tar, train exhaust, and something else mingling and filling each breath she gasped for. The click of the train-car wheels across the track oddly comforted her, a definite sign that she hadn't been flattened by the engine but in fact had been knocked off the tracks.

"You with me?" A low, rumbling voice filled her ears as much as she felt it through her very center. Her shuddering, shock-affected center.

"Y-y-yes." The chatter couldn't be helped, no matter how hard she clenched her jaw. But it wasn't hypothermic shivers that ran through her; it was so much more.

The weight shifted and she realized someone lay atop her, a very large, lean person, on the ground next to the railroad embankment. An involuntary moan left her lips. Did the man hear it? Did he think she never wanted him to leave her?

"I thought you were a goner back there." He gently rolled them both to their sides, still holding her protectively. Bright eyes filled her vision, a gloved hand cupped her chin.

"Who?" She couldn't manage more than the one syllable; the question *who are you?* really didn't matter, as she was still here, alive, intact. And yet it mattered a whole hell of a lot. Who was this savior?

"Here." Strong arms on either side of her, the weight gone, the sense of being lifted higher, higher, but in reality the man had only shifted her into a seated position on the ground, sitting next to her, his arm still wrapped around her shoulders. "Give yourself a few breaths before you try to stand up. Assess if you're hurting anywhere."

She listened to his voice, acknowledged she could listen to it all day, any day, and never grow bored of it.

"Are you in any pain?" He reiterated his concern as the last few cars passed, revealing a row of Silver Valley PD police cars on the other side of the tracks, back in the parking lot that stretched behind the library, diner and several other Silver Valley businesses.

"No. I'm…I'm okay." She wiggled her toes, her fingers, and mentally moved up her anatomy. Her butt and shoulders were sore on the left side—the large man had somehow cushioned the rest of her from the impact upon stony ground, but since he'd saved her life, she was inclined to agree with him.

"Who are you?" At least her voice sounded stronger. She'd never met him, she was certain, but there was something familiar about him, as if they did know one another. Suspicion stole into her sense of security. Did he know the laptop thief—was he part of some kind of criminal network?

Gray eyes narrowed, thin lines fanning out from their corners. "I'm someone you can trust."

She wiped a shaky hand over her mouth. "That's something after almost being—" She cut off abruptly.

Shudders started to wrack her body and tears spilled onto her cheeks. She'd been that close to dying. To losing it all, forever.

In one moment the importance of her worries and hopes to raise money for the library, to expand its services, her homeless shelter efforts—they all evaporated into what she'd almost become. Oblivion. She looked around her and vowed to never take another day for granted, no matter how cold or how aggravated she was by a laptop thief. It could all be gone as quick as she could say "choo choo."

"Come on." He lifted her to her feet and hugged her to his side. Only when he motioned with his free arm did she notice the pair of police officers who'd walked up to them, followed by EMTs.

"This woman is on the verge of shock." Her rescuer's voice held a note of steel she hadn't noticed as he'd made sure she'd survived their tumble. She turned to thank him but he was gone. Her brain felt like she was thinking in a fog and Portia didn't argue as the EMTs each took an arm and carefully walked her back to the parking area. She wanted to squeeze her eyes shut when they had to briefly traverse the tracks again, but at least it wasn't more than a few paces.

As she received first aid for a couple of cuts and bruises and then was taken to the ER against her desires, as a safeguard, her equilibrium returned. Portia had a lot to do when she got back to the library, but what she wanted to know more than anything was who the man was who'd saved her. And why she could still feel the imprint of his hands, his arms around her as they fell through the air and hit the hard ground, hours later. The matter of the person who'd led her so close to death didn't elude her. Portia wanted to know who she was and wanted the woman to face full criminal charges for all she'd done. But the overarching curiosity that kept her from drowning in the shock and despair of almost dying wasn't over the laptop thief. It was all about her rescuer, the man whose arms made her feel like no one could ever hurt her again.

And his eyes—the color of the Susquehanna in January. But unlike the cold slate of the river that ran through central Pennsylvania, where Silver Valley was nestled, the man's eyes had a warmth in them. And a sadness.

It must have been the shock, as he described it, that made a myriad of emotions assault her as she mentally replayed what had just happened. Because what else explained the instant, white-hot zap of attraction she'd felt for the man, her train-wreck savior?

And who *was* he?

Ludmila Markova wasn't happy. She'd have to circle back, in disguise this time, and drop the laptop off through the front door of the library, to leave it on the circulation desk. The book slot was too small for the computer, no doubt for added security. She'd have to act like a dopey kid who'd accidentally taken the laptop from the library property by accident.

Then she'd kill the librarian. Portia DiNapoli. She'd kept one eye on the bitch each time she'd entered the library, mostly just as herself, since this ignorant American town seemed to have a lot of library patrons. It made it easy for her to blend in.

She swore as she made herself down an entire quart of kefir. The protein was necessary to keep up her strength, and she missed the tang of her mother's home-made drink.

The thought of her mother, gunned down next to her brothers and sisters and Papa, brought tears to her eyes. She viciously swiped at them. No more. After this mission, she'd be free and have the funds to go wherever she wanted. Not back to Russia—never.

Using the tactics ingrained into her by the former KGB official who trained her, she shoved her worthless emotions aside and focused on what the rest of the day would look like. First a stop to the library. Then find the librarian and eliminate the worry of her testimony, no matter how unlikely.

"What do you mean you were almost hit by a train? I thought you were working the ROC distribution network case?"

Silver Valley PD detective Josh Avery looked at Kyle as if his colleague was a new recruit. Kyle's liaison with SVPD was a necessary part of working an op targeting criminal activity in Silver Valley. ROC was a menace to Silver Valley and instead of eradicating the crime ring's reach with the takedown of a human trafficking ring, they'd found themselves looking down the barrel of ROC setting up Silver Valley to be its epicenter of heroin distribution in central Pennsylvania, Maryland and parts of New Jersey. Several of the SVPD detectives and officers were cut into Trail Hiker ops on a need-to-know basis, and often a Trail Hiker agent was paired with a single point of contact at SVPD to minimize leaks and maximize both law enforcement agencies' ability to solve cases. Kyle came into SVPD to debrief Josh, after he was sure Portia was okay and being taken care of by the EMTs. Again, his focus was too heavy on the Portia side for his agent liking.

"I was. I am." Kyle weighed what to say next, even though Josh was his SVPD liaison for this particular Trail Hiker case. But they were working as a team. "I was conducting surveillance, the same kind you do every day, on the library's back entrance. Another agent had the front door covered. When trouble showed up in the way of an intruder—Markova—trying to pry open the locked exit-only door, I paid attention. I never expected the librarian to take off after the assailant, though."

"It's not like we can warn civilians about top-secret ROC details, not if we want to keep our covert ops secret." Josh's face revealed his concern.

"That's the double-edged sword of this work, isn't it? Providing safety for all by tracking the bad guys we can't talk about." Kyle leaned back in the chair across from Josh's desk, in the detective's office. "Who knew a librarian could run that fast?"

"I haven't seen the official report come across yet. Are you sure it was the head librarian, Portia? Or one of her assistants?"

"It was Portia. And we're lucky Markova didn't knife her on the spot at the library." No sense pretending he didn't know who Portia was. "You know Portia?"

"She's my fiancée's best friend." Josh grinned. "Don't get sucked into any librarian stereotypes. Portia doesn't take crap from anyone."

Two strikes against his attempts at staying unseen today. He avoided public venues with any law enforcement agencies, or LEAs, as much as possible while doing his initial surveillance of Markova and ROC. But both Portia and Markova had seen him on the railroad tracks. Portia might believe he was a simple Good Samaritan, as could Markova. But a former FSB agent operated on the belief that there were no coincidences. Chances were that Markova suspected she'd been marked. His days in his undercover guise as a homeless man were numbered now, because Markova was as good as an enemy agent got. She'd put him with his disguise with little trouble. "Hell. Can't one go anywhere in this town without running into another connection."

"It's not that bad. We're bigger than you think, not just because we're over twenty thousand last count. And you could run into the same people in a city of millions, especially in our profession. It happens."

"But it's not supposed to. Not if I'm doing my job right." Kyle's mission was to stay under the radar of a casual observer. He knew that Portia probably hadn't noticed him in the library. He wore various disguises whenever he went there, to keep himself free to be himself during off-hours. He should have worn a disguise this morning, too, but with daylight surveillance, he wasn't as worried—it was easier to pass off someone as inconsequential, normal, during busier working hours.

Josh nodded. He got it—he was an SVPD detective, yes, but also a Trail Hiker Agent as needed, per case. Right now they were using all agencies and means available to eradicate the crime through which ROC had infiltrated Silver Valley.

Kyle happened to have drawn the case of the stolen freight shipments, which amounted to millions of dollars of lost high-end technology goods in the past six months. Televisions, luxury audio systems and scores of top-of-the-line computer systems had been stolen. It'd blossomed into more when he discovered that heroin shipments were part of the ROC clandestine network, too. "I've narrowed down the place where they exchange possible hits and heroin drops to the library. I just haven't spotted them doing it yet."

"You still think it's with the library's computer internal system?"

"I did. But now, I'm not so sure. I've sat surveillance on Markova and the library for almost three weeks with no new leads." The lack of movement on the case had given him too much time to think about Portia.

He wondered if she'd needed stitches, if she was released from the ER yet.

*Not your problem.*

Josh shook his head. "This is the hardest part. Waiting out the losers to make a wrong move so that we can put all of us out of our misery."

"Yeah." Kyle didn't know Josh that well but knew that he'd recently been involved in a big sting against ROC. "How long did you wait before you saved all those Ukrainian women?" He referred to the human trafficking ROC had conducted in Silver Valley last year. Josh had also been instrumental in helping the wife of a notorious ROC operative get out of a domestic violence situation. He'd told Kyle about it in one of their many liaisons like today's.

"It felt like forever but it came together quickly, once things started falling in place. You know the drill—hurry up and wait. And then be ready to go full throttle."

"Hmph." Kyle tried to review the work he'd done

the past weeks, most of it surveillance, but he couldn't stop the image of Portia's big brown eyes watching him earlier. If he weren't committed to remaining single, putting his career first, always, she'd be...no. He couldn't go there. If he did decide to date someone, as he'd been considering, it couldn't be Portia. Portia was too dangerous, because he barely knew her and couldn't shake her.

"You're still thinking about Portia, aren't you?" Josh's grin rankled Kyle but not as much as his uncanny ability to read him. Few could.

"Why do you ask?"

"I think it's the same expression I had on my face, oh, about six months ago. When I realized Annie was more than a childhood friend."

"Doubtful. I don't know anything about Portia Di-Napoli except that she's the town librarian, and also volunteers a lot of time at the Silver Valley homeless shelter. I can only hope she doesn't recognize me the next time I'm there. She's making my job more difficult."

Josh slapped him on the back. "You are so full of crap. You had to have done a quick background check on Portia as part of this case," Josh called him out without hesitation.

Kyle felt his face redden. "Of course I did. But what I mean is that I don't know her personally, at all."

Josh laughed. "You'll figure it out. It's nothing a pro like you can't handle, Kyle."

"Easy for you to say. You don't have to pass as a homeless person a few times a week." Contrary to his words, though, he'd learned more from his undercover work at the shelter than what the case demanded. He'd realized that Portia was a very compassionate, dedicated woman. The kind of woman a man didn't play with romantically.

*You're undercover at the shelter for the case, not Portia.*

"When are you going back in?" Josh referred to the Silver Valley homeless shelter.

"Tonight. I'll look nothing like this, of course." He motioned to his jeans and flannel shirt. "The other night, I found out that there are three new dealers in town. I need their names. Then I can track down their supplier more quickly with triangulation." And hopefully directly link it to ROC, but he wasn't holding his breath. ROC was notorious for its ability to evade law enforcement. But ROC wasn't used to the state-of-the-art technology and techniques employed by the Trail Hikers. ROC thought they were up against SVPD and the FBI, tough enough adversaries. "I've also got to get into the library to do a thorough search for evidence."

"I've seen your getup. You're right—you don't look anything like the homeless person you use for your cover." Josh paused. "You'll need a search warrant for the library, though."

"Unless we can convince the local librarian to let me in for a look-see." Kyle drummed his fingers on the table, alongside his coffee mug.

"Kyle, you can tell me to mind my own business, but what did you do before TH?" He'd lowered his voice, as the secrecy of the agency meant that the majority of SVPD officers and employees had no idea of its existence. They all thought Kyle was a visiting detective from out of state.

"I was a Marine." He wasn't going to spell it out—Josh wasn't stupid.

Josh's eyes narrowed. "I *knew* it. The US Marine Corps—it explains how cool you are, no matter what."

"And my lack of patience while conducting civilian stakeouts."

"Forget about that. What do you think they're passing in the library?"

"I don't know but from all indications, ROC sends thugs from New York into the library to drop intel for a local operative. Then they split. The local person in charge comes in, gets the information, then passes the information to their local network. It's what TH has put together after collecting information from all available agencies and sources."

"You think there's a tip-off going down soon, for certain?"

"I do. It makes sense, as it's been ten days since the last rash of trailer thefts." Two truckloads of computer equipment and one of wide-screen, high-technology televisions.

"I'm glad they're not doing anything more than knocking out the truck drivers," Josh said, expressing what worried Kyle. It was only a matter of time before ROC left behind their use of chloroform and used weapons that would leave more permanent wounds. Or worse. Escalation was part of ROC's methods. The minute one trucker didn't go down easily with a chloroform-soaked rag, they'd up the ante to let the other truckers in the region know they'd better give up their goods without a fight. His mind flashed back to the image of Portia facing down Markova, and the former FSB agent's knife. He hadn't ever felt that frightened for someone he didn't know. Hell, when was he going to admit to himself that Portia had gotten under his skin?

"You and I both know that they're used to making smaller PD's roll over and get out of their way. They're not afraid to hit at officers as needed. They don't like the press attention, but when it comes down to it, they don't really care. To them, money and power is what matters."

"Not on my watch," Josh said, expressing how Kyle felt.

"I have to admit, Josh, I never know what I'm going to find when I walk into a new PD. Silver Valley PD is solid," Kyle said without thinking and realized he was speaking from his heart. He took a long, hot gulp of coffee. For over a decade, he'd either been a Marine or Trail Hiker, protected the highest officials of government, conducted clandestine ops and never thought much about his dang heart. But since this morning, and coming head-to-head with Portia, he'd—

"Officer Avery? Portia DiNapoli is here to give a statement and she wants to talk to you." The receptionist stood at Josh's desk. "Should I bring her back here or tell her to wait?"

Josh looked at Kyle. "You okay with her seeing you here?"

Kyle wanted to see Portia, know she was okay. It was an unreasonable level of concern for someone he wasn't personally acquainted with. Best stop it before it began.

*You're already done for.*

"Naw, I'll take off before you talk to her."

"Can you have her wait a few, and I'll come get her?" Josh said to the receptionist.

"Sure thing."

After she was out of earshot, Josh looked at Kyle. "I know you're undercover for TH, but Portia doesn't have to know that. She could think you're a contractor or other LEA, working with SVPD on the ROC case, in general. It's no secret that we've got ROC problems in Silver Valley."

"I know. It's the details that are classified, not the big picture." Kyle's gut clenched. It'd be too easy to let Portia know what he did, that he was someone she could trust, as he'd told her. "But unless she absolutely has to know—"

"I hear you. And I'd do the same." Josh confirmed the conservative approach all undercover agents employed. It was always better to stick to the tightest parameters of operational security possible. Then you could loosen up as needed. But once the cat was out of the bag, i.e., a civilian such as Portia DiNapoli found out you were doing something classified or law enforcement related, you couldn't put it back.

Kyle stood. "I'll check in after my stint at the shelter tonight. Tomorrow morning work for you, unless something important happens?"

"Sure thing. By the way, Kyle? You're doing it again."

"What?"

Josh didn't say anything for a moment while he grinned at him. Kyle braced himself for what he knew was coming, and it wasn't unwarranted.

"One word, Kyle. One woman. P-o-r-t-i-a."

*Fuuuuuudge.*

\* \* \*

It took most of the morning for Portia to be cleared by the medical staff at Silver Valley Hospital, so she wasn't sure if Josh would be in when she showed up to file a report at SVPD at lunchtime. Annie was engaged to Josh and Portia knew that they enjoyed lunches together during the workweek. She suspected the "lunches" were sexy liaisons, but never pressed her friend on it. Not too much, anyway.

Holding her driver's license up to the security camera, she pushed the button outside the station entrance. She'd had tours of the police department with the library's murder mystery book club and remembered the protocol for civilians.

"Come on in, Ms. DiNapoli." The receptionist's quick acknowledgment didn't surprise her. Portia had been instructed to go straight to the station after she left the hospital, to file her report.

"Hi. Thanks for letting me in so quickly—it's still pretty cold out there." She began to unbutton her coat in the warm entryway. The receptionist nodded.

"You're here to see Detective Avery?"

"Yes."

"Do you know where his office is?" Portia noticed that the entryway had a lot of people coming and going.

"I do."

"Great. Just pass your bag through the scanner and step through the metal detector."

Portia turned to the security guard who led her through the procedure, clearing her to enter the main building.

Portia walked back to Josh's desk once the receptionist cleared her. She didn't have a lot of business at

SVPD, except to ask Josh, a high school classmate, if he'd read to the elementary school students when she'd been working at Silver Valley Elementary. And even then, she called or emailed him, didn't pay the police department a visit. The bustle and sense of many different officers and detectives in constant motion hit her. It matched what she'd read: Silver Valley was in the midst of a crime wave unlike any ever seen before.

A tall man at the end of one of the long corridors made her stomach flip in ridiculous anticipation. Walking away from her, toward the back exit, he could have been anyone. But her body sensed it was the man from the tracks. He was tall, with an angular build that only hinted at his sheer strength—the kind of power that enabled him to knock her out from an oncoming train. Short, military-style hair, a sandy blond. Her gaze travelled down his length. He carried a parka in one arm, the same color as the man who'd saved her wore. Without the extra goose down padding his frame seemed all the more impressive. His butt was all muscle in worn jeans, and his stride in his boots bespoke of stealth. It might not be him, but then he threw her a quick look over his shoulder. His eyes—silver like a wolf she'd seen once, visiting a wildlife preserve. He gave her a curt nod. As if he knew she'd been there all along. Her stomach leaped and she increased her pace, but he disappeared around the corner before she reached him. Clearly, he didn't want to talk to her. She paused right before she got to Josh's office. She'd been through a lot today, and she might be seeing things, seeing *someone* wherever she looked. What were the odds it was the same man who'd saved her from the tracks? The man who'd held her, made her feel safer than she had in a long, long time?

"Hey, Portia. Come on in." Josh Avery's smile was as genuine as his quick, warm hug. He kept a hand on her upper arm after he pulled back and peered into her eyes. "You okay? Really?"

Realization struck her yet again that the morning's events hadn't been a dream, or an almost-nightmare. She'd indeed missed being flattened by a locomotive, with no more than a second or two to spare.

"I'm good." She raked a shaky hand through her curls, not caring what she looked like. "I have some bruises that are going to be pretty ugly, but the man that knocked me off the tracks also protected me from the brunt of the fall, and the hard ground."

Josh motioned for her to sit in one of the seats in front of his desk and sank into his chair. "Did our receptionist get you any coffee or something else to drink?"

Portia waved her hand in dismissal. "No, I'm okay, really. I'm so wired from the adrenaline rush that I'm sure any more caffeine would launch me to the moon."

"Okay." Josh tapped on his keyboard and she watched as his eyes tracked the information on the screen.

"Thanks for making time to take my statement. I know the other police officers are just as able to, but I'd feel better talking to you." And she wouldn't have to explain her hunches—Josh had known her since they were kids and had never patronized her.

"Are you kidding? Annie would have my hide if I didn't take care of this. Besides, it's part of an ongoing investigation I'm working on."

"Really? You mean figuring out who's stealing our library laptops, or something bigger?"

"We'll never figure out who took all of your laptops, Portia. I'm afraid we don't have enough man-hours. But if you can find evidence on your security footage, you know to bring it in."

And she did, but their tapes had been wiped. "Um, speaking of that." Heat rode up her neck, over her face. "The recordings were erased. My staff and I tried to replay the last several weeks' worth, only to discover there was nothing there."

Josh's brows slammed together. "What do you mean 'nothing there'?"

"There's a file on the drive that only I have access to, and I open it up for the staff to watch regularly. We fast-forward through it, pause when we see something suspicious. So far we haven't had any luck figuring out who lifted three computers back in October, and the more recent thefts are even more confusing, as we locked our laptops up overnight. In the mornings, they were gone."

"Yes, I read the reports." Josh kept typing on his computer, taking notes. "Did you say you were able to retrieve the security footage back in the fall?"

Portia nodded. "Yes. But these last two weeks, even after double-checking the camera equipment, doing a trial run on the system, we still lost it all. There's no footage of the library for almost three weeks."

"And yet the video feed is still good? From the cameras to the monitor?"

She nodded. "Yes. Our security specialist monitors the feed all day long. And we have it set for Record, always. Something goes wrong during the archival loop."

Josh frowned. "If anyone understands the information technology around this, you do, Portia. I'm damned sorry this is happening at the local library. Have you noticed anything else unusual?"

She shook her head. "No. Except this morning, when I saw the woman trying to break into the back employee entrance. I should have called SVPD instead of taking her on myself." She inwardly cringed at her transgression. If she'd told Brindle to immediately call 9-1-1, the woman might be in custody.

*And you'd never have met the dream man.*

She squirmed in her seat. She'd met no one, knew no one.

"Can you give the sketch artist a good sense of the woman—you're sure it was a woman— who took off for the tracks?"

"Only her eyes—they were blue. And her mouth had bright red lipstick."

Josh paused in his note-taking. "I see why you think it's a woman."

"I can't be positive, Josh, but I've seen that woman before. And the fact that she had one of our laptops means she's been in the library at least once before."

Josh paused, as if weighing something crucial. "Look, I don't want to alarm you, but we're working against some bad apples right now."

"You mean ROC? Russian Organized Crime?"

Josh's stern expression broke into a chuckle. "You've been reading the local paper."

"Of course. As well as the police blotter reports on social media. But laptop theft hardly matches the kind of crime ROC participates in, doesn't it? I mean, they'd steal a shipment of computers, I'd imagine. There isn't enough money in a paltry laptop from a local library."

"I'm not going to discuss details of any case other than yours, Portia. What I'm trying to explain is that there are some very unsavory types running about. It's inevitable with the heroin trade and opioid epidemic. And that makes people unpredictable. Paranoid. If the woman you ran after has any suspicion that you might be able to identify her, that might put you at risk. I'm suggesting you be very careful. Don't travel alone anywhere at night."

"You mean the usual way a single woman lives, Josh?" She couldn't help but tease him. "I'm not getting a buddy to walk around Silver Valley—that's ridiculous. But I will be more aware of my surroundings, I promise."

"And you'll call in anything out of the ordinary, no more facing down a criminal on your own?"

"Guilty as charged. For the record, I told my staff to call 9-1-1 if they saw the situation go bad."

"Which they did." Josh's eyes narrowed. "We weren't able to get anything from the security footage, though. The woman knew what she was doing, with a hood and ski mask. I'm not doubting what you say you saw, Portia. But you were under duress, to say the least." Josh paused. "I know you saw a woman, but I can't tell you why I know. Not yet. It's part of the process of taking your report to question what you remember."

Portia nodded. "I get it." She rubbed her upper arms as if to ward off a chill in the well-heated office. "After she shoved me, and I took off after her, yes, but I was calm when we spoke outside the library, at the back exit. I saw red when I saw her on the security camera, trying to open it with a tool of some sort. Now I realize she seemed familiar to me, but of course she had that mask on, so I guess I could be wrong. I'm frustrated that I couldn't get the actual serial number of the laptop. We're missing more than one and it would be helpful to know which one the woman had. Each laptop has different storage capacities and software applications. If we knew which it was, it might help to know why she was trying to sneak into the back with it." The numbers were on the inside of the cases, along with library-specific bar codes. She leaned forward. "You know me, Josh. You've watched me grow up, for Pete's sake. If you're doubting my powers of observation, ask Annie." She had him and didn't feel the least bit bad about it. Portia had been the one to encourage Annie to reconnect with Josh on more than professional matters last summer.

"I'm not faulting your judgment, Portia. I'm questioning what you've just been through, how it may have altered your recollection."

"It hasn't, or else I'd still be in the ER, and you'd be questioning me there."

"True." Josh paused from typing in her account and leveled a look at her. "You're sure you're okay?"

Portia nodded. "Absolutely. The person, the man who…who saved my life, he bore the brunt of the fall." The memory of being in his arms wrapped around her, and it wasn't frightening. The woman who'd have happily left her to be hit by the train, that was scary. But the stranger…he was more.

"By the way, Josh, I was hoping you'd be able to help me out. The man who saved me—he wouldn't give me his name. At the very least, I owe him an apology. Do you know who it was?" She was counting on SVPD's stellar reputation that they'd questioned everyone at the scene, and the man had been the one to hand her over to the EMTs, who arrived after SVPD. But her memory of that was foggy—Josh was right, she'd had a shakeup.

"Aww, Portia, it sounds like a Good Samaritan." Josh's gaze slid from hers, and if the day hadn't already been confrontational enough, she'd call her old school buddy on it. But not now.

It didn't matter. If the man wanted her to know his name, he had plenty of opportunity to tell her. And she wasn't as obtuse as Josh might believe—Annie had told her that there were always cases and law enforcement operations that Josh couldn't talk about. Maybe the man was part of that.

Or maybe she just had a special place in her heart for a hot man, around her age, who had saved her life.

# Chapter 3

Portia ignored the ER doctor's suggestion to take it easy for the rest of the day and went back to the library for the rest of the afternoon, after she left SVPD. Sure, the almost-being-killed scene on the railroad tracks had shaken her up for a bit, but there was work to be done at the library, and she had to pull her shift at the homeless shelter tonight. With the record-breaking low temperatures, the fifty-bed facility had been overflowing for two weeks solid. As exhausted as she imagined she was going to feel by later this evening, she knew she had a warm bed to go back to, a roof over her head from any snow flurries. The homeless of Silver Valley and surrounding Harrisburg area had few choices. Silver Valley Homeless Mission was one of them.

The reminder of her empty bed stung in a way it hadn't since she'd broken up with Rob. She had her own bed to sleep in, her own place, but it was always more fulfilling to share it with someone. Rob had been the only man she'd lived with for a short time. The other men she'd dated had, like her, enjoyed their own apartments when they weren't spending time together. Sometimes she wondered if she was destined to be single her entire life. She'd never met a man who'd made her feel she wanted to be with him, live with him, make a lifelong commitment.

Which was another reason why the train track rescue dude intrigued her. How was it that a man she'd never met had left more of an impression on her than guys she'd dated for months at a time?

She grabbed a quick dinner at the local diner, next to the library, before heading to the shelter. It was no more than twenty-five feet to the restaurant and yet she found herself looking over her shoulder, paying extra attention to the patrons entering and leaving the establishment. And she hated the laptop thief for stealing her sense of safety.

Immediately her mind flung back to the stranger, how he'd appeared from nowhere and disappeared as easily.

"Hey, Portia. How are you, honey?" The diner's lead waitress greeted her and grabbed a menu. Molly was a Silver Valley mainstay, the woman who served up hot soup or Belgian waffles when you needed them most. Molly sat her at a single booth, knowing how Portia enjoyed eating in the back corner of the diner, with a table to spread her books out on. "I heard you had a little excitement today."

"I did, and it's over." Portia shrugged out of her parka and hung it on the hook adjacent the bench seat.

"I called my parents right after, so that they wouldn't find out on social media or the online paper." Molly knew her parents, the entire DiNapoli family in fact.

Molly waited for her to sit. "That was smart. I'm surprised your parents aren't here with you now."

Portia smiled, still too worn out to laugh. "Trust me, I had to convince my mother that I'm totally fine. I promised her I was coming here to eat, then spending time at the shelter, where the other volunteers are like my second family."

"It's turned out okay, but honey, you were almost killed. Don't treat it so lightly, give yourself a little time to process. I'm so glad you're okay. That's all that matters."

"I appreciate that." And she did, but she couldn't keep dwelling on the frightening part of the situation or she'd never feel safe in Silver Valley again. "I see the chef made a batch of pepper pot pie." She referred to a local central Pennsylvania dish, which was actually a beef or chicken soup with square noodles, not a pastry-crust pie with filling.

"He did, and it smells divine in the kitchen tonight."

"I'll take that, and my usual."

Molly laughed, shaking her head. "I envy your ability to consume grilled cheese so regularly and not gain an inch."

"I'm on my feet all day." And today she'd earned all the comfort food she could manage to eat. She'd never forget how close she'd come to death, nor the enigmatic man who'd saved her life.

"Do you want hot tea, honey?"

"Yes, please." Molly walked away and Portia counted her blessings. Her parents were still in the area and she saw them fairly regularly, but her two siblings had moved away to Boston and Austin, Texas, respectively. Her brother worked with the FBI and her sister was a medical researcher. Their family times were great when they happened, but they were infrequent. It was nice to come into a diner and be treated like she belonged. Just like it was great to look forward to going to the homeless shelter tonight. Since her high school friend Lani had OD'd, Portia had found herself craving more human connection than what work provided. She wondered if her need to be with others would only intensify after her near-death experience today.

Certainly her obsession over her rescuer indicated she might need more human contact.

As she ate her pepper pot pie and sandwich dripping with Gouda and cheddar, she studied her handheld tablet. In a medium-sized town like Silver Valley, charities often combined events to help individual nonprofits to raise exponentially more cash. Since she'd been the one to suggest marrying the homeless shelter's fundraising efforts to the library gala, Portia knew her professional reputation was at stake. If the gala raised the same amount as last year, that meant less money for the library, as they'd agreed to give the homeless shelter 25 percent of the funds raised. There was less than a month left, and so far they had sold the same number of tickets as last year. She needed to figure out how to sell more by the RSVP deadline, two weeks away. The gala was to be at the end of the month, and would include a Silver Valley ice sculpture festival and contest. She was grateful for five weeks in January this year.

The homeless shelter was a short ten-minute walk from the diner, but it was located at the end of town, where the buildings thinned and the northern wind was a force to lean into. She'd traded her shoes for snow boots and wore her warmest down parka, but nothing seemed enough to stay warm in the sub-zero windchill.

The shelter was a modest craftsman-style home that had been converted to a fifty-bed mission by an anonymous donor three years ago. The porch and entry, usually full with patrons waiting until the last minute to go in for the night, stood empty. It was totally because of the cold, no question.

Still, a shiver raced up her spine and Portia knew a moment of sheer terror as she stared into the dark shadows of the porch. And then made herself look at the windows, aglow with light and promising warmth.

But she couldn't shake the frigid snare of fear that stabbed at her previous sense of safety, of surety about Silver Valley's place in the world. Would she ever regain it?

Kyle hoped tonight's surveillance at the homeless shelter would lead him to whomever might know when and by what means the next heroin shipment was coming in. On a cold night like this, addicts who normally avoided the shelters for fear of getting arrested for carrying illegal substances were sure to come in. He wanted to know who the newest dealers were, and where to find them.

Kyle checked in early to the shelter, well before the time he knew Portia normally showed up. Just in case she did. He'd expect her to go home and take the night off, after what she'd been through today.

Who was he kidding? Portia would no more likely bail on a volunteer shift than he'd quit an undercover op. Wasn't one of the things that he found so attractive about her the dedication she appeared to have to her work, her community? He tried to mentally brace himself to focus on finding someone else to date, to be with. Yet his gut instinct seemed to laugh at him, as if what he felt toward Portia were predestined, beyond his control.

He tried to breathe through his mouth, to not inhale the scent of his unwashed clothes. Part of his successful capture of intelligence regarding ROC's heroin and illegal-goods shipment operation was blending in, no matter the circumstance. As a homeless man, that meant stinking as if he'd been on the streets for several days.

He'd refuse to bathe here, unlike most of the men and women who gratefully accepted a hot shower. He couldn't risk anyone seeing him without the dirty wig or baggy clothes. He promised the intake person that he'd shower before bed. The mission also offered gently used but clean pajamas, to change into and wear so that their dirty clothes could be washed. Kyle found it easiest to play the role of the reluctant shelter-seeker. No one bothered him, save for the social workers who always tried to convince him to let them help him.

He'd found an old, scraggly wig at a used clothing store and wet it thoroughly, doused it with dirt, rubbed it around the attic of the house he rented, until it was sufficiently matted. No one would recognize him as the man who'd knocked Silver Valley's librarian off the local train tracks, in front of an oncoming train, just hours ago.

He scratched his head, hating the wig, and wished he hadn't shaved and had his hair cut. He'd had to, in order to hang around the library and not draw unwarranted attention. He'd needed to blend in, which he did by wearing different types of clothing each day, his wardrobe flexible to accommodate the needs of a farmer, teacher, professional or what he really was. An undercover agent.

After pouring a cup of hot coffee from the urn set up in the dining room area, he settled into a worn sofa and prepared to listen and learn. Observe. It was his job to do so.

A gust of polar air rushed into the room as the front door opened with a bang. His nape tingled and he silently swore to himself. It wasn't a premonition or anything portending danger. It was what he'd labeled his Portia Radar. He'd had to call it something, because as a good undercover agent, he couldn't afford to ignore how he reacted to people.

Before her shiny brunette hair that curled around her face and hung to her shoulders appeared, before the overhead lights reflected off her doe-brown eyes, before her confident, super-feminine laughter bounced off the dining room walls, he knew Portia was here.

A sense of urgency to get the ROC op wrapped up, Ludmila Markova locked up, gripped him. It wasn't so that he'd feel free to pursue Portia, because Kyle didn't do anything long-term, and Portia DiNapoli wasn't the one-night-stand type. Rather, she wasn't *his* one-and-done type. She was the woman that came to mind on the rare occasion he imagined what his "forever" woman would look like, if he were the type to settle down.

Hell. He had to get out of Silver Valley as quickly

as he could. Something about this place had wrapped around him, gotten under his skin.

And they'd never been properly introduced.

"Here you go, Mr. Turner." Portia handed the neatly folded pile of bed linens and towels to the man, still bundled up in his worn puffer down coat that she'd bet was from circa 1995. But it still kept him warm, and that was all that mattered. Still, she was glad he was at the mission tonight.

"Thank you, Portia. You're very kind."

"Just doing my job."

"They give you a raise yet?" He winked at her from behind his thick eyeglasses as he turned to head to his assigned bed. Mr. Turner, as well as most of the clients, she'd assume, knew who the volunteers were. The paid shelter workers included a social worker and counselor, as well as an accountant and grant writer, and were the ones who could get prescriptions filled as needed, medical care when warranted.

As much as Portia remained committed to her time here, she knew her vocation was in library science. Neither social work nor grant writing appealed to her. Her passion lay with seeing patrons find the book that they'd searched for, or a child figuring out that a novel was way better than the film version of their favorite story.

When she walked through the dining room, en route to the library, she couldn't escape the feeling she was being watched. Plain silly, as of course there were several pairs of eyes on her. Several different groups of people gathered around the family-style tables, drinking coffee or tea or hot chocolate. Alcohol and illegal drugs were strictly prohibited at the shelter, but she wouldn't be surprised if some of the hot drinks were spiked.

Portia ignored the urge to sit at one of the tables and find out more about the clients. Her shift was more than half over and she hadn't even started on the library. Before she left the dining area, though, she decided to get a cup of tea. The hot water urn was too tempting to pass up on such a cold night. Even with the house heated, the modern heating units couldn't keep up with the windchill. She pulled a bag of ginger tea from her pocket, ripped open the envelope and dunked the sachet into a thick paper cup. As she watched the boiling water turn golden, the creepy sense of being observed crawled up her back, her neck, and made her scalp tingle. This wasn't her introverted self being aware of the night's clients watching her. It was more.

Portia kept her back to the dining area, where at least twenty people sat around. The hum of their conversations hadn't waned, so it wasn't as if everyone had gone quiet and was staring at her, waiting for her to turn around and face them for an unknown reason. She heard the rush of liquid through the overhead piping, indicating that several overnight visitors were taking advantage of hot running water. Yet she couldn't shake her awareness of being watched in an unfriendly way.

Keeping her movements as casual as possible, she squeezed the tea bag with the paper envelope and threw it out. Hot drink in both hands, she turned carefully toward the door. As she neared the library's entrance, she risked a quick glance about the room. First she swept the dining room at large. No one paid her any attention.

Same with the people chatting in various easy chairs and sofas around the perimeter of the room.

Except for one man, who was sitting in the club chair next to the library entrance. He wasn't looking at her now; in fact, he'd looked away the second her gaze hit him. But not quickly enough. Not before she saw the flash of familiar gray eyes that gave away more than the fact they were watching her.

Her stomach flipped and her body froze. The man who'd rescued her was sitting Right. Here. Right. Now.

Impossible. This man in front of her had shaggy, dirty hair. He appeared filthy, from his worn clothing to the grime under his nails, lying casually atop the chair's upholstered arms.

Yet he had the same cut to his chin, the cleft almost as mesmerizing as his unusual eyes. Portia tried to make her legs move, tried to think and get herself to where she needed to be. But the shelter library's usual lure of a peaceful couple of volunteer hours was nothing compared to figuring out how the hell the man who'd rescued her this afternoon had managed to invade her every thought.

She shook her head and blinked. Forced her gaze elsewhere. Moved one foot in front of the other until she was in the safety of her beloved books. And away from the man who'd rattled her.

She set her tea down and noticed her hands were trembling. So not like her. Maybe she'd hit her head and didn't remember it? But the EMTs, and then the ER staff, would have found a lump during their examination of her, wouldn't they have? Unless she'd had no swelling but in fact had a concussion, or maybe even a hematoma. That was it—she had a hematoma and was about to have a brain bleed.

What else could explain the way her body had reacted to a complete stranger earlier today, a stranger who'd saved her freaking life? And how else to explain her reaction just now, to a homeless man who had nothing to do with what she'd been through? Self-recrimination slammed against her conscience. It was one thing to indulge in harmless fantasy at her own expense. But she'd just mistaken a homeless patron of the shelter, someone who came here out of extreme need, someone with a backstory that had to be pretty ugly to bring them to this point in circumstance, for a man she had an inexplicable draw to. A man she didn't even know.

Portia began to sort and stack the piles of books that were laid out on the few tables scattered around the small room. Maybe keeping her focus on what she knew would bring her sanity back. Otherwise she was going to have to return to the ER. And what would she tell them? That an unexpected attraction to a complete stranger, at the most terrifying moment of her life, was messing with her normally organized, methodical thoughts?

Kyle thought once, twice, three times about giving up and walking into the shelter's makeshift library and telling Portia DiNapoli who he was, what he was doing. Or at least offer a more broad-stroke explanation and tell her he was working with SVPD. ROC's presence in Silver Valley wasn't classified, and in fact only the details of his case were. But he stopped himself. Portia had been through enough. She was an innocent civilian in all of this, and any further contact with her invited trouble. He'd never forgive himself if her involvement with him in any way led to harm, or worse. This was an aspect of the case he'd not counted on: finding out that he cared for a woman he barely knew. And it wasn't just a sexual attraction, though that was front and center. There was something potent between him and Portia, something he'd never experienced with anyone else.

She'd recognized him, he was certain. And worse, by the way she'd halted midstep and locked her attention on to him, he suspected she felt it, too. The most surprising and intense awareness that seemed to connect them in a way he sure couldn't explain.

He grabbed another cup of coffee and headed to the middle of the dining room. He may as well use his time as he always did: listening for any indications of another heroin drop, or notice that another large commercial goods shipment was en route. As he pulled out a chair, he saw a dark shape flit across the frosted windows that lined the back wall of the room. Normally they overlooked a well-kept garden and yard, judging from the photos he'd found online. But in the current winter, it looked like a frozen tundra. The other night, he'd marveled at the way the moon reflected across the crystalline snowpack. But tonight the windows were foggy from the large amount of folks and need for increased heating in the shelter. The motion detector lights had lit up, allowing him to see the quick-moving shadow. His gut raised the alarm, clenching as it always had in Afghanistan, telling him that an attack or explosion was imminent. He'd never questioned his body's third eye of sorts—it was something he'd had as a kid, growing up in a less than desirable neighborhood in San Jose until his father bought an almond farm, and had only grown sharper with his Marine and then Trail Hiker training.

His sensitivity to danger was on full alert. He'd bet his powers of observation that the shadow was Ludmila Markova's, or another thug sent by ROC. The only room accessible from the backyard was the library, which was in fact the former screened-in porch. It'd been built up and insulated to become the library, but the door remained.

An entry point for someone with nefarious intent.

He didn't hesitate. He excused himself before he ever sat down, and headed straight for one of the private restrooms. Once locked inside, he used his phone to alert Josh at SVPD and his boss at TH Headquarters. They'd know to call in backup for him, and to keep it on the down-low until he relayed further information.

He left the restroom and went into the shelter's library, closing the door behind him. Portia jerked up from the pile of books she was bent over, her eyes widened from hearing the door click shut. She opened her mouth, and he saw her chest rise, and he concluded in a split second that she wasn't about to offer a friendly greeting.

Portia was about to scream.

# Chapter 4

Ludmila was about to make Portia DiNapoli pay for messing with her, the stupid fool. The librarian actually thought she'd run her off this morning, and she'd had to let her go, find her own cover. She'd come too close to the local police spotting her. As it was they'd seen her running away, but luckily for her, the train provided the divide she'd needed and she'd found cover among Silver Valley's many tiny alleyways and courtyard-style homes. When the law enforcement presence lessened, she'd circled back to her vehicle, a small economy car, just like all the others she rented and traded back in on a regular basis. Using different pseudonyms made her very difficult if not flat-out impossible to trace. The people she worked for provided nothing but the best in the way of forged documents and identification.

She'd had to spend the rest of the day in the mobile home she rented in a rundown trailer park outside town. It was pretty much abandoned and when she'd researched it, she discovered it had been the site of a cult that tried to take over the town. Silver Valley didn't impress her, with its openness and the ridiculously friendly people. Finding out they'd been victims of a cult until it'd been taken out at the very last minute only increased her derision. What good was this freedom they spoke about if they allowed outsiders like those people into their communities? Not that she cared. All Ludmila wanted was her own freedom from anyone ever telling her what to do, how to live, ever again. She'd escaped the FSB, virtually impossible for being such a well-trained agent. They didn't let their assets go, not alive. She'd escape ROC, too. All she needed was a little more time to pull one over on Ivanov. It was a shame she wouldn't be around to see the ROC boss's face when he realized she'd duped him.

Of course, her neighbors' welcoming nature worked in her favor. No one suspected her of being a lethal ROC operative. Fools.

The librarian hadn't come back to work today until much later, and then ate at the diner. She lived near there. Americans ate a lot of fattening food and very often—something she at once envied and reviled. As a top FSB agent, she'd needed to be in top form, and now working what she hoped was her last time for anyone but herself, her physicality was one of her best tools.

It was too tempting to drop the laptop today, to get it out of her hands and ready for the next operator. But it was too risky. No matter—she had until the end of the week. Her employer was unforgiving but reasonable about the length of time she was given to complete her job. And she'd gotten lucky—the shipment arriving in refrigerator trucks from destinations down south, close to the Mexican border, had been halted halfway across the country due to a blizzard. It bought her time. And her life, some might say, but she wasn't going to let anyone take her life from her. She had to keep going for the sake of her murdered family.

Finally she spied DiNapoli as she left the diner. As soon as feasible, she slipped into the night, following her down the sidewalks of Silver Valley. Dressed as an elderly woman, she was prepared to indicate she lived in a nearby apartment and had only come out to get a meal or a hot beverage at the nearby coffee shop. But she didn't expect anyone to bother her. It was still early enough in the evening for an older person to be out.

She watched DiNapoli turn a corner and cut behind a laundry to pick up her trail more efficiently. The do-gooder was heading for the homeless shelter. Of course she was. It had been part of the job to check out DiNapoli, observe her daily routine so that she'd know when to take advantage of it with the laptop placement. The woman spent a lot of time at the shelter, and from what she'd overheard, also at the library, doing things for others who weren't even her relatives. So as an ROC agent, she scoped the shelter out on a night the librarian wasn't there. Posing as a lost homeless woman had been easy. And had allowed her to commit the entire building to memory, room by room. She'd known immediately the room with all the books and magazines was DiNapoli's doing. It was organized just like the town library, but on a smaller scale. The room opened onto the courtyard—perfect for her plan.

Volunteerism was singularly distasteful to her. If there wasn't a payment, why do it?

DiNapoli paused in front of the shelter and unexpectedly looked around the street. She had to duck into an alcove but was certain the librarian hadn't seen her. The early winter darkness was her ally.

As soon as she confirmed DiNapoli was in the big house that the town used as a homeless shelter, she formulated her plan. She'd break into the shelter wherever the librarian worked and kill her there. Or better yet, she might be able to lure Portia outside, like she'd inadvertently done this morning. Portia DiNapoli was a naive, pampered woman, who wouldn't know the workings of an AK-47 if she were forced to watch an online video about it. She'd never outwit a former FSB agent and current ROC mastermind.

She felt no guilt, not a drop of remorse as she removed her pistol from her parka and prepared to take out Silver Valley's beloved librarian with one shot between her eyes. The woman would die as she lived—with her books.

Portia gasped at the intrusion, the sheer boldness of the intruder who barged into the shelter library and shut off the lights. He'd actually locked the door to the small room behind him. But then she recognized him, his gray eyes, the homeless man who reminded her of the sexy stranger who'd held her close only twelve hours ago. She stopped fighting her intuition that something bad was about to happen. She opened her mouth and prepared to give the loudest scream of her li—

The man moved faster than she blinked, and before she registered his intent, he was next to her, his hand over her mouth. Portia's instincts kicked into hyperdrive as she at once shoved her heel onto the man's instep, attempted to bite his hand and elbowed his ribs.

Her defensive tactics didn't yield a single *ouch*. He was a rock. "Portia DiNapoli, I'm a friend and colleague of Detective Josh Avery's. You know it's me, the man who shoved you off the tracks earlier today. You're in danger and I have to get you out of here ASAP. You have to trust me."

His voice, low and urgent against her ear, made something deep inside her still. It was the same voice; she'd know it anywhere. Or else she had completely lost touch with reality, in which case she was about to be killed by a stalker.

She tugged on his forearm. Slowly, he moved his hand away from her mouth. For as dirty as his hands had looked in the dining room, they were smooth and didn't smell. The scent of coffee clung to his skin, and she caught a whiff of the same scent from this morning. It wasn't a cologne or soap. It was *him*. The musk that she'd been unable to let go of.

"Why do you think I'm in danger?" She remained primed, her back still to his front, ready to lurch for the door and scream bloody hell.

"Like I told you this morning, I'm someone you can trust. But I can't explain it all right now. We don't have time."

She turned on her heel, still in the circle of his arms, and looked up at him. Only the shaft of moonlight revealed his shape, his largeness compared to her. But she knew it was him.

"It is you. But if I can trust you, why am I in danger for the second time in one day?"

The sound of the back door being rattled echoed across the room, and they both stilled, only their breaths between them.

"I want you to stay behind me. Do not come out of here until I come get you. And you can't go back into the dining room or you risk involving everyone else here."

"I'm calling 9-1-1." She was tired of people trying to break into her place of work, places that until now she'd always felt secure in.

"Already done." He put both hands on her shoulders as the door shuddered and she felt the cold air wrap around her legs. "Stay here, behind this shelf."

She didn't see a need to fight him. And what was she going to do, take out the intruder with a book?

He was gone and she hunkered down behind the one long shelf that split the room, the bookshelf between her and the door—and whomever was breaking in. Too late she realized her phone was in her purse—and secured in a volunteer locker. She'd never needed it before, never felt unsafe at the homeless mission. Even if there was an unruly overnight guest, the security guard had always been more than enough to handle it. Always.

Until now.

He knew Markova's tactics. Her weapon would be drawn, ready to take Portia out with one shot. She might make it look like a drug deal gone bad by leaving a packet of heroin with the body, a common ploy by organized crime, but he doubted it. Markova came from a long line of FSB agents, going back to the KGB.

Kyle kept his footsteps soft and swift, mimicking a

female's. He slid into the spot under the low window, next to the door. Markova didn't rely on her primitive tactics from this morning at the library, but instead he heard a succession of clicks, the tumblers freeing the catch. The door swung outward and he waited. It'd be so easy to take her out here, have her arrested and arraigned by a federal court on several counts, including overstaying her original visa, identity fraud and murder. Ludmila Markova was implicated in at least six unsolved ROC-related homicides.

But he didn't know how ROC was passing shipment information yet. He had to scare her off, keep her alive and active until Trail Hikers and SVPD brought the entire op down.

Her silhouette flashed up on the open door, at the precise angle of his line of sight. The handheld pistol was pointed up, but he knew she'd lower it and shoot with zero hesitation.

One boot-clad foot stepped into the room, and he struck. He moved swiftly, using the element of surprise for the split second it lasted. Twisting his hands around her ankle, he ignored her muffled cry of pain and yanked, hard, until she hit her ass on the hard concrete porch. He leaped to his feet and kicked the pistol out of her hand before he dropped onto her, pressing his knees to her chest, holding her arms flat. When she bucked to grab his head with her legs, he was ahead of her, leaning too close to her face, where her soulless eyes glittered under the moon. She'd taken out the motion detector light but couldn't stop Mother Nature. As he peered into her gaze, he noted that she, too, wore a wig and, in fact, was bundled in oversize clothing.

But he'd know her moves, her eyes, anywhere. She was his target.

"Get off me, you stinking pig!" Her voice was low and ugly.

He wanted to shout in victory that she thought he was a homeless person. But it'd be short-lived. In the moment she took him at face value, but later, when she flashed back over the events, she'd figure out he was in the same business she was, except he wanted to save the world and keep people safe. Not watch innocent people die for the sake of the profit made off heroin or whatever the hell ROC had her smuggling for them.

"You're not looking so good yourself. Get the hell out of here. Don't come back."

She spit in his face but he'd already lifted off her, stood between her and the pistol that had slid under the eaves. Markova scrambled to her feet, and without a weapon, took off to the nearest exit from the courtyard. The small wooden gate flapped against the house next door as she shoved it open, never slowing her stride.

Kyle pocketed the weapon carefully, knowing a pro like Markova had worn gloves, but still hoping there might be prints on the pistol.

He'd defeated ROC again, in another battle, just as he had this morning on the train tracks, no matter how convoluted the mission had been. But he hadn't won the war, and now Portia was Markova's prime target.

Portia heard no words exchanged, but she did hear thuds and gasps for air. Each thwack made her jump and it was hard, so hard, waiting and not reacting.

*Trust.*

The sound of a mewling like an injured cat rent the room, quickly followed by the sounds of fast footsteps.

A quietly spoken but fierce string of swear words, then steady footsteps as he returned.

"You can stand up. All's clear." His face was partially illuminated by his phone, into which he tapped a message. Who was he telling about what had just happened?

"That's it? You let the bad guy get away?" She rubbed the tops of her arms, chilled not only by the back door being open so long and letting the precious heat out, but from the prospect that she'd survived another near miss.

Steel-gray eyes found hers. The colors on the phone screen danced across his face, but his eyes were uncompromising in how he watched her. "I scared them away is more like it. And for the record—you're being targeted by some very bad people. I need to get you out of here."

A knock, then a loud "Portia? You in there?" sounded from the dining room. Gary, one of the other volunteers, was concerned.

Portia turned. "Let me unlock the door at least."

"No!" His hand was on her arm, stopping her. "Not an option. We're leaving out this back door, now."

"But I need my coat, my purse—"

"And I need to keep you alive." His words, exacting and scary in their connotation, seemed at odds with his stance, the expression she could make out in the dim phone light. "Damn it." He quickly tapped on his phone, held it to his ear. They were in the dark again.

More pounding. More people were outside the library room door. "Portia, are you okay? Open up!"

Some of the patrons must have alerted the security guard that she'd been followed into the room by this man. And she didn't know his name.

"Josh, it's Kyle. I have Portia DiNapoli with me and I have to extract us both from the homeless shelter, ASAP. Can you talk to her and tell her I'm good?"

She heard a man's voice answer, but it could be any man. When her rescuer held his phone to her ear, she saw the name across the top—Detective Josh Avery, SVPD.

"Hello?"

"Portia, it's Josh. You must do whatever Kyle tells you. It's a life-or-death situation." Josh's voice conveyed what his words didn't. He was worried for her.

She handed the phone back to the man Kyle.

"Where are we going, Kyle?"

# Chapter 5

Kyle took his keys out of his pocket before he threw his coat over Portia's shoulders and checked out her feet. "I know my jacket stinks, but it'll keep you warm. At least you have boots on tonight. Let's go."

She was a silent, quick partner next to him as they exited the house and ran alongside the walls that were shadowed from the moonlight's reach. He noted that Markova's footprints led to where he'd chased her off— the front of the building, away from the back part of the shelter, where the guests slept. Not that the ROC henchman had wanted anyone but Portia.

Portia stayed with him, thank God.

He'd wanted to take out Markova then and there, but couldn't. He had to have her alive to be able to track her movements, to figure out ROC's next move. But his problem was that Markova had come to wipe out her witness from this morning. The woman who trustingly ran with him, up to the wrought-iron gate that swung out onto the street. The snow around the gate was virgin, so no chance that Markova was lurking at this edge of the property. Yet.

He cleared the area, visually scoured it for any interlopers. Just an empty winter street in downtown Silver Valley, but he knew Markova or another ROC thug could be lying in wait anywhere. Fortunately his vehicle was directly in front of them. He'd planted it hours earlier, during daylight, before he'd assumed his homeless cover.

"Come on. This is my truck." He didn't wait but trusted, this time, that she'd follow without hesitation. He hit his key fob and the lights blinked twice quickly in succession. As he rounded the back, quickly checked under the chassis for explosives and then opened the driver's door, he noted that Portia had already slid into the passenger seat.

He didn't speak until they'd driven away and he'd employed countermeasures to ensure they weren't being followed.

"Thank you."

"For what? Blindly following you to my probable death?"

He laughed, the release of pent-up tension but also from her dry humor in such a dour circumstance.

"I promise you, Portia, you're not in danger from me." He pulled to a stop at a red light and turned to her, held out his hand. "Kyle King."

She looked like she might slap him away, but instead grasped his hand with hers. Her grip was not only firm but surprisingly large, for a woman.

"Portia DiNapoli. But you already knew that." She shook once, then withdrew. Not before she saw his expression at her grip. "Don't look so surprised. I threw shot put in college."

"You look like a runner, and you almost caught your thief this morning."

"I ran in high sch—wait. It *was* you. I'm not crazy." Her bemusement unsettled him. A distraught, scared civilian, he could handle. But Portia's steady thoughtfulness threw him off.

Portia fought to calm herself as Kyle sped through the icy streets. She'd always found the silence of a Silver Valley winter night soothing, but no longer. A lot of things were going to affect her differently after facing down the woman with the knife this morning.

Who was this man who called himself Kyle King? Was that really his name? His profile was exactly as she remembered it, against the morning sky, next to the train tracks as he held her. Rugged but with enough sexiness to make her feel the pulse between her legs wake up and remind her that it'd been too long since she'd been with a man.

But he was about more than the unrelenting sexual attraction she felt for him. This man, this Kyle, was on a mission of some sort. She'd seen that expression on the face of her friends that worked at SVPD, including Josh. And she'd seen it reflected back at her when she was hell-bent on making a community event happen, like the gala.

This mission, or whatever Kyle was about, had nothing to do with warm and fuzzy things like a charity event, though.

Before her nerves blew her anxiety into a full-blown panic attack, she forced herself to take action.

"Can I borrow your phone?" Portia was certain she'd heard Josh's voice on the other end of his cell earlier, but she'd been a little stressed. She prided herself on being a details woman. If she wasn't as safe as Kyle wanted her to believe, she wanted to find out.

"Sure." He pressed the home button with his fore-finger, unlocking the cell phone. Portia wasted no time punching in Annie's number. It was one of the few she still knew by heart, thanks to the ease of a smartphone.

"Hello?" Annie sounded cautious, as Kyle King's number clearly wasn't in her phone.

"Annie, it's Portia. I can't explain a whole lot now, but do you happen to know where Josh is right now?"

"He's next to me. Why? Do you need to talk to him?"

"Yes."

The sound of muffled laughter reached her and heat rushed over her face. Annie and Josh were inseparable since they'd decided to make a go of their relationship and got engaged.

"Portia, Josh here. Everything going okay with Kyle?"

*Phew.*

"Yes. I had to double-check and make sure it was you I spoke to."

To his credit, Josh didn't laugh at her. "I get it. I'd do the same. Where are you two now?"

She surreptitiously looked at Kyle, whose focus remained on the road, with no hint that he was listening. Not that he could help overhearing, though. "We're heading out of town, toward the catering barn." The town proper fell behind them and they traversed the road that cut like a pale blue ribbon through worn farm fields, blanketed in feet of snow that had fallen over the last month.

"If you're with Kyle, you're safe, Portia. He'll fill you in on what he can."

"Got it. Thanks, Josh."

"No problem. Call anytime, as always. Do you want to speak to Annie again?"

"No, that's okay. I'll catch up with her later in the week. Bye." She disconnected and wished it were already Friday and she was having dinner and a drink with Annie. Their standing girls' night hadn't changed, except for the frequency, since Annie had fallen in love with Josh. Portia slid the phone back across the wide console toward Kyle.

"Feel better?" Kyle's voice was too alive. Too full of sexy vibration.

"Yes. No. How would you feel if a complete stranger first saved you from becoming a human Frisbee earlier in the day, then protected you from some unknown intruder the same night?"

"I'd feel pretty damned lucky, Portia." The lines that bracketed his mouth deepened and she sensed he fought a smile.

"Good for you, Kyle. But I'm a librarian, not a… What are you? Do you work for SVPD?"

"Something like that. I'm a private contractor, law enforcement. I get called in for the cases that require a little more finesse and time than the local LEAs can provide."

"So you're here because of ROC."

He maneuvered the truck around a tight turn before he pulled over to the shoulder and put it in Park. Kyle turned to fully face her, and the sense of comfort she'd started to feel shattered in the face of the sheer power he exuded. From his eyes that missed nothing to his hands that had held her, saved her twice today, to his athletic physique, Kyle King embodied competence and awareness.

"What do you know about ROC, Portia?" Kyle spoke the words with deadly precision, keeping his voice low and purposeful. Gone was the man who'd told her she could trust him. In his place, a predator.

"What's not to know? I read that ROC is fighting a huge battle with local LEAs, all up and down the Eastern Seaboard. Since Silver Valley is in the midst of the logistical hub for the East Coast, it was only a matter of time before ROC's crime affected our town." As she spoke, she noticed that he sat back a bit, his shoulders relaxed.

And he let out a low belly laugh.

"What's so freaking funny, Kyle?" She was almost too tired to get angry at his response. Almost.

He shook his head. "You read about it. The article in the *Silver Valley View*, am I right?"

"What's wrong with that?"

"Nothing. I admire how well-informed you are. And for the record, that article is about 95 percent accurate."

"What's the 5 percent that's wrong?"

"Oh, nothing's wrong. Not at all. But they're missing some crucial facts that are classified. Only SVPD and folks like myself are in on the most critical facts."

That made sense. And frankly, she didn't want to know the other facts the paper hadn't had. Although—

"Don't even bother asking me, Portia."

\* \* \*

"I wasn't going to ask you anything." She bit her lip, angry at herself for showing her thoughts so obviously that he'd read her expression. Heat rushed to her cheeks. "I wanted to tell you that I lost a high school friend to a heroin overdose just before the holidays. It hasn't even been three months yet. I hold ROC responsible for making it so easy for her, and the other victims of this awful scourge, to get the drugs. Not to mention how they cut them with lethal ingredients like fentanyl."

"I'm sorry, Portia."

"Keeping my community the safe place I've always known it to be is what matters to me."

"That's what I'm here for, too." He stared at her and she was immediately aware of being alone with him, on the abandoned road, in the dark. If she wanted to run, she'd never make it back to town before getting hypothermia. They were at least five miles out into the countryside.

"Why are we stopped?"

"I'm not going to hurt you, Portia." Low and seductive, his voice circled her mind, set parts of her on fire that she'd neglected since breaking up with Rob. But even after a good bit of foreplay, Rob had never lit her up the way Kyle did.

"Then why have you parked here?"

"I had to make sure we weren't followed." He hesitated and she knew he was holding something back. Maybe one of those confidential facts he'd mentioned?

"What happened to the person who tried to break into the homeless shelter? Why were they doing that?"

He sighed. It wasn't just an expulsion of air into the

interior. It was as if Kyle wrapped years of longing into his breath, his sigh.

"This morning, when I, ah, shoved you off the tracks—the woman whom you were chasing is a suspected ROC thug. That's more information than I should be telling you, but you asked, and you've done your research." A quick flash of white as he grinned. "My concern then, and now, is that she would come back for you. You identified her, saw her face-on behind the library and then on the tracks."

"That's crazy! I saw her, yes, but she had a ski mask on. I could never in good conscience identify her or have a reliable sketch made of her." Portia's heart began to pound, partially from the fear of being stalked by such a dedicated criminal, and by her growing awareness of being alone with Kyle King. The man was vouched for by Josh, so he was safe, trustworthy. And she'd known that at her gut level, anyhow. If he'd wanted to hurt her, he wouldn't have put himself at risk to save her, twice.

Kyle looked through the windshield as if soaking in the view. When his gaze reclaimed hers, she knew he'd been preparing to give her the news no civilian ever wants to hear.

"Portia, you can't go back to your apartment in town. It's not safe. The fact that you were tracked to the homeless shelter tells me that the ROC thug wants you off their radar."

"Off—as in dead, you mean." She swallowed. "This is unexpected."

His expression changed from the professional whatever-he-was law enforcement person to something far more approachable. Too easy to interpret.

Kyle looked like he cared.

"I know this has to be tough on you. But it'll be a lot more than tough if you wind up dead, another victim of ROC and its attempt to use Silver Valley as its playground."

"So ROC picked Silver Valley as its headquarters in this area?" She'd read the articles thoroughly, and while they stated that ROC's various criminal activities were embedded in central Pennsylvania, she couldn't get her mind wrapped around her hometown being overtaken by organized crime.

"*Headquarters* is too strong of a word. As a main hub, yes. And..." She watched his mouth close, his generous lips thin from the pressure of his thoughts. Disappointment flared deep in her belly. Until she saw the moonlight hit his eyes and illuminate his pupils, dilated against his silver irises. Her regret turned to anticipation as quickly as a flame engulfed dried paper.

Kyle wanted her, too.

# Chapter 6

Kyle wasn't a rookie when it came to wanting a woman, and he sure as hell knew when he needed to turn and walk away. But that had been before, with other women. Portia was different. Kyle could fight the erection that strained his battered jeans, he could ignore the heat that ignited each time he set eyes on Portia. And who was he kidding? The warmth that Portia stoked in him lasted all day, hours after he'd been around her.

But breathing the same air as her in the confines of the old truck's front seats made being anything but a human being, aware of every single nuance in her expression, impossible.

Kyle leaned in to kiss her, watched her eyes soak him up, her gaze settle on his lips—

A hard tug on the top of his head halted him midmotion.

"What the—" He reached up to discover his wig had caught on the rim of the cab's sunroof. *"Fuuuuudge."*

Portia's giggle startled him. It was the first time he'd seen her react without reservation or the guard she kept up around him. And while he knew her defensive stance was important to her well-being, and he in fact would be the first to encourage it, he still reveled in the warmth that rushed over him.

"Who would guess that a wig would save me from a huge mistake?" He spoke his thought aloud: an even bigger mistake. The wariness was back in her eyes and she shrank against the passenger door.

"I'm not used to being referred to as a 'mistake.'" Challenge emanated from her deep brown eyes.

"Portia, it's not you—it's me."

She snorted. "I've heard that one before. Look, spare us both and cut to the chase. Where are we going? I'll need to stop at my place to pack. That's what you're getting at, right? That I can't be seen in town for a few days or I'll be killed by some ROC thug."

His breath escaped in a sharp exhale, as if he'd been gut-kicked. It didn't surprise him, though, that the woman in front of him was incredibly perceptive.

"You're awfully astute and adaptable for a civilian."

"Don't you mean 'for a librarian'?"

"No, I didn't mean that at all." He removed the wig, scratched his head. His hair was close-cropped but it still itched after having a synthetic cap with dirty nylon atop it. "You're remarkable. You went after Mar—that woman without a second thought, all to get the laptop back for the library. It wasn't the smartest move from a safety standpoint, but it took guts." And an excellent level of physical fitness that agents worked hard to maintain. "Are you sure you're not in law enforcement, too?"

She fought it for a second before the grin split her face. "Not at all, but do you think I could be?"

He laughed, more from relief that she was conversing with him, letting go of his stupid comment about the almost-kiss being a mistake. "You're certainly strong and fit enough for it. But working in law enforcement has to be a passion. Like your community work."

"How do you know what my passion is?"

She'd caught him.

"I, er, had to run a background check on you when I began surveillance on the library."

She straightened up, leaned in toward the dash, toward him, watched him closely. "And when, exactly, was that?"

"A month ago."

"Son of a…" She trailed off and he swore he heard the synapses firing in her brain. "That's why your eyes looked so familiar. But I didn't recognize you on the tracks. Or rather, off them."

"A good thing. It's my job to stay under the radar."

"Why wasn't I told there was a case going on right under my nose? I didn't have to know all the details, but maybe I could have helped."

"Which is why we don't tell civilians more than absolutely necessary. You said yourself you read exposes on ROC and how we're fighting it in Silver Valley and all of Harrisburg. It's difficult to know who to trust. And there's no reason to bring innocent civilians into a potentially lethal case. That's what we're trying to avoid."

"Who else besides you has been watching the library?"

He shrugged, tried to appear as nonchalant as possible. And knew he was utterly failing in front of her. What was it with Portia? He'd lied and gotten away with his undercover disguises in front of other people close to him over the years. Yet Portia had immediately pegged him in the homeless shelter, and she didn't take any of his standard lines now. Portia was different.

"SVPD has plainclothes officers circulate through, and there may be other…contract employees like me who keep an eye on things." He wasn't about to reveal anything about Trail Hikers, or any specifics.

"Fair enough. I imagine you'll let me know if you're FBI or another agency when you realize you can trust me." She sniffed and he glanced at the dashboard clock.

"We've got to go." He was certain no one had followed them out here, and he was safe to go back to his apartment. "I have a place for you to stay tonight, but then you'll need something more long-term."

"What? I can't miss work."

"You have no choice. You show up at the library or anywhere in town right now, you risk being killed. ROC doesn't screw around, Portia."

"But what about my purse, my clothes? I need my contacts, my prescriptions—"

"I'll take care of that. I can take care of the shelter and get your purse, phone, whatever." He'd send in an undercover cop or ask a favor from another TH colleague. "You mentioned that Annie is your best friend? We can ask Josh to go with her to your apartment and pack a suitcase. You're looking at two to four weeks of hiding out, Portia."

"This is absolutely ridiculous. In this day and age, with all the technology available, can't SVPD put a security camera or two in my apartment, have a patrol keep an eye on my place? You already said the library's being watched."

"We're keeping surveillance on it. And yet you still were almost killed yesterday, because of your judgment that you could catch a thief." He turned to face the steering wheel and shifted the car into gear. "Trust me, Portia, you're going to thank me for this when it's all said and done."

And he vowed she would thank him. That he wouldn't screw it all up by letting his dick call the shots around her.

Portia took in Kyle's small apartment atop Silver Valley's favorite coffee shop, Cup o' Joe's. "I never knew this apartment existed, and I've lived here my entire life." And he'd been living in the building next to hers.

"So you remember when the coffee shop, this building, was a bank?"

"I do." She watched him, wondered how long he'd been here. How had she overlooked him in the library? The air throbbed with the pure masculinity radiating off him and created a potent sexual aura she found difficult to ignore.

In fact, she'd done anything but ignore it since he'd held her in his arms after saving her life this morning.

"Holy crap," she said to herself as she sipped the weak tea he'd made her. He'd boiled the water in a mug in his microwave and she'd used one of her teabags that she'd stuck in her pocket for the shelter.

"What?"

"It's only been twelve hours since we met. Since that train almost—" She couldn't finish around the huge toad in her throat. Tears ran down her cheeks and she swiped at them. "Sorry. I'm not usually so emotional." She sniffed.

The sofa sagged as he sat next to her and she held her mug out to prevent the warm liquid from spilling.

"Here." He took the mug and placed it on the scarred coffee table. The furniture was all rather ratty and indicative of coming with the place. Kyle King was a man on the move. Did he have a real home, anywhere?

"I'm fine."

"Sure you are." Warm arms came around her and she stiffened but Kyle didn't move as his body heat seeped into her and she accepted defeat. Relaxing into the hug, she leaned her head against his shoulder.

"I'm not the weepy type."

"Of course you're not." Hands smoothed her back, her shoulders, pulled her close. As much as the sexual tension between them was a constant companion, this wasn't a come-on. It was pure comfort and solace. Portia closed her eyes and decided to surrender, to give into the soothing attention. For a few minutes.

"Was today a typical day for you? As far as fighting off the bad guys?"

"No. A typical day for me is boring, actually. Lots of waiting, watching. A good amount of time with my laptop, helping, ah, my colleagues put together information."

"It's okay that you don't tell me everything, you know. I get it. My brother's in a similar job."

"Oh?"

"And you know I won't tell you what he does. I

can't." She heard her voice slur, felt the weight of the hardest day of her life since losing her close friend Lani close in on her.

"No." The vibration of his voice rumbled through her and she could have pulled herself from the under-tow of exhaustion. "You don't have to tell me anything you don't want to, Portia."

"Why do I feel that relates to more?"

"Hmm?"

She leaned up and looked at him. "Are you telling me that you won't do anything with or to me that I don't want, too?"

The laughter crinkles at the sides of his eyes smoothed and his hold tightened on her, as if he needed her to know his deepest secrets.

"I've never taken what I haven't asked for first, Portia."

"I know that. And for the record? I trusted you be-fore you got me out of the homeless shelter. Probably from the minute you side-tackled me off the tracks."

He kissed her softly on her forehead, and while she longed to turn the chaste kiss into more, she didn't want to lose this special closeness. This was what she'd been trying to put a finger on when she'd wondered if she'd always be single. *Intimacy.* She wanted to savor it as long as she could.

Kyle couldn't recall the last time a woman had fallen asleep in his arms. He'd planned to put Portia in his bed and take the sofa, but she was out cold, and he didn't want to risk waking her. She'd been through a lot. So much that he was shocked she hadn't had a meltdown of some sort. Most civilians would have. Heck, a lot of agents struggled with compounding events. Anyone would. To have a near miss like what happened on the train tracks was big enough, but then to find out you were being personally targeted by a lethal organized crime group?

He gently laid her down on the sofa, noting how small she looked asleep. As if her personality, at rest, made up for half her size. The soft, worn blanket he used as an afghan on the rare nights when he streamed a show covered her perfectly. But the scratchy throw pillow wouldn't do. He took it and left it on his bed as he brought his pillow back out and tucked it carefully under her head.

Her hair was silky and springy under his fingers and he fought to not run both hands through it. That would be downright creepy, as Portia was sound asleep. He settled for taking a last look at her, noting the way her long lashes contrasted sharply against her high cheekbones, and how full and rosy her lips were.

As he crouched next to her, he smelled not the scent of her floral perfume but something earthier.

*Crap.* He needed a shower, as he was still in his homeless garb, sans the wig. He stood up and walked back to the bathroom. Had he really been about to kiss Portia while decked out in the filthiest clothing and wig possible?

Humility was a good thing. He switched on the water in the small stall and considered himself lucky to be humbled by the likes of Portia DiNapoli. It reminded him that even he, after years of undercover work and ops against organized crime, wasn't immune to being blindsided by his hormones.

Except, his connection with Portia felt deeper than any potent chemistry he'd ever shared with a woman before. Which made it deadly. Distractions were anathema to any law enforcement agent, especially when working such an explosive case. Neither he nor Portia could afford the chance that their attraction could cost him the case, or worse, her life.

He stripped out of the smelly clothes and shoved them into one of the extra plastic bags he kept under the sink for the wastebasket. He'd toss them. His cover was blown tonight when he'd fought off and scared away Markova. Even if the ROC operative didn't recognize him, she was very good at what she did. Which meant her intuition would alert her, let her know if she encountered him at the mission again.

Damn it. He still had to remain focused on Markova, but it was no longer solely to dismantle the ROC shipment and heroin schedule. It had turned into a way to save Portia's life.

Which meant he'd be seeing more of Portia, something he couldn't afford. He'd call Josh first thing tomorrow morning. SVPD, or someone else at Trail Hikers, needed to take over Portia's safety, because in addition to the case being lethal to her, Portia was also lethal to Kyle's carefully built life. A life that allowed him to move freely from mission to mission, with no emotional ties binding him or his agent work.

And he had California to look forward to. He was only in Silver Valley for the next two or three weeks, enough time to take this ROC op down. There wasn't a future here, on his own or with Portia. He'd best remember that.

The alley was long, dark, with only a huge wall at the end. Portia was trapped, the woman with the evil eyes no more than ten yards behind her. She willed herself to jump, reach for the top of the wall. In an instant she was in the air, flying, until her feet landed on the solid top of the roof.

The sound of metal scraping against the brick wall caught her attention and she hesitated, looked down. Icy blue eyes met her gaze as the woman climbed the wall with the aid of the long-bladed knife. The weapon that could have killed Portia behind the library, and then on the train tracks. The laptop thief smiled and her teeth looked like a rabid animal's. Too late, Portia recognized her mistake. She didn't trust her instinct to keep running, and now the killer was inches away, Portia's fear keeping her from flying off the wall. If she'd listened to Kyle and stayed put, she'd be okay. And now she didn't know where he was.

With a start Portia jerked awake when a shout rang out. She sat up, struggling against the bedclothes. She panicked when faced with the pitch dark, not knowing where she was. In that same instant, she recalled it wasn't her apartment but Kyle's.

"Portia." Strong hands on her shoulders, then smoothing the hair from her sweaty brow. "You're safe. You're with me, Kyle. You've had a nightmare."

Mutely, she nodded. Had that scream been in her mind or had it been her? She swallowed, the rough soreness of it validating that yes, she'd yelled in her sleep.

"Sorry." Her voice was wispy and didn't begin to convey the depth of emotions she'd just plumbed.

He knelt in front of her, but kept a good distance. She got it. As much as she didn't know him, she was a stranger to Kyle, too. She couldn't keep a smile from splitting through her angst.

"That's more like it." Kyle's voice reflected relief, encouragement. And soothed her.

"It's funny that we've gone through so much together in less than twenty-four hours, and yet we don't know one another. But I feel like I've known you my entire life. Is this normal for your kind of work?"

Kyle's breath sucked in, and she waited to hear his exhale. He didn't speak for a good while as she leaned against the sofa back, crossing her legs under her.

"Taking down a criminal ring like ROC is the definition of intense. So yes, it's not uncommon for very strong feelings to surface. It's its own kind of intimacy, I guess you could say." Kyle leaned away from her, shook his head. "But what you and I are feeling isn't usual. It's different."

She peeked at him from under her lashes. "And you're not very happy about that."

"It's not my prerogative to have any feelings about it. I have a job to do, and now we've got the added complication of your life being on the line. It's not like we're at an island resort, where we could have some fun with this, this smoke between us."

"Smoke? Do you mean chemistry?"

"No. I mean smokin' hot heat, babe." The honesty of his bare assessment made all of her most intimate parts tingle, but she saw his quick grin.

"You're joking."

He stood up and stretched. "Actually, no, I'm not. It's nothing to take lightly, but we can't explore whatever kind of connection we're feeling. Feelings are distractions, Portia. In my line of work, they get people killed."

In her life, feelings got her heart crushed. Not anything she wanted to do again, for sure.

"Can't you call Josh and have him guard me, or send over another cop to do the same, while you're chasing down the bad woman?"

"Is that what you dreamed about?" He'd gone still, standing at the end of the coffee table.

She nodded. "Yeah. It was a classic anxiety dream, and more intense than I usually have because of yesterday. I get anxiety dreams all the time. Usually I have to take an exam for a class I didn't attend all year."

"Did you ever skip a class in your entire life?" That flash of white again. His grin could make any woman want to rip her clothes off and encourage him to do the same.

"As a matter of fact, I did."

"I don't believe you."

She shrugged. "You don't have to. I know it's true. Last semester, senior year of college." It'd been her elective class, ballet, that she'd purposefully missed in order to take advantage of a local politician's meet-and-greet. "That's when I started to realize I wanted to be active in my community. Not necessarily in politics, but something that would make a difference."

His grin twisted ruefully. "The last semester of school doesn't count, not really."

"And I suppose you skipped class all the time?"

"Never. My scholarship was at stake, and the cost of the class exorbitant. I would never have risked it."

"So you're the pot calling the kettle—"

"No, I'm the kettle who recognized another kettle."

"Point taken." She tugged the covers back up around

her, not wanting him to think she expected more conversation. "I'm fine, Kyle. You can go back to bed."

"I'm just down the hall if you need me. You can still take my bed and I'll sleep here."

"That's all right, but thank you anyway."

"You're welcome. See you in the a.m." He'd already begun to return to his room. Once she was left alone again, sleep didn't waste time returning. This time it was dreamless.

# Chapter 7

Kyle called Josh the next morning, only speaking freely because he was using his TH secure cell phone.

"It's not SVPD's job to provide personal security, Kyle. You know that." Josh sounded annoyed and Kyle knew he'd probably woken up his buddy. The sun had barely breached the horizon when he'd called. Portia was still fast asleep on the ancient sofa. She was going to have a crick in her neck, for certain.

"She needs guarding until Markova is out of the picture."

"Don't you mean until ROC is out of Silver Valley?" Josh took a wider perspective in his Trail Hiker responsibilities, not focused in on one target like Kyle had to be.

"No. I'd bet Markova hasn't told her superiors any- thing about the train track incident, or about the laptops, or her attempted break-in and murder last night. I have no doubt she would have killed Portia on the spot if she had a chance to." He relayed how he'd kept the weapon, and why he believed Portia was in mortal danger. "Markova's doing this on her own, and doesn't want anyone to think she's incompetent."

"Then if we're only worried about one potential murderer, Portia can stay safe with basic countermeasures."

"You mean on her own?" Kyle's insides became as twisted as the web of ROC crime that riddled central Pennsylvania. He knew what the protocol was for protecting innocent civilians. There wasn't much, actually, because the local LEAs were stretched too thin to provide personal security. And TH agents were operatives, not bodyguards. But Portia...

"You're doing it on the phone, man." Josh's voice in his ear yanked him out of the dank mental rabbit hole. "Portia's a big girl. If you want, I have an idea on where she can stay for the next week or two while we ramp up our efforts against ROC."

"Where's that?"

"I have a family friend who invested in a beautiful piece of property that's alongside the Appalachian Trail. Scenic views, privacy, an unexpected place for a town librarian. Anyway, they need someone to housesit while they're on an extended vacation down south. You know, away from this dang winter."

It had been brutally cold, but Kyle hadn't noticed it for the past few days. Not since his case had become so wrapped around Portia DiNapoli. He was in a world of trouble and he knew it. His attraction to her refused to listen to his best mental reasoning.

"The place is available right now?"

"Yes." Josh gave him the address. "Before you go there, bring Portia here so that we can tell her a little more about what she's up against. She can make her own decision about where to stay until we catch Markova and take down the crime ring."

"She'll think she can remain in her apartment." And he hated that she did.

"Not once we fill her in on more than what she read in the paper. The train tracks would be enough to scare away most people, but Portia's always had steel in her spine."

Kyle chuckled. "So I'm not the only one who's noticed it?"

"Hell no. When you meet Annie, ask her. She's known Portia just as long as I have. She'll fill you in."

Only after they'd agreed to talk in a bit and disconnected did Kyle realize he hadn't corrected Josh on his assumption that he'd be doing anything social in Silver Valley. He and Josh had struck up an easy friendship that wasn't just business, as they'd told one another a bit here and there about their personal lives. As a rule, Kyle kept to work and sleep for the entirety of a mission, only allowing himself a social outlet like grabbing a beer once his job was done and he'd left a place. That was fine when his residence had been in New York City and he'd taken shorter Trail Hiker assignments all over the globe as they came up. Trail Hikers paid lucratively and allowed him to enjoy New York when he wasn't on a mission, and kept a nice loft on the Lower East Side. But he'd been in Silver Valley for over a month, with no end in sight to the current op. And now he'd met Portia.

Was she the reason that he felt more at home in Silver Valley than any other place in over a decade? The last few days he'd tried to convince himself that Pennsylvania wasn't for him, but something had changed. The town made sense to him, and he was invested in getting ROC the hell out of it. Not in his usual way—he was an agent and of course wanted to protect innocent civilians wherever the job took him. But he'd inexplicably become more invested in Silver Valley.

*You're still going back to California.*

He was. His purchase of the small lot adjacent an almond orchard had been his way of promising himself there was more to life than his undercover work, in case he ever tired of it. As the years went by, he also came to the realization that agents couldn't keep up the pace of operations he had much past the age of thirty-five to forty. Sure, there were Trail Hiker and FBI agents twenty, twenty-five years his senior. But they mostly conceded the heavy physical demands of specific ops to the more junior agents. It was life.

And he loved it out west, he really did. Who would willingly accept these freakishly cold winters, the sticky humidity of the summer? Last summer he'd sworn to himself he'd not spend another hot August on the East Coast. Give him the dry air, sunny clime and endless beach of California any day.

Kyle walked out to his kitchen to brew a pot of coffee, but the scent of roasted beans hit him before he left his room. Portia stood in the kitchen, her hands wrapped around one of his mugs, a catlike grin on her face. Her hair tumbled around her scrubbed skin, still damp.

"You took a shower." He hadn't heard or noticed that while talking to Josh. Not very agent-like on his part.

"Good morning to you, too. Yes, I showered. And I'm afraid I used your extra towel—you only have what's in that tiny linen closet, I assume?"

"Yeah." He helped himself to coffee, ignored how she moved far out of his reach. He opened the refrigerator to find the creamer gone. He noticed she'd borrowed his robe, too. And fought the urge to tug at the belt around her waist, open the garment and gain access to her luscious breasts.

"Here you go." Portia held the plastic container out to him. "I wouldn't have pegged you for a chocolate-mint creamer dude."

He couldn't keep the grin off his face. "It was 75 percent off at the grocery. Left over from Christmas."

"You don't have to justify your sweet tooth to me, Agent King. Is that the right title for you?"

"Not at all. It's Kyle. Always." He faced her, allowed his first sip of coffee to be mixed with the delicious sight of Portia in his kitchen. Warmth pulsed through his chest, down his belly and right to his dick. He wanted to brush it away, tell himself that it was just a beautiful woman's effect on him. That it was merely the creamy skin of her cleavage, visible above the V of the robe, the tops of her breasts rounded and highly kissable. As were her mouth, her long throat. But it was *Portia's* energy that wrapped around him, made it feel as if she belonged in his kitchen. With him.

"Okay." She eyed him and he had the startling awareness that he was being studied in a way he knew too well. The same way he watched a criminal target.

He knew Portia wasn't a killer, but why was she looking at him as if she were going to take him out?

Portia had awakened to an ache in her neck from the rickety old sofa, but couldn't deny she'd had the most solid nine hours of sleep since she didn't know when. The blanket she'd tossed back was a clear sign that Kyle had made her comfortable before he left her alone to rest.

As she stared at him, her body so attuned to the sheer strength available in every inch of his frame, she acknowledged that her attraction to this man wasn't going away anytime soon. And that it might be more than a physical connection. Kyle was the first man she'd wanted to know all about, from what kind of kid he'd been to how many women he'd loved, in forever. But he saw her as a job, someone he had to protect.

"How long are you going to have to babysit me?"

His brows shot up. "Ah, that's an interesting question. I just got off the phone with Josh and we're coming up with a solution. You'll have a place to stay for the duration."

"Duration?" *Please don't let it affect the gala.*

"Two, three weeks. Maybe a month, but heaven help us all if it takes that long to drive these losers out of Silver Valley."

"The gala's in two weeks. I can't stop working on it, or miss it. It's taken a year to plan." She'd booked the new venue for this year's bigger, more lucrative fundraiser the week before last year's event.

"You can keep working on it from a distance. How much in-person time does a dance take?"

"It's not a 'dance.' It's the largest charity event in the

Susquehanna region, held right here in Silver Valley. We're expecting almost a thousand guests."

"Great. Among those hundreds of guests, there has to be at least a few people who could take over for you, help you out?"

"No. Not this late." She ran through the list of items yet to finish. It was always tight, this close. Organizing the silent auction items took her an entire weekend last year; this year's contributions were twice as valuable and numbered a third more. "There's a lot of coordination that happens last minute, too. I have to be on-site."

Kyle put his coffee mug down and she mentally smacked her forehead for even noticing the hair on his forearm, the size of his capable hands. Hands that had saved her yesterday, and that she wanted to find out more about. Like for instance, how they'd feel on her breasts, or pressing her buttocks as he brought her pelvis up against his.

She was in deep water with this man, and she'd only known his name since last night.

"Don't worry, Portia, you'll figure it all out. And if we're lucky, it won't be an issue—the case will be finished before you have to be more visible again." The conciliatory softness that played over his hard features made the tight ball of sexual awareness in her belly loosen and spread through her, across her breasts and down to the place between her legs that began to throb for him. Her rational mind didn't even bother trying to fight her want, her need.

When Portia became this mesmerized by a man, she rarely let it go. Not until she explored her desire, found out if it was passing or more substantial. And she'd never felt this strongly this quickly about any other man. Ever.

Mistaking her quiet stare for disagreement, he stepped toward her. "Seriously. It's not anything you can control, the hiding-out part. It's to keep you safe, and the resources we'd need to let you keep up your regular routine can go toward catching the bad guys. It'll work out, Portia."

"I know that. I'm fighting it, but you have to understand I only want what's best for Silver Valley." And she did. If half of what she'd read was true, then Kyle and Josh knew so much more.

The combination of feeling overwhelmed at having to do something she'd never done before, hiding out, and feeling that she somehow had a part in it because she'd stupidly chased the laptop thief instead of leaving it all to the police, wore her out. And made her push past her inhibitions. So what if she barely knew Kyle? They could both die at the hands of ROC, and would she want to die wondering what it would be like to be in this man's arms? To have him in hers?

"Portia..." Kyle spoke her name in a warning tone. His eyes shone bright silver even though the kitchen had light from only the stovetop light and the initial spill of dawn light that crept across the vintage linoleum.

"Don't you ever get tired of being the mysterious man behind the scenes of a case, Kyle?"

"There's nothing mysterious about my work." His breath hitched and she placed her hands on his chest, only his thin, long-sleeved T-shirt between her fingers and his steel-cut chest. His hands came up and wrapped around her wrists, but his touch was gentle, and he didn't try to stop her.

Portia stood on her tiptoes and moved until her face was a whisper from his, noses almost touching, mouths sinfully close. "Let me know you, Kyle. Remove a layer of your mystery for me."

Her excitement ratcheted and she gave him one heartbeat, two, certain he'd snap his agent face back in place and tell her to stop. Tell her that this was a bad idea, a "mistake."

When he didn't, Portia closed the tiny gap between them.

His lips were warm, supple, firm, and Kyle only held back for a nanosecond before he let go of her wrists and buried his hands in her hair, held her face at the perfect angle to allow them to deepen the kiss. She teased the outside of his lips with hers, loving how he let her take the lead while fully responding to every lick and nibble. When his tongue came out to greet hers, she caved and fully opened her mouth, needing him to explore her, too.

Kyle didn't disappoint as he kissed her, tasted her, plunged into every nook of her mouth. It was more than she could have fantasized, the pure, sexual power of their embrace. Portia's hands gripped his T-shirt, but when that wasn't enough, she reached up and clung to his neck, pulling his head down closer.

The kiss lasted minutes but Portia wasn't fooled. This kiss, this intimacy with the man she barely knew, had life-changing abilities. No one had ever kissed her so thoroughly, had turned her on so quickly and intensely that she wouldn't have fought it if Kyle suggested they take it back to his bedroom. Or on the counter.

He lifted his head and she couldn't stop the protest that her voice emitted, a high-pitched cry that left nothing to his imagination, she was certain.

"Portia." His ragged breathing only served to stoke her desire, make her hotter than she'd thought possible. But she remembered his words from inside the truck last night and pulled back, put her hands on his chest again and gently pushed him away.

"Do you still think I'm a mistake, Kyle?"

"You're not a mistake, Portia." He held her, reluctant to let her go, to end this but the only way it would go was problematic for both of them. Her eyes were half lidded, their brown depths willing him back into the warmth of what pulsed between them. Besides his erection. He placed his hands on her shoulders and took a half step back, needing the space to think. "It's what we'll have to face after we take this to the most obvious, and yeah, hot as hell conclusion."

"You're leaving Silver Valley after the ROC mission is over." Her small white teeth peeked out as she gnawed on her lower lip, still swollen from their kissing. "We're both adults, we know where we stand."

"Babe, I want to agree with you. You know I do." He grasped her hand and placed it on his erection, needing her to know he wasn't coming from a place of intellect. He cared about Portia. Too much for someone he'd only just kissed.

"Kyle!" Her breath caught in a sexy growl and she closed her hand around him through his jeans but he pulled away then.

"We've got something that doesn't come along every day, Portia, but we won't have anything if you get killed because of being involved with me. Or if I get taken out, how would you feel? Isn't it better to stop it before we get in too deep?"

She smiled softly and shook her head. "It's funny— just two days ago I would be the one saying this to you. But after coming so close to dying, after seeing what kind of work you do, even just this little glimpse of it, I think I've changed my mind."

"How so?"

"I think that life is short, and sometimes it's the best thing ever to just go for it. To not overthink things so much, to enjoy life one day at a time. Not worry about the future."

Her words were balm to him, and he didn't disagree. But it didn't change the fact that he had to keep her safe and take out Markova. No short order.

"Tell you what, Portia. Let's table this discussion for now. I've got to get you to the safe house and I have a lot of intel data to analyze."

She watched him and his respect deepened for her as she stood her ground, didn't try to convince him to go to bed with her now. As if she, too, knew that sometimes the deepest needs had to wait.

"Then let's get the day going. I want to be a help to this case, not your worry."

He turned to place his laptop and phone in his bag, and heard her feet walk back to the bathroom where he assumed she was getting dressed. This was another first for him. Making the adult decision he loathed, turning away from what he knew would be an explosive union with Portia.

Comfort washed over him and at first he didn't recognize the emotion. Until he heard Portia humming as she dressed behind the closed bathroom door.

Hope. He had hope that somehow, someway, things might take a very good turn with Portia.

# Chapter 8

Kyle and Portia didn't waste any more time alone in his apartment. As soon as she was dressed and had her few items in a bag, they left. It wasn't just his desire to be alone with Portia that gave him a sense of urgency, either. He never forgot that Portia had a huge target on her back. As sure as he was they hadn't been followed, and despite the high level of technological security he'd wired the place with, Markova wouldn't give up until she found Portia and divested herself of her witness.

"I don't see what going into SVPD is going to accomplish." Portia argued with him, but she didn't fight getting back into the truck, once he cleared the parking area and surroundings.

"We'll talk to Josh and see where you can stay for the time being."

"Why Josh?"

Kyle gritted his teeth. "He's my point of contact for this case. And without getting into it, you absolutely cannot talk to anyone else about this, Portia." He trusted Josh to reiterate the warning. And yet he also hated that he had to talk in work terms with her at all. This was hard—doing his job with a woman he was more attracted to than anyone else.

"I understand the need for confidentiality. But that doesn't extend to me. I'm the one someone wants to kill!"

He looked over at her after he parked at the police station. While she appeared calm and all together, he knew this was incredibly difficult for her. It would be for anyone, even a tough-as-nails woman like Portia. Her cries during the nightmare had wrenched him awake.

"That's why we're here. You're safe, and I'm going to keep it that way." He waited for her beautiful brown eyes to meet his, to see his sincerity. She managed a smile.

"I know. And I'm sorry, Kyle. I'm being a brat because, well, because I'm sexually frustrated." She let out a self-deprecating laugh. "And that's not something I'd normally admit to anyone!"

He reached over and squeezed her thigh, a friendly reassurance to hopefully break the tension between them. He didn't expect her to cover his hand with hers. The warmth of the skin-on-skin contact stilled him as heat rushed straight to his groin.

When was he going to learn to be extra careful around Portia? The woman wasn't just another civilian witness to protect, nor a casual friend. They had a deeper connection that he couldn't screw around with.

"Kyle." She swallowed, licked her lips. Both signs of nervousness, yet all he paid attention to was how ruby-red her lips were and the fullness of the lower lip. The memory of their kiss seared right through to his dick and he had to make an effort not to groan. In the police station parking lot, no less. Where was his professional bearing?

Right where he'd left it the minute he'd noticed Portia as more than the Silver Valley librarian.

"Kyle." She pressed her other hand under his, gave him an answering squeeze. "Thank you. And if you're anything like me, you're wondering why you're not being totally all about business around me. I'm wondering it, too. I don't usually kiss a guy I hardly know, and I'm not used to such a strong attraction dropping in on me out of the blue." She lifted his hand to her mouth and kissed it. "You're a good man, and I trust your law enforcement instincts. As much as it kills me to say it, if you think I need to disappear from town for a bit, then I do. As long as I can keep working on the gala from a distance. I'll be able to use the internet, I hope."

He stared at her, momentarily stunned into silence. He was darn sure Portia had never been through a clandestine op, had probably never had the occasion to fire a weapon, unless she hunted like many folks in this part of the country did. She was an innocent to the different circles of hell his line of work provided him with on a daily basis. And yet, she'd been the one to step up and call whatever was going on between them what it was. No denial, no hiding it like so many others would.

It made him all the more committed to her. To protecting her, from Markova, yes, but also from himself.

"Portia, you have more balls than a lot of the agents

I work with, and let me tell you, there's no one stronger than an undercover agent most days."

She grinned. "I'm a bit of a control freak, I'll admit. I love the organizational side of library science, and it spills over into my personal life. I've had some…some betrayals and unexpected difficulties with men in the past. I find it preferable to be open right from the get-go, don't you?"

"Whatever you say." He leaned over and kissed her firmly on the lips, a seal of his intent to keep her safe. "Let's get inside."

"I don't need counseling," Portia grumbled at her best friend, who happened to be a police psychologist. Annie Fiero worked for SVPD and also did contract work for other law enforcement agencies.

Annie was at the station when she and Kyle had arrived.

They sat in the nicer waiting area of the police station, reserved for interviewing victims. "And I wasn't a victim." She refused to wear that mantle. Sure, she'd been shoved by the laptop thief, but she'd been on the railroad tracks due to her own decisions. And the almost-attack last night at the homeless shelter was something she didn't want to think about.

"I haven't said a thing." Annie handed her a paper cup from the specialty coffee shop downtown, and Portia bit back the instinct to tell her she'd spent the last night sleeping over it. "I got you a London Fog. The stuff they have here in the station is swill."

"So you knew I was coming back in."

"Of course. I happen to be engaged to one of the men in charge of this portion of the case."

Portia gratefully accepted the drink, her favorite. As Annie knew. "Thanks." She sipped, the warm smoothness of the vanilla flavor mixing with the bergamot and immediately calming her. "This is my go-to comfort drink."

"I know. And before I forget, I brought in a few changes of clothes for you, along with your laptop. It's all in Josh's office."

"Thanks."

"Anytime." Annie smiled, eased back into the easy chair across from the one Portia perched on. "Josh says you came close to getting hit by the train yesterday, and then at the shelter last night you could have been killed. I'm so glad Kyle was there."

"How do you know him?" Was she the last person to meet the sexiest man she'd ever seen walk the streets of Silver Valley? And the most mysterious, at least to her.

Annie's expression faltered, became guarded. "He's a work colleague of Josh's."

"You can quit with the 'it's police business' attitude. It's okay if you can't tell me." She put her cup down so that she could slide back in the chair, just as Annie had. As soon as she did, she realized how tired she felt. It had been a long morning. The time with Kyle this morning had been glorious, if not totally what she wanted. She wanted to have Kyle in every way possible, but not at the expense of his job or this case. When they came together, if they did, she wanted it to be without the weight of worry she saw in his eyes whenever he mentioned the risks to her.

"I'm not pulling the 'it's classified' routine. But some cases are tougher than others, and this one is the mother of all cases Josh has ever worked on, from what I can tell."

"I'm glad you're working at SVPD now. It means a lot to have you here this morning. It's been a rough day or so. How's the yarn shop?" Annie had taken over her grandmother's small business when the woman had suffered a stroke this past summer. Ezzie had returned and ran her shop again but Annie helped her grandmother in between fulfilling contracts for SVPD as a police psychologist. She'd worked for NYPD for several years before coming back to Silver Valley when Ezzie had her stroke. While working the yarn shop's register, Annie had encountered a woman she'd suspected had been a victim of domestic violence, so she reported it to Detective Josh Avery, now her fiancé.

"Grandma Ezzie is doing fine with the new shopkeepers I hired for her. I'm actually here full-time now, with the recent uptick in investigations."

"The ROC stuff, you mean."

"How much do you know about ROC? We've only talked about it in terms of when Lani OD'd, with the heroin distribution network."

"I read the paper. Everyone knows about it unless they're living with blinders." She couldn't stop the shudder that rolled over her. "What the heck is happening, Annie? Where is the Silver Valley you, Josh and I grew up in?"

"It's still here." Annie leaned forward. "And look, so are we. We're stronger than any group of criminals."

"I don't know. Tell that to Lani's family."

A cloud passed over Annie's expression, the same darkness Portia fought hard to avoid whenever she thought of Lani. They'd lost a few other high school classmates already, to car accidents or premature disease. But to lose one to a heroin epidemic hit her harder. Mostly because she felt it could have been prevented.

"It's tough, as we still don't have answers as to where the fentanyl came from." Annie looked at her. "I don't want to talk about that right now, Portia. I want to know how you're doing, really."

Portia took in a deep breath, held it, forcefully exhaled. "I'm okay. It's probably not totally hit me yet, but I'll get through this."

"You will." Annie looked thoughtful, though, and Portia couldn't help wonder what she knew that she wasn't sharing.

"What's going on, Annie?"

"Nothing more than the usual, since ROC came to town. I want you to know that SVPD will do everything to keep you safe. I'll do whatever it takes to protect you."

"That's quite all right. I've seemed to have made a friend out of someone I've never met before."

"Kyle."

"Yes."

She'd known Annie since they were in second grade, and she knew her friend's moods. Something was on Annie's mind, but she wasn't going to give it up.

And as emotionally spent as she felt, Portia gained tremendous strength from being with her dear friend. And Kyle—Kyle's presence had kept her sane through life threatening circumstances.

"You don't have to say anything, Portia. I see it on your face."

"What's that?"

"You've got a crush on your protector."

"You know me well, but not as much as you think. Yes, there's something there, but it's not a crush, Annie. This is big. I've just been through so much that I don't want to mistake extreme gratitude for...for..." She didn't know what to name it.

"You don't have to do anything but focus on today, Portia. My only suggestion is that you don't let the fact you've known him such a short time prevent you from exploring your feelings. I knew Josh for forever, but when the time was right, our relationship took off and well, you know what happened."

"I do." Annie and Josh were as deeply dedicated to one another as long-married couples, and they'd only been together for the last half year or so.

Could Portia even wish for what her friend had, with a man she'd only just met?

Portia's head swam from all that had transpired but was surprised to find she felt comfortable in Josh's office at SVPD for the second time in twenty-four hours. She couldn't ignore that it no doubt had a lot to do with having Kyle at her side.

"Hello again, Portia." Josh handed her the large laptop bag and purse. "Annie got these for you. She went to your apartment and added more clothes, stuff from your bathroom. I'm sorry you're dealing with more than just a random library-computer theft. Kyle's informed you that it's best that you don't go back to your apartment or the library for a week or two?" Josh looked from her to Kyle as if trying to figure out the extent of what they'd talked about.

"I told her that you and I were coming up with a plan." Kyle looked up from his phone; he'd been texting someone. Portia realized she'd never wondered if he was single, available. She'd let her desire carry her away, because she'd wanted to believe kissing Kyle was a good option. Hadn't she learned from Robert that powerful men rarely had anything less than a bevy of women on their heels? Yet Kyle hadn't struck her as being involved with someone else. He was too focused on her whenever their eyes met. As if she were the only woman he'd ever seen. A delicious feeling, actually.

"Did Kyle mention the house?"

"What house?" She shook herself out of her Kyle daze. "Is it in Silver Valley?"

"On the outskirts. It's a friend of my family's place. They're wintering in Florida, and they've left the keys with me. Annie and I have used it as a getaway from time to time, and I check it out regularly to make sure it's secure. It's up behind its own gated fence, right past the walk-on for the Appalachian Trail."

Portia knew the area and had a friend or two who'd bought land there once they married and decided to start a family. "Sounds beautiful. And very boring."

Kyle's laugh made her jump. "You work in a library. Don't you appreciate a more serene space?"

"Don't mistake quiet for uneventful. The library is anything but peaceful. Recent events notwithstanding, our daily foot traffic is enough to rival any local retail shop. Inquiries about the town and local area are constant, and it's a rare day that I can close up on time." She shifted in the utilitarian SVPD chair. "I could easily rent a house, or own one, for the price I pay for my apartment in town. Silver Valley's not huge like New York City, of course. But I can walk to wherever I need to go, whenever. The part of town Josh is talking about requires a car and I have to plan for an hour round-trip for any errands. It's a full twenty-five minutes just to the grocery store from there."

"Which makes it the perfect place to keep you out of trouble." Kyle looked up from his phone and she allowed the shock of his silver eyes to shoot through her, swirl around in her belly and branch out to every inch of her. "Safety is the priority, Portia."

Josh cleared his throat. "It won't be for long, Portia. Kyle's an expert at what he does and he'll have this case wrapped up in no time."

Kyle remained silent, but she sensed communication between them.

"At the risk of being told I can't know, what exactly is Kyle's job?" She looked at Kyle the entire time.

"Glad you asked. We're going to head over to the conference room about now, and fill you in on some basics. You have a right to know who is protecting you, and for the sake of our operation against ROC, you'll benefit from some background."

Kyle looked up from his texting to respond. "She'll be here in two."

Josh nodded and stood up, indicating that Portia and Kyle should do the same. "Great. Shall we?"

Portia followed the two men out of the small office, down the corridor and into the conference room. She saw a tall, salt-and-pepper-haired man waiting for them at the head of the table. He was in civilian clothes, but with a weapon holstered at his waist.

"Chief," Josh called, and then turned back to usher Portia into the room. "This is Portia DiNapoli, our town librarian."

"Good morning, Portia. Colt Todd." He held his hand out and she shook it.

"Good morning, Chief. We've met several times, at the annual fund-raising gala."

He nodded. "Yes, we have."

Portia waited for him to say more, but he looked past her, toward the door, and his interest was riveted.

"Hello, everybody. Kyle, Josh, Colt." A woman with silver hair in a chic bob strode into the room with a combination of strength and grace that Portia immediately liked. And she was vaguely familiar. Hadn't Portia seen her with SVPD Chief Colt Todd at last year's gala? There'd been hundreds of attendees, so her memory could be faulty. Her laser-focused blue gaze landed on Portia.

"You must be Portia." Everything about this woman screamed total expert, in whatever she did. Confidence and comfort in her own skin radiated from her. "I'm Claudia Michele."

They shook hands, and everyone took seats at the glossy wood table. Portia had been to enough library conferences, book conventions and other business events to know when it was her place to listen and learn.

"We've asked Claudia to come into the station to help explain a different part of the case that you won't read about in the paper," Kyle said quietly. "Claudia's my boss, by the way."

Claudia nodded. "I run a special type of classified law enforcement agency that employs people from all over the world to take on the most difficult cases. We don't take the place of local or even federal law enforcement, but we get in and help where it's challenging, or even impossible, for local LEAs to operate."

"Like CIA and FBI?" Portia didn't want to appear too green in this world she knew nothing about.

Claudia shook her head. "No, not at all. We're more under the radar than either of those agencies, believe it or not." She motioned with her head at Kyle. "Take Kyle. He and I share that we're Marine Corps veterans, and we used what we learned in the military to become fully employed as undercover agents. I don't personally work many cases, as my job is to keep the entire team at my agency running, but I've worked alongside a good number of our agents."

"I'm here to help with ROC's heroin operation in Silver Valley. To infiltrate it and destroy it." Kyle commanded the attention of everyone in the room with his steady, quiet words. "You've gotten caught up in it, unfortunately. Normally we do everything to engage a criminal away from civilians, but it's impossible with the heroin scourge. It's in every city and small town across America."

"It's been all-consuming," Claudia added. "Kyle's worked the ROC crimes that have hit the East Coast especially hard, but when we figured out that ROC was using Silver Valley as its central drug distribution hub, I brought him here."

"I was working out of New York City for the past eight years, ever since I joined." Kyle's expression remained impassive, but in his eyes she saw a flash of concern. Did she imagine it or was Kyle trying to tell her something? "I've been living in Silver Valley, posing as various persons, for the last few months."

"So that's why I didn't immediately recognize you on the train tracks."

His grin broke through. "Off the tracks, and yes."

Heat rushed to her face, not just from his smile. From remembering how close she'd come to losing it all yesterday.

"We're sorry you had to go through that, Portia." Claudia looked at Colt Todd.

"Yes, we're very grateful to Kyle for being there and stepping up. But it's imperative that you understand we don't want you engaging any suspect again until we close this case." Chief Todd's concern was etched in the lines between his brows. "And since I don't have enough officers to spare one for guard duty, we're asking you to lie low for a bit. I'll make sure your paycheck isn't affected, of course."

"Thank you. And I promise I'm not going to give you any trouble—I want to help any way that I can. But I do have to do my work with the gala. Its success this year is more important than ever, with our public funding being slashed every which way. And I'm hoping to earn a nice gift for the homeless mission, too."

"Certainly you can keep working on the gala. We'll provide you with the proper security equipment to scramble your Wi-Fi and internet footprints. I have a special interest in your charity work, as Colt and I enjoyed the gala so much last year." Portia remembered the couple, how attune to one another they'd been. As they were now, but it simmered under their professional demeanors. She wondered at their history, but it wasn't the time to ask.

"Kyle mentioned this could take several more weeks. Can you give me any better idea of the timeline?"

"Annie asks me that all the time about my cases," Josh said. "As with any case, especially undercover, we can't be definitive about how long it'll take. I'm sorry, Portia. One bright spot is that you'll continue to receive your salary. We had the approval signed by a county representative, because you need police protection."

"Rest assured we're working to come up with a solution as quickly as possible." Claudia nodded to Kyle. "Did you bring the nondisclosure forms?"

"Here you go." Kyle slid a folder across the table, toward Portia. "It's up to you, but if you'd like to know a little more about who I'm working for, you need to sign the agreement."

"It's not just for your edification. What we do is need-to-know, but also, Portia, we may ask you for more insight as to how your library works, how you store the laptops, how you maintain your inventory for all your technology."

"Will I get a chance to do any of the surveillance with Kyle?" She felt Kyle's glare and ignored it. Of course he wouldn't want her anywhere near him while he worked. He was a protector, through and through.

Claudia smiled. "No, I can't promise that. Why don't you read over the paperwork and then decide how much you want to know?"

The room grew quiet, but then the three others struck up a low conversation as Portia read over the agreement. It stated she'd never reveal anything she learned from TH, Inc. That had to be the agency Kyle worked for. The one Claudia ran. She signed where appropriate, and the chief witnessed it.

"Okay, so now to put us on the same page, Kyle, Josh, Colt and I all work for Trail Hikers. That's the

TH you see on the document." Claudia went on to explain that the shadow government agency was responsible, behind the scenes, for helping law enforcement agencies at home in the US and abroad. Claudia was a retired Marine Corps General, and she'd taken on the agency right after leaving military service.

"Are all TH agents former military?"

"No, but it's a natural transition, especially for special operatives like SEALs and, of course, intelligence specialists. For every undercover agent working the field, we have at least a dozen personnel working intelligence analysis, communications technology, administrative duties to include travel schedules and logistics, and counterintelligence."

At Portia's blank look, Claudia smiled. "We have a team making sure no one figures out who we are and what we're doing here in Silver Valley. We adopted the name Trail Hikers to fit in with the Appalachian Trail, of course."

"Thank you for the explanation." Portia felt a little bit shaky. She didn't regret signing the papers and finding out more, and she wanted to do whatever she could to help bring ROC down. But it was sobering to realize what was required to keep a country, a state or a town safe. "And thank all of you for doing what you do. I had no idea, beyond what I read online, in papers and in other news sources." She looked them each in the eye, made sure they knew she wasn't speaking platitudes.

"Thank you, Portia. Do you have any questions for us?" Claudia looked ready to go and Portia couldn't imagine how full the woman's schedule was. Unlike running a library, Claudia's job involved life-and-death situations.

"Not a question, but a commitment. I'll stay at the house you've got for me for as long as it takes." She mentally squeezed her eyes shut against the risk to the gala, to her job. The safety of Silver Valley was paramount. "And if you need me to do anything that would help you catch the woman after me, or anyone else, you can count on me."

"Civilians don't participate in law enforcement operations." Kyle's stern admonition sliced across the, until now, cordial ambience. "Stay in the house and you'll be doing your part."

"Thank you for bringing that up, Kyle," Claudia said. "I wanted to point out that it would be most beneficial for you to check in on Portia from time to time. You've got the most expertise with the case, you know how to make sure you're not being trailed and Portia knows you."

Portia's insides immediately froze and flamed hot. What was she getting herself into?

# *Chapter 9*

"I don't like that I won't have my own vehicle to get away in." Portia knew she sounded like a broken record, but it felt good to express her opinion. Not that it was going to change her situation.

"I wouldn't like that, either." Kyle drew to a stop at a traffic light. They were in a nondescript, unmarked police car, to keep Portia's movements under wraps. Kyle had explained that switching up vehicles kept the bad guys guessing. She knew that Kyle must have to keep a low profile, too, but didn't ask him about it. She got it—some of his and Josh's work wasn't any of her business.

Except when it was. "So I'm supposed to hang out with no contact with the outside world until you catch the woman who wants to kill me?"

"Pretty much." They crossed the Interstate 81 overpass and sped into what Portia thought of as the rural part of Silver Valley. Away from the town proper and the main commercial highway that ran around it, they entered the more mountainous, wooded area of the town's outer limits.

"How much longer?" She hadn't paid too much attention when Kyle asked Josh more specific questions about the house. It was hard to imagine she was being plucked from her normally independent life and had to basically hole up like a doomsdayer for the next several days, if not weeks.

"You said you knew the area." Kyle was being very short, deliberate in his words. She didn't like it. She wanted him to bare at least a tiny bit of his soul to her.

"I do, but you have the GPS on it." She took a deep breath as if she were about to plunge into the icy Susquehanna. "Why don't you tell me a little bit about yourself, Kyle?"

Kyle almost swerved the dang car as Portia's request hit him right where he knew she wanted it to. In his soft spot, which was expanding at an alarming rate since he'd met her.

Hell, since he'd first laid eyes on her over a month ago.

"There's not a lot to know."

"Are you going to make me ask it all? Where are you from?" She sounded genuinely interested. When was the last time anyone asked him about himself? Other than for a security clearance?

"I was born and raised in Northern California. My family owned almond farms." Still did, but his dad was getting ready to sell them off, unless he or his brother stepped up to do it. "It was a great way to burn off steam as a kid, helping Dad out during harvest. I knew I wanted to join the Marines from the time I was in high school."

"Your family supported you doing that?"

"Yeah. Not right at first—my mother was freaked out, with the war in full swing after Nine Eleven. But both she and Dad understood my desire to serve. And it provided me with the means to an education, which I got after I left active duty."

"Where did you go to school?"

He looked at her. Yup, big brown eyes soaked up each drop of what he said, as if it mattered to her.

"Boston College."

"Really? I thought you'd go back to the West Coast. To be near your family."

"I got a great deal from the college, scholarship-wise. They matched my GI Bill benefits." The Yellow Ribbon Program had been a godsend, allowing him to go to a top-notch school. By then he'd been tapped by Trail Hikers and knew what his options were after he earned his degree. "What about you, Portia?"

"Nothing nearly as exciting, trust me. I went away to school, but 'away' for me was Penn State, only two hours from here. It was good, though, to have that time out of Silver Valley."

"Did you ever consider living anywhere else?"

"No. This area's in my blood." She gazed out the window and he wanted to watch her expression all day. Except he was driving and didn't think she'd appreciate him running them off the road.

"Have you traveled a lot?"

"Yes. My parents were big on the National Park

scene and took us to many of them each summer, usually for a good week or two. My mother is still a teacher, and has the whole summer off. Dad works for the state, in Harrisburg, so he gets a decent vacation, too."

"We couldn't take off on vacations with the farm to worry about. But we did day trips, especially in winter. Lake Tahoe's only a few hours away from where I grew up, so we went skiing regularly."

"You sound like you miss it."

"I do. As a matter of fact, after this case is solved, I'm taking a month's leave back at home."

"Will you ever move back?"

"That's the plan. Claudia is okay with me moving my home base out west. It'll open me up for assignments not only there but in Asia." It'd be great for his resume, whether he stayed with Trail Hikers for the time being or decided to leave law enforcement.

"So you can retire from the agency, have a pension?" Spoken like a local librarian. Lifelong security would be her primary concern, and he understood it perfectly. He'd had the same questions when he'd joined the Marines.

"Yes. My time in the Marine Corps gets tacked on, too, so I only need sixteen years with Trail Hikers, and I'm at seven now. It's a good option, but part of me would love to start a private investigative firm."

"In California."

"Yes." He didn't want to talk about himself one second more. He'd had a mental safe spot to retreat to these past years, and it'd always been California. He didn't see himself taking over the almond farm, but he'd happily support his brother in doing so. And he'd also enjoy building his own home and office on a portion of his family property. It'd had been his parents' dream when they'd sunk all they owned into the prime real estate, which had exponentially increased in value over the years.

"Here we go." He turned into an asphalt-paved drive, more like a tiny country road. It shot straight back to a copse of evergreens, obscuring anything beyond it from the main road. Only after they'd driven under about a half mile of oak and maple trees did the house come into view.

"Wow." Portia's word hung between them, expressing his reaction, too.

The house looked like a modest A-frame at first glance, albeit huge with an extensive wraparound porch with railings heavily crusted with several inches of icy snow. As his vehicle neared the building, two additional wings emerged, slung low on either side of the main house. He had a twinge of longing in his gut. It reminded him of the mountains surrounding Lake Tahoe, of the ski chalets school friends escaped to during winter break.

He pulled up to the garage door and killed the engine. "I need to do a thorough walk-about. Let's get inside and figure out whatever you need to know to live here."

She laughed. "I think I can manage that on my own, Kyle." The wariness in her eyes didn't match the curve of her lips, though. Had he said something that bothered her, with all his talk of California? The life of a farmer wasn't luxurious, but his family had always thrived. Maybe hers had struggled at times?

"Yes, but you need to learn the first lesson of a good

law enforcement op. Trading information. You know a lot about me now. I still don't even know what you do on a daily basis."

"Oh." Her lips, slightly parted, created a cold-air balloon with her breath.

"Come on, let's get inside. It's freezing out here."

The warm golden hues in exposed wood beams were welcoming and soothing to the eye. Granite and stainless steel stamped the kitchen with a gourmet feel, and the river-stone hearth beckoned for a night of reading while sipping hot chocolate or a hot toddy. Portia appreciated the contemporary sensibilities in the otherwise cozy, traditional home.

But what won her over were the views. Each and every room of the house seemed to have a view of the surrounding hills and rolling mountains that provided the footbed of the Appalachian Trail.

They stopped in the kitchen and she put her purse and laptop on the expansive counter. "I don't think I ever thanked Josh for taking Annie to get this back to me, or for the extra clothes."

"You've had a lot on your mind." He walked up to her and the spacious room morphed to the inches between them. Cool gray eyes appraised her and it was as if this man, a mere stranger only a day ago, read her better than she'd ever done her favorite Dickens stories. "You keep saying you're fine, Portia, but trust me. I've got years of the kind of day you had yesterday behind me, and it was a long day for me. It'd be completely normal for you to think you're losing it a little bit. Or to feel frightened."

She blinked, but didn't break his eye contact. "I

admit I was shaky yesterday, but this…this feels better." She meant the house, the sense of security being away from where the woman had tried to kill her—twice—or knowing that SVPD—no, Kyle—was looking out for her; all of these things made her anxiety melt away. But it'd be a lie. She felt better because Kyle was here. Still.

*He's going back to California eventually.*

So what? She didn't want anything lasting. Not after the Robert mess. And wasn't it healthy to connect with someone on a sexual level, after such life-threatening events?

"You've got that look again, Portia." The white gleam of his grin told her he was on the same frequency. Which sent thrills from her skin to her deepest, most intimate parts.

"What look?" Her voice sounded breathy and begging for his kiss again, at least to her ears.

He leaned over and stroked her cheek, his finger tracing an electric trail from her cheekbone to her earlobe. Then he moved his hand to her nape. "Like you want to kiss me again."

"I—"

"Do you?"

"Yes."

"You've got to know that I'm a full-partnership kind of guy, Portia. Since you kissed me last time, it's my turn to kiss you."

"Aren't we kissing each other?" she said in a whisper, as she watched his mouth move around his words, saw the flick of his tongue against his teeth. Her knees were wobbly, sure, but it was the insistent hot pulse between her legs that shook her. She'd do anything this man let her, allow him to do whatever he wanted. Portia wanted Kyle as she'd never wanted another man. It didn't make sense; she barely knew him—

His fingers touched her temple. "Stop, Portia. You're thinking too much. If either of us stops to think this out, take it to its logical conclusion, we're going to miss out."

"Yes." Her lips throbbed, too, wanting this kiss to start so that it could never end.

"I'm going to kiss you now, Portia. Is that okay?" His breath warmed her face, and she loved the intimacy of his scent mingling with cinnamon and maybe a linger of the morning's coffee. Other than his hand on her neck, they weren't touching. She swayed and her pelvis moved with her, needing to know if he was as turned on as she.

"Stop talking, Kyle."

His chuckle was the last thing she heard before he hauled her against him, grabbed her ass and held her as he pressed his erection—his wonderfully hard and straining erection—into her heat. Layers of clothes didn't prevent the shock of it from reverberating through her, making her toes clench and unclench in her boots. Her arms went around his neck as his mouth covered hers and sensation assaulted her, blowing away any concerns she had about this being a short-term affair. Any affair with Kyle would be welcome and, in her current state, medically necessary. Because as they kissed, as their tongues stroked, their mouths sucked, their hands explored, Portia felt what she hadn't since before she'd become an ROC target, since before she'd met and been used by Robert.

Portia felt alive. Kyle's touch reminded her that

she loved life, and couldn't wait to see what each day brought.

Today, it handed her Kyle.

Kyle never mixed sex and work. It was a bad combo, not only because of the risk of missing a danger signal but also because emotions ran rampant during a high-stake mission. He'd always preferred to keep his personal commitments completely separate from his duty, which meant he had long-term relationships with women he rarely saw. Since that got old, he'd let go of even trying to form more than a brief sexual bond when opportunity arose.

Portia was different. This wouldn't be just sex and he knew it. He also knew that he'd told her he was leaving after he brought ROC down, going back to California, where he'd pick up the rest of his life.

She'd made it clear she was a Pennsylvania woman, highly educated and well-traveled, at least within North America, but not interested in going anywhere else permanently. Silver Valley was Portia's home, as the tree-nut farms of Northern California were his.

Her kiss was magic, no other word for it. He'd been hard for her all morning, but when she'd turned and looked at him in the kitchen, he'd been unable to maintain his professional demeanor.

"Kyle." She spoke against his mouth as he moved his hand to between her legs, cupped her, intimated with a wiggle of his fingers what he wanted to do once he got her skirt and panties off. Would she even wear panties, or was it a thong, a G-string? He pressed his forehead against hers. He needed oxygen.

"If we keep doing this, Portia, I need all of you. It's been a while, and—"

She silenced him by licking around his lips with her hot, furtive tongue. He wanted to know what it'd feel like on his dick, how she'd take him in her mouth and use it to bring him to full release. When she reached down and stroked him through his jeans, he felt like he was fifteen again and ready to lose it before they even got started. He wrenched his mouth from hers.

"Now, Portia. Here."

"We need a condom." She turned in his arms and grabbed her purse, unzipped it.

He reached into his jacket inside pocket and pulled out the strip of condoms he'd taken from his medicine chest this morning. As much as he'd berated himself for even contemplating involving Portia in his frenetic life, he felt nothing but gratitude.

"Here," they both said at the same time, as she held up a similar strip of protection. Their eyes met and the heat between them evaporated into gales of laughter.

"When did you have time to get condoms?" He hadn't seen her leave his place, but she could have, when he was in the shower. The drugstore was a two-minute walk, tops, from his apartment building.

"After yesterday, at the tracks." Her already flushed face turned a deep crimson. Something warred in her eyes, as if she were on the verge of telling him her deepest secret. "I haven't been held like that, like when you saved my life, in a long time. Maybe forever. It got me thinking that I've been a bit of a…a recluse for too long. It's my way of being prepared, of making an affirmative step toward the life I want."

When her lips formed the word *want*, humor left as

quickly as it'd appeared, and he was a lightning rod full of charged particles—for Portia. All he saw, all he felt, all he wanted was Portia. To be with her, inside her, moving her toward the enjoyment he longed to see her experience.

The insistence of Kyle's lips on hers, the way his fingers dug into her just a bit beyond sexual need, let her know that his desire ran as deep as hers. It wasn't a time for anything but enjoying the present moment with him. They both knew it could end at any second.

The strips of condoms made soft splats as they hit the counter and floor, but not before Kyle had torn off one.

"Do you want to go to a…bedroom?" She didn't know the house, didn't personally care where they came together. All she wanted was him, wherever.

"What do you want?" he asked against her mouth before dragging his to her throat, his hands adeptly circling her waist and lifting her onto the island. "Tell me, Portia."

But she couldn't speak as his hand unzipped her coat and he helped her get her arms out of the sleeves. He shrugged out of his parka, too, and let it drop to the floor. Struck by the urgency of the moment, Portia raised her sweater and shirt over her head, throwing them onto the counter. Clad in only her bra and skirt, she still felt overdressed. She wanted to be skin-on-skin with Kyle.

"You're stunning." His eyes glittered with promise as he looked at her breasts, which spilled over her lacy pink demi-cup bra. He lowered his head and trailed his tongue along the plump skin, the moist heat of him hardening her nipples and making her squirm with desire on the counter. She wanted his tongue everywhere at once—in her mouth, on her breasts, between her legs.

His chuckle vibrated against her and he expertly undid her bra clasp with one hand, while the other gently pinched her nipple. Portia thought she was going to climax on the spot.

"Kyle!" She reached down, trying to get to his belt, but he leaned back, laughed again.

"Patience." As she watched, he unbuckled his belt and shoved out of his pants and underwear in one move. He still wore a button-down shirt and she went to work on unfastening it. Kyle took advantage of her busy fingers to gently blow in her ear, nibble at her lobe.

As soon as his shirtfront was open, he helped by getting out of it and then lifting his undershirt over his head. Portia greedily watched him, saw how his pecs flexed under smooth skin. She leaned over and sucked his nipple into her mouth, but his skin was so taut, he was so chiseled, that it wasn't much more than a nip. But it was enough to make him hiss, and she smiled as he gripped her head and tugged until her mouth was accessible.

This time the kiss wasn't tentative or an invitation. It was full-on passion, with intent to take it as far as they could. When he hauled her up against him, holding her legs, her breasts flattened against his chest, Portia's skin blazed as if he'd touched her everywhere. She linked her feet over his ass and reveled in the erotic sensations that rocked her. Their kiss was a whirl of tongues and gasps and tiny bites and more. It was a promise, a vow that this would be the hottest sex of her life.

Still holding her against him, her arms around his neck, Kyle walked them to the sofa in front of the fireplace and bank of windows that overlooked the rolling Appalachian Mountains. She'd have plenty of time to take in the view in the countless hours and days alone she knew she faced. Right now, she had Kyle and he was all she wanted.

He knelt next to the sofa and set her down. Anticipating their union, she moved to grasp his incredible erection but he stopped her.

"Not yet, Portia. You first."

Before her head had even landed on a throw pillow, he'd spread her legs, held her at the sensitive top of her thighs and covered her sex with his mouth. Never had she been this turned on so quickly. It was as if they'd engaged in leisurely foreplay for hours and now she was primed and ready to come as his tongue did wicked things to her most private folds. Yet they'd only been in the house for what, ten minutes, tops?

He lifted his mouth from her and she looked into his eyes as she moaned her distress at the sudden loss of stimulation.

"Stop thinking. It's you, me and this." He lowered his head, and this time she didn't think about anything but how his mouth felt on her. She reached down, ran her fingers through his short hair and couldn't stop it, wouldn't. The rolling orgasm hit her from her center and exploded out to every nerve ending. Her scream of release echoed around them in the mountain home, as tears streamed down her cheeks. The release was beyond complete.

And they'd only just begun.

* * *

Kyle held on to his erection, refusing to let Portia's cries undo him right then and there, while she pulsed under his mouth. He tasted, smelled, felt nothing but Portia, and it was exquisite. But the best was yet to come. He almost laughed at his mental pun but thought better of it. He wanted this to be perfect for Portia.

Because she was so damned perfect for him.

He leaned up and kissed her forehead, smoothed back her hair. She opened her eyes and, instead of the languorous expression he expected, she grinned.

"You still have that condom?"

He couldn't stop his answering grin if he wanted to. He ripped open the packet and donned protection before he hovered over her, their bodies so close. Portia was freaking beautiful.

"Kyle, stop teasing me. Please. Now."

He'd never paused before, never felt such a need to soak it all in, appreciate every moment. He'd never been with a woman who'd taken him from sexual interest to unstoppable need like this, either.

"You ready, babe?" He gave her one last kiss before he plunged into her, savoring every inch of her sweet hotness as she closed around him. It was as if they'd done this a thousand times and yet, somewhere deep inside of him, he knew that every time with Portia would feel like the first time. Exciting, sexy, special.

Before he went down the feelings rabbit hole, his physical need took over and he pulled out, then thrust in again, harder this time, deeper. Portia's heels lifted to his shoulders and he about died then and there, but managed to channel the turn-on into thrust after thrust, her sighs and moans affirmation that this was so, so good for her, too.

He wanted it to last all morning, all afternoon. He wanted to shove into Portia again and again, never breaking the intimate contact. When she cried out for the second time and pulsed around him, he couldn't fight his release. It wasn't like it had ever been with any other woman before.

With Portia, he'd found his mate. And it was the worst possible time to have found her.

## Chapter 10

Kyle and Portia adopted a silent agreement after they'd given into their need for one another a few days ago. She told him that she understood that he needed space to work on the case, and he knew she didn't want to distract him. They slept in separate rooms, he in a guest room and her in the master suite, and avoided being alone together for too long. It worked out, as Kyle was gone for at least fifteen hours a day, keeping track of Markova. He only left when he turned over her surveillance to another Trail Hiker, and arrived at the house each night, well past when Portia had gone to bed. The times they saw one another, usually in the kitchen over breakfast, she'd been quiet, a more reserved version of the woman he knew she was.

Guilt hassled him at every turn. He wanted to draw her out, make her stay here more enjoyable, but if he did, he'd risk getting in too deep with her again. Never a good idea during a case as heavy as ROC.

On the evening that marked the first week since he'd brought Portia to the country house, Kyle knew she needed more than the phone calls with Annie. Brindle was filling in for Portia, with a temporary staffer acting as her librarian assistant, so Portia didn't have any library work to do. He knew she spent hours each day on the gala, but still worried about her. Portia was a woman who thrived on community involvement. She was the epitome of community and she'd been shoved into a strange house, even though it was a beautiful one at that, with no end in sight.

He couldn't shake his sense of culpability over her needing to stay in the strange house, yet keeping her safe remained his priority.

He found her laptop and stacks of papers splayed on the coffee table that separated the huge fireplace from the cozy oversize sofa. But no Portia. A quick glance at the French doors proved they were closed, that she was somewhere in the house. He walked down the hall that led to the bedrooms and saw that the light in hers was on, and heard water running from the master suite. She was taking a shower. Just like she'd done every other evening, after her late-afternoon workout.

Relief was impossible to ignore, and it was exactly the emotion that buoyed his steps back to the kitchen, where he began to set up dinner. The local Greek place was a favorite of hers; she'd told him as much over the deli sandwiches and tomato soup she'd made last night. He told himself he'd stopped and ordered the meal because keeping her fed and her strength up was part of his job.

But he knew it was complete BS. Portia's smile was something he was willing to go to untold ends for, he was finding out.

Soft feet padded on the oak flooring, followed by the scent of her shower soap, or maybe it was her shampoo. Something vanilla but with extra spice added in.

Not that he wanted to pay attention to her that closely. Not touching her this last week had been excruciating, but by a silent agreement they'd both kept things platonic.

"That smells incredible. I didn't know you cook—" She froze in place in front of the island, her mouth agape at the spread of spanakopita, freshly chopped Greek salad with creamy feta dressing, and skewered chicken and lamb.

"You went to Greek Delight!" She regained her composure and reached for the foil packet he'd pulled out of the takeout paper bag. "These toasted pitas are the best."

"You said you liked Greek, so I thought I'd treat."

Her eyes narrowed. "I thought you told me that all of my living expenses were paid for by Trail Hikers. For the duration of your case."

He cleared his throat. "They are. It is."

"But you paid for this out of your pocket?"

"I did." Crap, the way she said it, combined with the quizzical way her brow arched, made it sound like he'd planned a date with her. Or something.

He opened his mouth to allay her misconception but was blindsided by her as she quickly reached up and gave him a sound peck on his cheek. Her lips were smooth and her hair sopping from the shower. The kiss was totally casual, but she may as well have scorched his cheek with a hot brand.

Portia didn't notice that he was dumbstruck as she beamed at him. "Thank you so much. This is very sweet of you."

Now she thought he was sweet. He fought a groan.

"You're experiencing the hardship here, Portia. You've been grabbed from your regular life and forced to live in a strange house with no official deadline. It's the least I can do."

"All you have to do is say 'you're welcome,' Kyle. Don't worry, I'm not misconstruing it for something like a romantic gesture."

"Good. I mean, good that we're on the same page." Hell, how had he gone from a man in charge of a huge secret government stakeout to sounding like a fumbling adolescent? Something about Portia brought out his full range of emotions. Feelings he was more comfortable neatly compartmentalizing and storing far away from the scrutiny of daylight. Or an inquisitive librarian.

"Let's serve it up and enjoy it in front of the fire. It's gotten really cold today—have you noticed it?"

"Heck yeah. I was waiting all day for the woman who's targeted you to show up." At her questioning glance, he continued. "Outside the library."

"Let me guess, you were disguised as a homeless man, without the benefit of your better winter coat?"

"Something like that." He helped himself to several of the lamb skewers and noted that she piled her plate with the salad. They took silverware and napkins and settled on the sofa.

"Here, let me clear my stuff up a bit." Portia balanced her plate in one hand and shoved the papers away from where they sat.

"Don't worry about it." He set his plate in a clear spot and stood back up. "What can I get you to drink?"

"The sparkling water is fine. Thank you."

When he returned with their drinks, he saw that she'd ignored him and cleared her clutter to one side of the cocktail table. She'd also switched on the fireplace, a gas insert. As he sat on the cushion next to hers, he knew that all too easily he could get very used to this.

"Is it always this cold in central Pennsylvania in January?" He dug into his food as he waited for her answer.

"Not this bad, no, but we get our share of bitter cold. This year's been a little worse with the polar vortex deal." She referred to the weather phenomenon that had the local meteorologists all abuzz. The air currents formed in a way that allowed pure arctic air from the North Pole to be channeled south, as far down as the center of North America. That included Pennsylvania, which was currently in a deep freeze.

"It has gotten colder today, by twenty degrees. This salad, by the way, is delicious. You were right."

She eyed his tiny portion of greens, compared to his much larger stack of meat. "You didn't trust my judgment, did you?"

"Hey, don't be so defensive. Salad is known to be chick food. You can't blame me for wondering if you're big on rabbit food like a lot of women are."

She shook her head and grabbed one of his chicken kebabs. "Vegetables are for everyone. And no, I'm not against heavier fare—you saw me polish off that sandwich last night, and I told you I love Buffalo chicken wings."

"You did."

They weren't flirting; they weren't talking about the case, or anything super weighty. And he was happier than he could remember ever being. His mind tried to grab onto what he'd used as his happy place, mentally, these past few years. It'd always been the hope of returning to California, to the year-round sunshine and much more reasonable weather.

But right now, the polar vortex–cursed Silver Valley, Pennsylvania, felt incredible.

Portia savored every last bit of the Greek takeout, almost as much as she did being so close to a man who made her feel things she'd not thought she was capable of. The great sex they'd shared almost a week ago was almost supernatural in its quality, no question. Yet sharing a meal with Kyle proved more intimate to her. As a single woman who spent so much time out of her apartment, working at the library or homeless shelter, she was used to quick meals, most of them alone. Breaking a pita with Kyle proved absolutely the sexiest thing she figured they'd done together.

Not that she'd tell him. By a silent agreement, they'd avoided touching one another since they'd given in to the very strong tension between them. That was still there, but they'd managed to sidestep it.

She was okay with that. Portia didn't want it on her conscience that she'd distracted Kyle in any way from his ROC mission. It was bad enough that he felt he had to protect her by staying here.

"What are you thinking about, Portia?"

She sighed. Should she tell him? "I'm thinking that you're going to ignore what I'll say, but at the risk of repeating myself, you do not have to come back here each night. I know you go out to work at all hours, and driving up here has to be a pain. Your apartment is in the center of town, so much more convenient."

He wiped his mouth with a paper napkin, crumpled it and threw it on his empty plate. Leaning back into the sofa, he stretched his arms across the back of it and let out a long breath. "That is what I call good grub."

She couldn't help but laugh, which only made her more exasperated. "Did you even hear a word I said?"

Silver eyes, so intense, on her. The heat climbed up her throat and face, just like it did every single time he looked at her. He had to know how he affected her. Yet he never took advantage of it, which she gave him kudos for. "I hear every word, Portia. I hear how you take your showers, how you stay in the stall a while as you dry yourself off, then how you open the bathroom door to help let the steam out of the room. Do you want to know anything else that I notice?"

She swallowed. This was going off the rails again, too quickly for her. Their companionable meal was a safer space. Safe from the tantalizing memories of how it felt to have his hands on her...and his tongue.

*Stop.*

"No, that's enough. I believe you." She forced a smile before she stood up to clear the plates. His arm shot out and his hand gently circled her wrist. "Leave it. And I'm sorry. I'm trying to keep things cool between us."

She sank back into the comfy cushion and faced him. "I appreciate that. It's not easy living in such close proximity after we, ah, had the time we had the first day here."

He watched her, but his arm was back at his side. "No, it's not. I never want you to feel used, Portia."

"I'm an adult. What we shared was mutual. Do you feel used?"

"No, ah, I… Yes, it was mutual." She loved that she'd flustered him. "But I'm leaving Silver Valley after we take down ROC. Especially after I break up the heroin distribution and we capture Markova."

"Markova—that's the woman who wants me dead?" His eyes answered, narrowing and growing angry. "Don't be mad at yourself that you slipped her name, Kyle. I heard nothing."

"It's not something you needed to know, but yes, her name is Markova." He rubbed his temples. "This case has turned into way more than I expected when I first heard of Silver Valley."

"I know that. You've made your reason for being in what I'm sure you consider Podunk, USA." She wouldn't stop her defensiveness over Silver Valley. "I've seen a lot of the US, you know, and I travel overseas every summer for at least ten days, usually two weeks. There are plenty of other places I'd be comfortable living, but nothing compares to Silver Valley. It might just be a place you have to deal with while in the middle of a work gig, but it's a source of great strength for a lot of people."

"Whoa, I didn't mean to get you riled up over this, Portia. I'm going back to California because that's my home. Or it was, until I left for the Marines right out of high school. I get your devotion to this area, really, I do. It's evident in everything you do, you know.

From the library to the homeless shelter, to all the kids I saw you help out who were doing research for high school papers. And you're terrific with the seniors who come in and have a zillion questions about technology." He paused, and she watched in complete shock as he began to chuckle. "Do you know, one day I was hanging around the computers and I watched you help this one older gentleman order a gift for his lady friend at the senior center. He'd found out it'd be less expensive from an online retailer and you patiently led him through all the steps."

"I had no idea you were there." She remembered it as if it were yesterday, because the said gentleman was Mr. Nolan, the retired schoolteacher who'd taught her French classes through high school. He was a community pillar and he'd come in a few weeks before Christmas to order that particular gift. "You've been here since before the holidays? I know you told me that at one point—I just didn't put it together until now."

"Why would you?" His gaze was appreciative and she blushed. It was one thing to know she turned him on, but to realize that he'd seen her in her element, completely unguarded, was a bit overwhelming. "I was just another patron as far as you knew. No one you'd notice."

But Kyle was a man she'd always notice. He had to be very good at his job if he'd escaped her observation until the train track rescue.

He nodded at her work, stacked on the end of the coffee table. "How goes the gala planning? Anything you need me to take care of while I'm out and about?"

"No way. I'd never ask you to do anything but what you're here to do. Save Silver Valley from ROC."

He looked at her like she'd missed something in their conversation. "Ah, you know that I'm just one of many law enforcement types working to make that happen, right?"

Another thing she'd picked up about him, as he'd held her in the shadow of the train that could have killed her: his sincere humility.

"Yes, but you're the one who saved my life and for some reason feel responsible to make sure I'm safe, a week out. Josh has known me my entire life, and while I know he cares, as does Annie, he didn't volunteer to check on me regularly."

"Because he's in uniform, and more visible in the community. He can't send SVPD units out to patrol the area without raising eyebrows. We don't want anything to appear out of the ordinary."

She tore her gaze from him to watch the blue flames in the glass-covered hearth. Her body was too aware of him, but worse, her heart was getting in too deep with Kyle. With a man who was headed for the West Coast the minute the investigation wrapped up.

"Are we going to be able to have the gala?" She voiced her worst fear, as far as her community work went. The other anxiety, over never finding a man like Kyle again, someone who got her right from the get-go, she buried deep.

The cushions moved as he leaned forward on his knees to look at her. "I'm doing everything to ensure you can. But it has to be airtight as far as security is concerned. Why don't we go over the plans together?"

Disbelief made her laugh. "You're kidding." She looked at him and sucked in a deep breath at the light in his eyes. Her heart reacted, too, making her feel as though she'd just run ten kilometers in the bitter cold. "What about a charity ball is interesting to you?" He worked in the most exciting profession she could think of. "There isn't an adrenaline rush involved in planning a silent auction and dance for two to three hundred people, trust me."

The lines around his eyes deepened, but he didn't smile completely. "I'm not an adrenaline junkie, believe it or not. Sure, I've been in tight spots, but that was more likely when I was in the Marine Corps. My job as an agent involves a lot of watching, listening, waiting. And I read a heck of a lot of intelligence reports and criminal profiles. When I'm not actually in the field, I spend eight hours a day at my laptop, wherever I am."

"So while the Trail Hiker headquarters is here, in Silver Valley, the employees don't all work and live here?"

He shook his head. "No, not at all. The staff here exists to keep the agency running, to coordinate the missions."

"And for Claudia to tell her bosses what's going on."

He didn't reply to her comment—she didn't expect him to. "I know that most all of what you do is very classified, and I'm not looking for information I don't have a right to. I suspect you've probably told me a little more than I really need to know, right?"

"Maybe. Claudia wouldn't have told you the basic premise of Trail Hikers, or my role in this particular op, unless she thought it necessary and that you are trustworthy. And don't forget she had you sign the nondisclosure forms."

"You already knew my background when you started surveillance on the library?"

"Yes. Which means, of course, that Claudia had access to the same information."

"Does everyone in your office have access to these files on me?" She was all for supporting law enforcement and helping get rid of the bad guy, or in this case, woman. But having her most personal data out there was disconcerting. As a librarian, she understood the power of information.

"No, quite the contrary. I know you've never been in the military, but as with any government entity, release of classified material is on a need-to-know basis. So other than me, and my supervisor, no one else can read the files. Unless they start to work the same case, or something related to it."

"That makes sense. And yes, I did know that. I regularly read several national newspapers, along with all the local press."

"Yeah, a lot makes it into the papers that shouldn't." He raised a brow. "You probably don't agree, as an information manager."

"Actually I have no problem with the concept of classified information—as long as it's handled that way for the right purpose."

"There's a lot more to you than a lot of people see, Portia." His scrutiny had gone personal again, exactly what she'd hoped to avoid. Unless they were going to make this either a full-fledged fling, or Kyle was going to stay in Silver Valley after ROC was removed, she couldn't let her heart go there.

# Chapter 11

Kyle hated to leave Portia again the next morning, but she hadn't seemed fazed. She'd all but shooed him out of the huge house, reassuring him that she'd be safe. It'd taken her no time to master the intricate surveillance system Trail Hikers had installed, but he never forgot who their adversary was. Ludmila Markova knew her way around the most sophisticated technology. His one solace was that he knew Trail Hikers had the best equipment the US government had to offer.

It was his job to protect her, no matter what Trail Hikers or SVPD policy was about providing personal security. Sure, he couldn't stop his mission, but he could damn sure make certain Portia never faced Markova again. To ensure it, he had to get to the bottom of the case ASAP. Markova was the person with the answers as to how the heroin was getting into Silver

Valley, and when. He had two objectives: take out Markova and break up the heroin distribution ring.

His first stop in town was to meet with Claudia at TH headquarters. He made certain he wasn't followed and took precautions with his appearance. Winter and cold weather made it easier, with hats and hoods being commonplace. He entered the building with a card, then passed through three additional security checkpoints that included fingerprint, facial and retina identification. TH hadn't utilized such strident measures during its initial setup, but as their adversaries grew more technologically astute, so had the agency.

"Hi, Kyle." The receptionist tapped on his smart tablet and Kyle knew that Claudia had been informed of his arrival. "Claudia's in a meeting but will be available in five minutes."

"I'll wait." He took a seat in the minimalist but comfortable lounge area. Time with the director of Trail Hikers was precious and he wouldn't be here if he didn't need to.

After the exact time specified, he was escorted to her office and waited for the receptionist to close the several-inches-thick steel door behind him. The entire office building was a fortress, with the agents effectively working in vaults due to the classified nature of the Trail Hiker mission. They would assist international, federal, state and local law enforcement as needed, always maintaining complete anonymity except for the LEA personnel who were also TH. Trail Hiker agents avoided discovery at all costs. What the mission statement didn't reveal was that TH only took on the most difficult and deadly cases, the ones that had to be stopped in their tracks immediately or monitored for the long haul, for the safety of innocent civilians.

"Kyle. Have a seat." Claudia ran a hand through her signature gray hair, and her attractiveness wasn't lost on him, even though she was twenty years his senior. At least. More importantly she was his boss, a fearless leader whom he'd been thrilled to work for when he first learned of the possibility. He'd never worked with Claudia while still a Marine, but her legacy to the Corps was inimitable. To the present day, Marine Corps Intelligence Officers were trained with techniques she'd perfected when she was still a junior officer, before she made General, and long before her retirement as a two-star.

"Yes, ma'am." He never got used to calling her by her first name, no matter that the work environment demanded it. There wasn't the hardline ranking in Trail Hikers like he'd experienced in the military. They were all colleagues, agents all working together for a common cause. Of course there were ranks and definite leaders here, but to minimize the chances of exposure, they didn't refer to one another with anything other than their first names.

"You've got Portia settled at the Olsen house." A statement. Claudia came as close to an omniscient presence as anyone he'd ever met.

"Yes. I'll go back at night to check on her, when I'm not working."

Claudia swiveled in her chair and rapidly typed on her keyboard. He couldn't see her computer display but knew from other times he'd worked a case with her that her monstrous monitor would reflect Claudia's comprehensive assessment of the case.

"It looks pretty tight, security-wise." Cool eyes peered around the monitor at him. "Does she know how to use a weapon?"

"I didn't ask her, but I'd doubt it."

"Why? You're in Pennsylvania. She doesn't have a license to carry in the background check we ran, but she may have hunted before, or gone to a firing range. Find out. I'd like to equip her and you with a few extra firearms, just in case."

"Portia's not a Trail Hiker." He was, and he'd be doing any firing of weapons as needed.

"No, but she knows enough about the case, and of course she's the one Markova's targeting. Have you told Portia anything about her adversary?"

"No. All Portia knows is that ROC is in place in Silver Valley and refusing to leave, and she knows Markova's name. She knows I'm here to help bring the heroin operation down, break up their logistics."

Claudia nodded. "I'm not sure what you pulled up on Portia when you did your background check, but in the profile I have here, it talks about one of her high school friends succumbing to heroin. Annie knew the woman, too."

He hadn't read that part in his file, and he'd been too busy the last week to reread Portia's dossier. He was living with her—that was all he needed. And it made him more aware of Portia as a human being than he had been. Portia had a fire in her belly for charity work. No doubt her high school friend's overdose only further motivated her.

"I do know from her file that she was involved with a local politician. It didn't work out."

Claudia snorted. "Because she ended it, which was a

good move on her part. Robert Donovan is a slickster. He's even accepted donations from out of state donors to include a Mr. D. Ivanov." She met Kyle's gaze again and he registered the same level of disgust.

Dima Ivanov was the head of East Coast ROC, the big kahuna of ROC criminals. He'd alluded capture, even though he'd been in Silver Valley at least a half dozen times in the past eighteen months. Problem was, no one reported him when he was in town. The locals would only see him as a tourist passing through, and frightened anyone who thought they recognized him into keeping quiet. Ivanov knew well enough to keep up a disguise from the local LEAs.

"Is Donovan in with ROC for this operation?" He referred to the heroin distribution chain. It wasn't beyond politicians to convince or at least try to convince LEAs to look the other way when it preserved a solid donor.

"No, not from what we've seen, but nothing would surprise me." Claudia frowned. "You and I have seen so much destruction around the globe caused by greed. I hate that it's come to Silver Valley."

"We're on it, boss."

"We are. So after you find out if Portia can fire a weapon, and train her if she can't, take some extra arms out to the house. Feel free to use our firing range."

"We don't involve civilians in our cases." No way was he training Portia how to fire a weapon. She was a librarian, the town's Mother Theresa of the homeless. Not an undercover agent.

*You're getting in too deep.*

Maybe he already was.

"Portia's already involved, Kyle." She peered at him from her desk. "Are your emotions becoming involved,

Kyle?" Her astute query was underscored by the blaze of comprehension in her blue eyes.

"No. Maybe. Yeah."

"There's no harm in caring for someone, but it can't affect your mission. It would be rough to reassign you this deep in, but I can make it happen if you'd like."

"No, I'm going to finish this."

"Good." She nodded. "Are you still considering the move to California?"

"As long as the offer to launch the West Coast Trail Hiker office still stands." And even if it didn't, he still wanted to go back to his native state. Didn't he?

He'd thought of it, planned for it for the last year or two. It was as much a part of his everyday awareness as his job. But he hadn't thought about California lately.

Not since he'd held a certain Silver Valley librarian in his arms as he knocked her off the train tracks.

It'd come close for Markova last week at the homeless shelter. So the librarian had a protector—no matter. At some point, the woman would have to go back to work, and then she'd make her move, more exactingly this time. Following her from the library had been foolish, the action of an amateur.

She was not a rookie, as Americans liked to say. FSB training was for only the very best, and when she'd joined them, she'd been young, strong and full of idealistic Russian dreams.

Now she knew they were all lies, but in America with Ivanov, she'd found her place, found a way to use her abilities while still helping her fellow nationals who'd come here looking for a way out. All of them were misfits as far as the Russian government was concerned, all FSB or other government agency throw-aways.

Using her best teenage boy disguise, she'd hung out in the local comic book store since three thirty, the time when high school students liked to relax, she'd noticed. Certain that the man she'd encountered on the train tracks, and again in the homeless shelter, was no-where in the vicinity, she left the store, entered the li-brary and headed to the classic fiction shelves. There, on the Russian translation shelf, somewhere between *The Brothers Karamazov* and *Anna Karenina*, she sur-reptitiously placed the USB stick on which she'd cop-ied the most detailed instructions from the site on the dark net. She put the memory device behind the aged volumes, out of sight of a browser. The Russian novels were so obvious a place they would be discounted by SVPD or FBI. They'd had another drop place closer to the front entrance but she'd changed it after the day the librarian chased her onto the train tracks.

Her immediate subordinate in ROC, in charge of the individual dealer logistics for the area, would come and get the stick in the next fifteen minutes.

Not wanting to appear obvious on any security foot-age that could be analyzed by the local police, and still wanting to drop off the laptop whose hard drive she'd wiped, she went back upstairs and spent the next sev-eral minutes browsing the periodicals. She wasn't to know who her handoff was, nor was it her concern. All that mattered was that he or she got the informa-tion she'd left.

A group of school-age children, along with a few parents, entered the library, and she used the crowd to her advantage. She pulled the laptop out of the bag and carefully left it on the circulation desk as she exited the library. She couldn't keep the grin off her face. The man who was tracking her would be in for a big surprise, and no doubt infuriated. Ludmila loved aggravating her tails. It was part of her job description as far as she was concerned.

The only thing she hadn't figured out was where Portia DiNapoli was. She hadn't been back in the library, from what Ludmila saw, since the very day she'd almost been flattened by the train.

Outside the library, the air froze the hairs in her nostrils, not unlike Moscow or Saint Petersburg. While she was prepared to work in any climate, anywhere, she had to admit that the cold was her friend, the constant companion of her youth in the block-style apartment building, a holdover from the Soviet era. She'd missed out on it, the glory days of her country. But here in America, she had a chance to see how the system could really work, when ROC's plan to take over the domestic economy came to fruition. At its core was fortifying the influx, distribution and sale of heroin. She was determined to see it work out.

A homeless man sat inside a threshold and she stepped over his feet. And thought about it. She turned back.

"There's a homeless place for you, next block up."

The man shrugged and huddled more deeply into his ragged coat. Ludmila answered with her own shrug and continued walking.

She lit up a cigarette as she walked in the frozen winter twilight of Silver Valley. The smoke fit her disguise perfectly, but also calmed the adrenaline that annoyingly surged through her system. Portia DiNapoli had to go, the sooner the better. Ludmila needed one chance, one straight line of sight, and she'd take the woman out.

Ludmila never left a witness behind, even when what they'd actually seen and could recall for the authorities was questionable. She worked on a zero-risk belief system. It was what had earned her top rankings in the FSB, and ensured her spot as a trusted agent for Ivanov in ROC. And this skill she'd developed so carefully, so thoroughly, was what would allow her to disappear from the face of the earth, take a new identity and leave this life behind for good. All she had left to do was kill Portia DiNapoli.

It was so delicious to think of finally taking out the town librarian she wondered for a fleeting moment if she'd ever be able to stop it—the killing. There was power in taking life, and Ludmila loved having power over people.

Kyle remotely snapped several photos with the miniature camera he'd placed in his ski cap, positioned so that the torn material appeared as any other hole in the fabric and not sporting a lens. The activation button was the crown on the cheap-looking watch he wore.

He'd immediately known it was Markova by the way she tried just a little too hard to appear like an American teen. Markova was good, but not perfect. First, she'd missed him sitting by the front door of the library on her way in. And just now, he was certain she hadn't known it was him. If she had, he'd be fighting for his life or have had to kill her to keep his.

Markova was all about her mission, her survival. He

got it, because he was, too, except his efforts benefited society. Unlike ROC.

He'd called in to another TH agent working the case inside the building to check out the library—everywhere that Markova had walked. All they'd discovered was that the laptop had been left on the circulation desk. It was already on its way to TH headquarters for analysis, but there wouldn't be anything on it. A professional like Markova didn't make those kinds of mistakes, and besides, he knew she'd meant it as a slap.

The question was if she'd left something else somewhere else in the library. He'd change out of his disguise and go in during after-hours to search the place.

As night fell early and snow began to fall, he faced his other conundrum. How was he going to keep his hands off Portia when all he'd wanted, all he craved, since they'd been together, was to be with her again?

Portia didn't go stir-crazy during the first full week of her imposed exile at the mountain home, but by the end of week two, she was beyond antsy. She promised Kyle she'd stay in the house, but surely that had to extend to the immediate property. It was close to nightfall, but she had at least another twenty minutes of sufficient daylight to take a break from the gala planning.

Once outside, her head cleared and the open air immediately soothed her jagged edges. Kyle had checked in on her each day, about midday, then at night, where he'd dutifully slept in a guest room, while she slept in another. He'd not made a move to touch her since their cataclysmic sex the first day she'd been brought here.

And she'd refrained from touching him, too. It was

a silent agreement, as they didn't discuss it. She wondered if his reason was the same as hers, though. Kyle made it clear he was going back to California, which made a relationship with him a nonstarter. Her home was Silver Valley.

Although, in a moment of sheer boredom, she'd looked up open library positions in the northern part of the state, where he'd mentioned he was from. And just as quickly shut the screen down, because in the fantasy of a life with Kyle lay madness.

As she walked off the expansive back deck and onto the concrete patio below, she saw the large cover over a pool, and the surrounding woods appeared frosted with the snow that had begun to fall about an hour ago. According to the weather reports, a flat-out blizzard was headed into the Susquehanna and Cumberland Valley areas. Since Silver Valley was smack-dab in the middle of them, they expected up to three feet, maybe more, in less than twenty-four hours.

She knew it could get ugly outside, but right now it was perfect. The wind hadn't picked up yet and the snowflakes pinged off her parka. Holding out her mittened hands to capture them, she saw that they were tiny ice particles. Standing under the deck, watching nature sprinkle the sparkling snowflakes all about her, it was difficult to imagine she was here because her life was threatened.

Thank God for Annie, who'd talked to her endlessly on the phone these past two weeks. Otherwise being a shut-in would lead to insanity, at the least.

Footsteps sounded on the ground near her and she froze. Kyle always came in through the front door, which was upstairs, on the house's main living area.

He hadn't been on the deck over her head or she would have heard his firm, steady steps.

She shrank back against the house, forcing her breathing to still and her thoughts to focus. Who was here with her?

# Chapter 12

Kyle spoke to Josh as he drove up to the house. In a few minutes, he'd be near Portia again. It was at once torture and relief. Relief to see her beautiful smile, know she was safe and unharmed. Torture to be as turned on as a man possibly could be and unable to do a darn thing about it.

"I just talked to Claudia, Kyle. The laptop was wiped, as you expected."

"Yup. It's Markova's way of letting us know she's a step ahead."

"But she's not. You saw her in the library, and the security footage verifies what you described." Josh's laugh sounded throughout the inside of the car, as Kyle used the hands-free phone. "You were spot-on about everything."

Kyle silently thanked Claudia for making sure the library's security feed had been linked to SVPD early in the surveillance operation. It exponentially cut their analysis time down.

"What about the other places she went? Tell me what you saw. I'm going back as soon as I check in on Portia, after the library closes." He couldn't inspect every inch of it as needed with patrons present.

"She walked by the literary fiction section, appeared to linger for a brief moment by the Russian books."

"Aren't you glad I told you where those were?" He poked at Josh, who'd been convinced ROC wasn't so nuanced. But he hadn't had to work against Russian FSB agents before. Kyle had.

"It just seems too obvious."

"And therefore classic. What did you see? Could you see her hands?"

"No, that's the problem. I see her reach up for maybe three seconds, that's it. If she put a piece of paper or a USB of any kind in there, it could be gone by now."

"Go over it again, and go through the next several minutes of footage for me. If you see someone go there, we have our transfer point." And the Silver Valley point of contact for ROC, besides Markova.

"Will do. Also, we just found out that there's definitely a large heroin shipment en route," Josh said with a sigh, which expressed his frustration. "It's the largest sent to the East Coast yet, and it's coming here, to Silver Valley."

They had to stop it. Neither man had to verbalize it.

"We're going to. Keep me posted and I'll check back with you after I get through the library."

"You know about the storm coming in, right?"

"I saw some messages on my phone." He had, but he'd been too busy, first working undercover at the library and then preoccupied with getting back here to check on Portia. He looked at his windshield wiper blades as he turned them off, pulling to a stop in the circular driveway.

"It's not just a storm, Kyle. They're expecting blizzard conditions by midnight, and it won't let up for as much as two days."

"So we need the information Markova left in the library tonight."

"Definitely."

"I'm on it." He disconnected as he killed the engine. It was six o'clock. The library closed in two hours. Enough time to grab a quick meal with Portia and get to the library and back in time for the storm. He did not want her alone at all, but especially during weather that Markova functioned exceptionally well in.

He pulled the couple of bags of groceries he'd brought out of the back and realized that they'd need more provisions to survive a few days, maybe even a week. This wasn't far enough north that they had snowplows standing by to promptly clear rural routes like the one that led to the mountain house. He'd make sure the snowmobile in the garage had enough fuel, and that there was propane for the backup generator.

As he stomped up to the front door, he sent up a thought of gratitude. One nice thing about such a fancy place was that it was set for any kind of weather.

"Hello!"

The greeting had been his usual way of letting Portia know he was here. He knew that he had a habit of stepping softly to avoid detection. A good thing when working undercover, but terrifying for someone like Portia who was alone in this huge house all day.

She didn't answer, and the first niggle of concern tugged at his gut. Portia might be in the shower, or the workout room in the basement. She'd made herself at home, utilizing every space and staying busy beyond her gala planning and the miniscule library work she did long-distance.

He dumped the bags on the island, where he noted she'd left her laptop open, a half-drank mug of tea next to it. He felt the cup—it was cold.

A worm of cold fear began to take root. *Nope, not going there*. She was fine.

But if she wasn't, if Markova had somehow found them, despite his evasion tactics, he couldn't run around shouting for Portia. He had to fight the instinct, not something he was used to. Normally he stayed cool under the toughest situations. But they hadn't involved Portia.

He silently walked to the French doors that led onto the enormous cedar deck, a full twenty feet above ground level. The structure held patio furniture, now covered with weatherproof protection, and a hot tub he vaguely remembered Josh mentioning.

No Portia.

But there were footprints leading to the steps that led to the concrete patio. It was impossible to peer between the slats, as they were laid tightly together. If Portia was down there, being held by Markova, he'd be walking into a trap from which he couldn't save Portia or himself.

Kyle quickly and silently retraced his steps back into the house and locked the French door behind him. He pulled his weapon as he ran back through the house, into the garage and then out the garage's side door. To his relief, there were no prints in the snow that had fallen between the house and the immediate line of trees. His weapon drawn, ready to fire, he pressed forward to the back, northwest corner of the house. Listening for scuffling, any vocalizations, he heard nothing.

He turned the corner with his .45 held in front, ready to fire at the first sign of Markova.

The space under the deck was pitch-dark, the last remaining daylight long gone. He'd not turned on the outside lights, but as he moved to the space farther under the deck, a motion detector light blazed blinding-white in his eyes. He heard a gasp and froze, blinking to regain his vision.

"Kyle!" Portia. Thank God.

"Where are you?" Damn the light.

"Why are you pointing a gun at me? I'm fine." He heard her steps, then she was at his side, away from where he pointed the gun. "Kyle."

Only when he looked into her eyes, allowed himself to accept that she was alone and safe, did he let out his breath. His vision returned and he scoured under the deck for anyone else.

"Kyle, I told you I'm alone. I came out to get a breath of fresh air. I'm so sorry if I worried you." She hugged herself. "Holy cannoli, you scared the heck out of me! I heard your footsteps but you weren't up on the deck, where I'd expect you to be if you came in and saw I was outside. I thought I was done for."

Kyle holstered his weapon and faced her. Snowflakes landed on her soft curls, the white sparkles contrasting with her brunette hair. "You've got a target between your eyes, Portia. Of course I was concerned."

"You seemed a lot more than 'concerned.'" She

made air quotes as her brows rose. "You need to be more careful, Kyle. For a minute there, I thought you cared."

He knew it was her nerves talking. He'd scared her, too, coming up on her like she was his target. "This isn't the time for this." Yet he didn't move. Didn't go anywhere, but instead stayed under the deck with her, where the ambient light from the motion detector allowed him to see her face without totally exposing them to anyone looking at the house.

"There was plenty of time earlier in the week." One side of her lush mouth curved up, and he couldn't take his gaze off the warmth in her eyes. Was it for him? Dare he hope it was?

"I'm not sorry for that, Portia. It was…fantastic. But I'm in the middle of a case. I can't be distracted. And at the end of it—"

"You're moving back to California. You already told me that." She stood her ground. He'd been about to say that he was an undercover law enforcement agent, she was a librarian, they lived in completely different worlds.

"That doesn't bother you?"

"What? That you're moving on? It's not my concern, is it?" She watched him in a way he understood. As if she were waiting until he couldn't take it anymore and admit that there was something deeper brewing between them than the ROC case or lust.

"It'd be your concern if you thought I'd change my mind."

"I'm not looking to change your mind, Kyle. And I know you're not trying to change me, either."

He wasn't, not at all. Because the woman in front

of him was far more than he'd ever dreamed existed.
The real deal. The full package—for him.

"Aw, hell." Much against his personal vow to leave
her alone, he had to have one more taste. Just a nip.
He reached for her at the same instant she touched his
face with her mittened hand. The rough texture of the
wool scraped against his cheek, but he didn't feel any
discomfort the minute his lips touched hers.

Portia's hand overshot Kyle's cheek and she used
the momentum to wrap it around his head, to tug him
close to her as their lips met. Her fright turned to mol-
ten desire as his tongue probed deep, filling her mouth
with his taste, his need.

His hands roamed down her back, pulling her in
close. The layers of clothing between them were too
much. They'd avoided one another all week and it had
proved too long. She could blame her emotions, being
alternatively scared for her life and then so relieved
to have Kyle's hard, reassuring form against her. But
it didn't account for the taught tension that strung between them since they'd made love that first time, since
she'd become aware of his presence in her life.

She kissed him with all she had. And never felt any
less than fully reciprocated as he whispered sexy words
against her lips, told her what he intended to do to her.
What he wanted her to do to him.

"Kyle." More kissing.

"Mmm?" Another lick.

"There's a hot tub upstairs, on the deck." She fantasized all week about being in it with him, had considered asking him to join her, purely platonically.

But their connection would never be anything but very sexual, incredibly sensual.

"Let's go." He grabbed her hand and tugged her behind as he led them up the stairs. He stopped at the French door. "I have to go in and get a condom, but I locked this door when I saw you were gone." Lines etched around his eyes, the light of the great room spilling a soft yellow glow over them through the door's windows.

"I'm sorry I worried you."

"It seems I did the same to you." He kissed her hard, then smiled. "I can think of no better way to let go of it, can you?"

"No. Here's the key." She handed him the set of house keys that included the one to the back-deck door.

"You carried them with you." He stared at them.

"As you advised. I did listen when you talked to me about safety, you know."

He looked like he had more to say but instead unlocked the door. "I'll be right back. You coming in to warm up first?"

She laughed. "I'm not feeling any of this cold right now. I'll get the hot tub ready."

He disappeared into the house and she took the lid off the spa, watched the steaming water begin to bubble once she found the switches. The snowfall had picked up and was a steady douse of white, piling up on the deck railing and steps where they'd just walked. She quickly unzipped her jacket and walked to the door to strip out of all of her clothes before she made a beeline for the warm water.

Sinking into it was pure bliss. She'd managed to work out each day in the house's high-end gym room, but missed her runs. So she'd pushed it on the tread-mill and elliptical machine, which made her muscles complain a bit. The soothing vibration of the pulsing water was almost as good as—no, it came nowhere near to sex. Not with Kyle, at any rate.

She heard the door click and looked up to see him stride naked across the deck. Kyle's nude body wasn't unfamiliar to her, yet to see his starkly masculine form, underscored by his raging erection, shot a bolt of pure lust through her. If it were any more tangible, the con-nection she felt to this man would part the water of the hot tub, cause the deck to quake. But she'd settle for making love to him again.

"You didn't waste any time, I see." The flash of his teeth indicated his pleasure as he simultaneously dropped the house keys and a strip of condoms on the deck next to the tub and himself into the water.

Portia couldn't speak. Mesmerized by how his broad shoulders dipped below the water, rivulets running over and down his skin as the steam wove around them, kept her from being able to do anything but stare. Her limbs had no problem reacting, however, as she found herself moving next to him, her fingers running across his skin, cupping his face.

"Where did you come from, Kyle?" She waited for his silver eyes to focus on her, saw the same arousal she enjoyed. And something deeper. Was it the sense of timelessness to their relationship that she felt?

"Snowflakes are sticking to your eyelashes." He held her face, too, as they knelt in the steaming water, keeping it shoulder level to stay warm as the storm intensified around them. When he lowered his head to kiss her, she met him halfway. As under the deck, their need exploded into a desire so fierce that Portia thought she'd never breathe again.

"Oh, Kyle, this is so much." She gasped out the words, unable to focus as his lips landed on her throat and his hands cupped her breasts. He suckled on one nipple, then the other, and as the frozen air hit her skin, it only made her hotter, more desperate to have him inside her.

"Patience, Portia." His mouth came back to hers and she expected he'd reach for the condoms, make short work of foreplay as they both so clearly wanted the ultimate connection. But he instead reached between her legs under the water and stroked her folds with his fingers. Before she got used to the intense sensuality he shoved one, two fingers inside her and caressed the deepest part of her. His caresses bespoke expertise, but so much more. She had no time to figure it out as an orgasm crested and took her out of herself. The only concrete sensation was the feel of Kyle's muscular shoulders under her hands as she held on to him, used him as an anchor in the turbulent onslaught of pleasure. Her cries escaped her throat with no effort from her, and she thought she'd immediately find an apartment to rent that had a hot tub on the deck when this was all over.

"Like that?" Breath from his sexy laugh tickled where he kissed her on her temple. Kyle nudged her cheek with his nose until their lips met again. As she kissed him, she reached for his erection, gripping him firmly and stroking with unquestionable intent.

"Babe." Kyle sat back on the spa's underwater bench and closed his eyes, his head leaned back against the edge as she worked her hands on him, straddled him.

Her body felt weightless, yet she'd never felt more empowered, been more aware of how her actions affected another human being.

But it wasn't just another human being or man—it was Kyle.

She kissed him as she moved her hand over his shaft and was rewarded with an open, fully exposed kiss that communicated his total need, total trust in her. His erection hardened further, a feat she'd have thought impossible.

His hands were on her shoulders and he gently pushed her away, his eyes heavy with lust. "Careful or it'll be over before we get to the best part, babe."

She laughed softly as he reached for the condoms, tore one off and stood on the spa bench. Only his knees were underwater, and she was transfixed by the water sluicing down his powerful thighs as snow pelted his chest. Kyle had huge, strong hands and even so his erection seemed too big for them. She swallowed, her mouth wanting something that would have to wait for another time.

Once he donned the protection, he sank back down and in one fluid movement pulled her, straddle-style, onto him, pelvis-to-pelvis. Maintaining eye contact, his hands gripped her hips, moved to her buttocks as he guided her over him, onto him, positioned himself at her entrance. The moment she closed her eyes, parted her lips in a sigh of want, he thrust into her, making her already sensitive sex on fire with need.

"Kyle!" She grasped his wrists, which were behind her back, and tilted her head to the snow-filled sky as he pumped into her with complete abandon, as she moved over him and pushed back with a ferocity that matched his. They may have been like that for an hour or a minute—it didn't matter, as time never did between them. But their connection, the thing that mattered very much, propelled them to the obvious conclusion as they both reached their releases at the same time, their cries of satisfaction muffled only by the now roaring wind.

Afterward she remained on top of him on the bench as the water bubbled and gently lapped around them. The snowfall had turned into a full-fledged blizzard as the wind drove the flakes into her skin, but she was more attune to Kyle's skin against hers, his breath returning to normal along with hers.

Inexplicably, she'd found her match in the undercover agent she'd known for barely two weeks.

# *Chapter 13*

Kyle left Portia within the hour, as darkness was complete and he was fighting against the snowstorm to get to the library, then return to the country estate before the roads became impassable.

At least this time he didn't have to dress as anyone but an undercover agent with much needed protection from the cold. And he'd accepted Portia's work keys, saving him a trip to Josh's desk at SVPD. Since they coordinated every aspect of the case, they'd agreed to leave most of what they'd need at SVPD. The less Kyle or any agent was seen going in and out of the actual TH headquarters, the better.

Certain he hadn't been followed, he parked his truck in the diner parking lot. There were only half a dozen cars as compared to the usual twenty or so. And the streets and sidewalks were deserted, save for a few intrepid souls scurrying into the local convenience pharmacy, no doubt to get that last loaf of bread or carton of milk. There were plenty of full-size grocery stores on the main pike, but the drugstore, with its few shelves of foodstuffs, was all the people who lived in the downtown area had within walking distance. Kyle knew it well, as he'd subsisted on plenty of its supplies these past weeks.

Maybe that was why he was reacting so intensely to Portia. Not the sex part, which would be out of this world with her no matter what, but the emotional intimacy. The time he was spending with her at that beautiful house, in the perfect natural setting, was the most he'd had to just *be* since he didn't know when. He'd been on this Silver Valley ROC assignment for a couple of months, but it was the culmination of years of following the criminal organization and its key players. He knew he wasn't alone in this, which made it more frustrating that LEA hadn't succeeded in toppling the nefarious empire yet.

As he entered the library through a side entrance, unseen from the front and not in view of the back parking lot, he tried to clear his mind, open his senses to whatever evidence might be available. But Portia's smile, her luminous eyes, the warmth of her, never left him.

He supposed he should get used to it. He imagined she was going to stay with him for a long while, all the way to California and the future he'd counted on for so long.

Whoa. He froze at the bottom of the library stairwell. This was the problem with accepting that he couldn't get a woman out of his soul. His imagination led him to believe she'd always be with him, any-where he went.

Portia wasn't leaving Silver Valley, and he sure as hell wasn't staying anywhere on the East Coast.

For now, he had a job to do. He made his way to the international fiction section and read the very familiar Russian Literature label at the base of the metal shelf. Replacing his winter gloves with latex, he quickly re-moved each volume, shaking the books in case a note had been left inside and thumbing through the pages, opening each work to make sure it was a book and did not contain a concealed hiding place. He'd gotten through at least two dozen novels, from Chekhov to Dostoyevsky, when he noticed the small object at the back of the shelf. It had been painted a cream color to blend in with the metal surface and his gut tightened. As he plucked it up with his fingers, he saw immedi-ately that it was a USB. Or at least was meant to look like one. He could do nothing with it until it was back at SVPD, the only "safe" place to take it. When work-ing against the kind of intelligent criminals he did, he had to always assume the worst. Which meant he as-sumed that the USB port could in actuality be a GPS tracking device, or other technology that could reveal his location.

He placed the device in a plastic evidence bag and pocketed it. Before he left, he continued his methodical search through each book, then replaced them, leav-ing them as he'd found them. No sense making extra work for the staff, or drawing unneeded attention to the Russian Literature section.

He pulled his phone out to text Josh, so that he could arrive at the library in an SVPD vehicle to retrieve the

USB stick. The face was lit up with weather warnings that urged residents to remain in place at home for the next forty-eight hours.

Two days of storm? It should concern him that the operation would be stymied for that long, or that ROC might still somehow get their heroin shipment delivered under the cover of blinding snow. Instead, he experienced a surge of anticipation. He'd get to be with Portia for two full days.

So much for keeping her at a safe distance.

She watched through the hole she'd rubbed out of the condensation on the diner window as the Silver Valley Police car pulled up and around the diner parking lot, saw it park next to the truck she'd noticed was often in the same spot. One thing none of them expected was that she'd take a job as a waitress, which allowed her to piece together who was who in this simple American town.

The man she'd fought with, thought about killing in the courtyard behind the homeless place, was in the truck. She was certain it was him—he'd come in here for coffee one time when she was on shift. She always took the night shift, as her real job required her to do all ROC duties in full daylight. She was the best at undercover work and they needed her where their other people couldn't operate. So the night, the darkness, was left to the amateurs, as far as she was concerned.

It was an amateur who'd not received the information she'd left in the library, not like he was supposed to. So it sat for another day, until tomorrow, when she'd have to make certain it was picked up. Otherwise Ivanov would have her head on the chopping block. Ivanov didn't like it when anyone screwed up, and this was a costly operation. She'd heard him tell his number two, a new man, since too many others had been either killed or incarcerated, that the sales from the heroin would take ROC to an operating value worth more than many governments.

It didn't matter to her, once this mission was complete. She'd have her new identity, and begin a new life somewhere else, far from this.

As the police officer and other man spoke inside the truck, she couldn't see their lips, couldn't begin to guess what it was about. But she knew the man was at least an undercover cop. Based on his hand-to-hand combat skills, he was former military or FBI, probably both. No matter. All she wanted from him now was to get to the librarian. He had personal interest in the woman or he wouldn't have worked so hard to keep Ludmila from her.

"Melissa, can you take care of table three?" Bob, her clueless night manager, addressed her by the pseudonym she'd carefully generated.

"Sure thing, boss." She prided herself on her faultless American accent, the red wig she wore, the way she walked just like the locals did. Without the constant sense of being followed that most Russians lived with each day. It was something she always lived with, because she knew ROC would cut her from the payroll the minute she was no longer needed. She wouldn't just lose a paycheck, though, but her life. Once an ROC operative, always ROC. There was no such thing as quitting or leaving the group. Which was why she'd planned her disappearance so thoroughly.

\* \* \*

Kyle and Josh sat at the Formica-topped dinette and bantered about the storm as the waitress approached. It was never smart to talk business anywhere but SVPD or TH headquarters, as they didn't know who could be listening.

"Can I get you something to drink?" The redhead's eyes didn't meet his and Kyle figured she wanted to be home for the storm, not taking care of a cop and his buddy in the midst of it.

"I'll have a coffee, black." He'd be up most of the night anyway, sorting through the data he'd downloaded onto his portable laptop in the truck.

"Same." Josh waited for the waitress to be out of earshot. "I'll get the stick to TH tomorrow for analysis. From what you just downloaded, it seems to me it's a normal old USB stick, though." Josh had encouraged Kyle to download whatever was on it.

"I don't think it's anything but a digital storage device, Josh. Which makes me want to put it back on the shelf. We'll catch the handoff."

"True." Josh sat back to give the waitress room to place his coffee cup. He watched her as she walked away. "I don't recognize her. Do you? Not that I know every server in here, but most at least look familiar."

"No. And yes, I'm thinking what you're thinking, but unless she's slapped a bug under the table, she can't hear us."

They both laughed. Kyle knew that as a mission drew to its successful end, tensions made it easy to be paranoid.

"The ROC operatives around here have gotten more

sophisticated, that's for sure. I wouldn't put it past them to have spotters in this diner, the coffeehouse down the road, maybe even the library." Josh's concern echoed Kyle's thoughts.

"They most likely do, but not in the library. There haven't been any new hires there in six months, and they began this particular branch of business only in the last two."

Neither of them spoke for a few minutes, lost in their thoughts.

"How long do you think it'll take you to figure out what's going on with the data?" Josh's voice was quiet, concern in his tone.

"I'll figure it out pretty quickly. Many of the ROC thugs use different idioms, but I've had training in most. Fortunately, they're not usually big on making their directives complicated."

"But they don't usually go to such extremes with their communications, either."

"True." Kyle finished his coffee. "I've got an information technology expert on hand, though. She'll see whatever I miss."

Josh slammed his cup down. "Portia's not law enforcement of any kind, Kyle."

"I hear you. But the information isn't classified on its own, you know. And if she can make it go faster, why not?"

Josh's face brightened. "One thing Portia enjoys is helping out. From what Annie's been telling me, Portia's bored to tears out there."

"She seems to keep herself busy, though. She's still

planning the gala." He noticed the waitress heading back to pour refills. Had she heard him say anything?

They continued their conversation after she walked away.

"Do you think she'll be able to attend it?"

"I'll make sure of it." He hadn't realized it until he'd said it aloud, but he was in fact going to get Portia to that gala if he had to take her himself. He'd worry about it looking too much like a date later.

Portia had never spent so much time without contact with other human beings in her life. And the one person she had access to, Kyle, was the very man she needed to protect herself from.

Sometimes life just wasn't fair. She walked around the house and checked every egress point as Kyle had shown her, making sure the doors and windows were secure. There was no telling when he'd be back, and she needed to get some rest. She had one week until the gala and just as much work to accomplish. It was easier when she was at the library, as she could see at a glance who'd dropped off auction items as they came in. As it was, she had to rely on her staff to email her, and since the gala was a charity event, it didn't trump daily operations. The extra cold winter had a booming effect on library patronage, as reading and watching DVDs were two cold-weather favorites.

As she checked the fasteners on a stair-landing window, she saw headlights approach down the long drive. Fear snuck around her carefully constructed serenity, reminded her that she'd almost died not only on the train tracks but had been targeted by the ROC woman at one of her safest places—the homeless shelter.

*Please let it be Kyle.* She repeated the mantra, not stopping until she recognized his shape as he got out of the same truck he'd driven her back here in. Relief was short-lived, however, as she watched through the curtain of wind-driven snow and saw him open his back door and pull out several objects. She prayed it was the snow, but the shape of one of them was undeniable.

Why had Kyle brought weapons to the house? She knew he carried a pistol, expected him to always have it on his person. He was law enforcement; it was part of his job. But if what she watched him carry toward the house were indeed a rifle and possibly other firearms, what did he expect to do with them?

She ran down the stairs to the front door and threw it open just as she heard the scratch of his key.

Kyle's face was lit by the foyer light that spilled from behind her. His expression barely registered surprise but she did note something more welcoming—pleasure?

"Here." He didn't greet her except to shove one of the objects at her, which she accepted. Her hands closed around a long barrel, confirming her suspicions.

"What are you doing, bringing these guns out here?" She had to shout over the roar of the wind. How he'd made it back from town safely was beyond her.

"Get in the house." He didn't have to shout—his voice sliced through the high pitch of the wind with little effort. And wrapped around her a little too tightly.

"I don't take orders from you, Kyle." Still, she backed up so that he could come in. He stomped his snow-covered boots on the front porch, and then again after he'd shut the door behind him, locking it with purpose. When he turned to face her, he shoved his hood back and took off his ski cap. His eyes found hers and he waited to make sure he had her attention. As if she'd ever be able to ignore him.

"I meant to tell you about these earlier. We're up against a cold-blooded assassin here. She won't hesitate to kill you. You don't have to like having weapons in the house, but right now we don't have a choice."

Portia's throat constricted against the retort she'd planned to hurl at him, to remind him that she was here willingly but her cooperation stopped short of housing an arsenal of killing machines. Unbidden tears flooded her vision and when she blinked, huge drops fell and ran down her cheeks.

"When you put it like that..." She gulped, steeled her spine. "I've never fired a gun before, but I'm sure you can show me how."

Her stomach sank at the prospect but she was determined to help where she could. If keeping herself safe helped Kyle spend more time on his work, and hastened the capture of ROC's major players, then so be it.

Kyle watched as her conflict played out in her expression. He fought his hands as they itched to drop the weapons and wipe away Portia's tears. To kiss her until she forgot her life was at risk.

But that wasn't what a good protector did. And he was her protector, even if it was a self-assignment.

"Let me get my coat off, and then we'll go through this. I thought you'd be asleep by now."

"I did, too, but the wind is louder than I've ever heard it. And I've lived—"

"Here your entire life. I know." He gave her what he hoped was a reassuring smile. "You've told me, and it's one of your many admirable traits." He hung his parka on the hooks just inside the door.

"Why is that?"

"You could have gone anywhere in the world, still could, but you brought your talents back to Silver Valley after you graduated."

Doubt clouded her eyes. "I keep forgetting that you know everything about me."

"Not everything, just the highlights of your resume. And maybe a little more." Like her birthday, the fact she'd dated a dirtbag politician last year and, much to his great gratitude, dropped the dude when she'd discovered he was a wanderer.

They walked to the kitchen, where he made use of the oversize island and nodded for her to set down the rifle, while he laid down two handguns, his backpack and his personal .45.

"None of these have any ammunition in them yet, that's in my backpack, but I'm going to show you how to check to make sure the chambers are clear and how to use each one. We'll do it in the morning, when you're most alert."

"Fair enough." He loved the steel in her voice. Portia was courageous if nothing else, and she was a lot else. In fact, she could easily become everything to the right man.

*It can't be you.*

"I'm going to stay up for a while, going through some evidence. I can work in the basement rec area if you need me to."

"Not at all. I don't hear much in my room, unless I walk out onto the balcony, and there won't be any of that tonight."

At the mention of the private deck, his jaw tightened. There weren't any stairs attached, and it was two stories up from the ground that sloped away, as the house was built halfway up a mountain. But still, someone trained in rock climbing or rappelling, or a highly trained burglar, could use it as an entrance point. He mentally saw how he'd do it, with the right equipment. How he'd scale the house wall with the aid of a rope he'd fasten to the deck with one carefully aimed throw. But instead of himself, he saw Ludmila Markova, her profile.

And his insides froze.

"Kyle, what's wrong?"

"Son of a bitch." Quickly he told Portia about the waitress at the diner. "I thought something was unusual about her, but she didn't have an accent and she was in a perfect disguise. But the profile—I know it was her."

"Can I know her name?"

He looked at her, weighed the risks. "Ludmila Markova is the name I have, who she was when she immigrated to the US almost three years ago. She's been working for ROC ever since, under many aliases." So many that he couldn't be certain of all the intelligence TH had on her. Random reports could mean something but could also be throwaway, useless information that was meant to distract American law enforcement.

"Ludmila Markova." Portia leaned her hip on the island. "She sounds like a Russian spy."

"As she was trained to be, most likely. But she's here now, and our problem until we figure out what she's protecting." He pulled his laptop from his backpack. "I have hundreds of pages of spreadsheets loaded on my computer that I'm going to spend the night looking at."

"I'd love to help if you'd like. I don't see myself being able to sleep through this." At that instant a huge gust hit the house and he felt the shudders vibrate through the hardwood floor under his stockinged feet.

Portia's eyes widened. "That had to be a seventy-mile-an-hour gust, at least, to make this big place feel it."

Kyle agreed. The house was the best money could build and he wouldn't have expected it to feel the effects of the storm at all.

As they stood in the kitchen, gazes locked, he felt the heat he'd been fighting return as strongly as the raging snowstorm. Portia felt it, too, and as he wavered between leaning in and kissing her or running down to the basement to keep them both safe from whatever it was that they shared, the lights flickered. Once, twice and then they were plunged into total darkness.

"Kyle?"

"Yeah?"

"Please tell me a house this fancy has a generator somewhere."

# Chapter 14

Kyle used the flashlight he kept in his backpack to find and start up the generator, located along one side of the sprawling house. Portia was relieved to know she'd still have access to Wi-Fi and her library system. Although if the rest of Silver Valley lost power, it was a moot point. The library had a generator but it was minimal, existing only to keep the emergency lights on. The computers and server that were the gateway to her work wouldn't be available.

"I have an extra battery charger in my room. I keep it in my bag. It has enough power to restart a dead car battery," she said as she scoured the columns of the spreadsheets on Kyle's laptop. "We don't have to worry about how long this takes."

They sat next to one another at the dining room table, she wrapped in a down throw and he in sweatpants and a long-sleeved thermal shirt, with a flannel shirt as an added layer. The house generator could handle the heating system but not at the constant rate needed to keep up with the plummeting temperatures.

"I'm sure we'll need it. It's going to take days to get through this information." She heard the despair in his voice.

"To summarize, you think that there's a heroin shipment inbound and it's going to be collected here, in Silver Valley?"

"Yes. We know it's inbound but we're not sure when or how. In the past, ROC has used shipping containers, mostly those on long-haul trucks instead of trains. They like to hide the drugs in with random goods being shipped here on a regular basis. Then they take out the truck driver and get the illicit drugs. We've found traces in everything from major appliance to kitty litter shipments."

"Okay. So we need to take a look at these spreadsheets and keep the big picture in mind. Figure out the commonalities, and if we can find a delivery timetable."

"Portia."

She looked up from his laptop. His eyes were on her, his expression soft. "What?"

"I did run it by Claudia to make sure I have the okay for you to see this information. But it isn't your job, babe. I've got it."

"Apparently you don't 'have' it, or you wouldn't look like you're about to pull your hair out." She ran her fingers through his hair and gave him a sound kiss on the lips, surprising herself with how easy it was to partner with this man. "And you have lovely hair, so let's get to it, shall we?"

* * *

"It was insane to think you could ever do this on your own, Kyle. You're looking for a needle in a haystack, you know." Portia spoke as if she were an expert at intelligence analysis, and Kyle's deadpan expression made her giggle.

"Um, yeah. That's why I got permission from Claudia to have you help me with this."

"At least the snowstorm will keep the trains from running, so that buys you some time, right?"

He nodded, his face taut with concentration in the light of the laptop screen.

"Wait—what did you say about a train?" His five o'clock shadow had turned into two-in-the-morning sexy scruff and she longed to touch it. To lick it. Portia blinked, and not just to keep the spreadsheets from blurring. She leaned back from the display, put some inches between her and Kyle.

"You're looking at the products carried on trains that pass through central Pennsylvania, and thus Silver Valley."

"How do you know this, from just looking at these spreadsheets?" His skepticism was punctuated by fatigue.

"You're in luck, Agent King. I happen to have a very good working knowledge of the resources and consumer goods that come in and through Silver Valley, as the graduating senior high school class participated in a nationwide survey on local economies."

"And?"

"These spreadsheets are set up in exactly the same way. Except instead of having every single train, container load and where it's from, this lists what each container will have." She skimmed over the count-less processed food, raw grain and other miscellaneous commodities. "We know they're including their heroin shipment in with regular goods, but it won't all be on one train. Which is smart, when you think of it. This way, if they get caught, they won't lose it all."

Kyle's expression morphed to reflect his enthusi-asm. "Can you tell which trains will have the drugs in them?"

Portia stared at the data, then smiled. "For sure. If you look at this column, it's the pounds per container of whichever good is being shipped. This column next to it, though, doesn't have a header like the others." She pointed at the container rows, and then the train, time of arrival, gross weight and commercial value columns. "This column header has a summation sign, and look at the numbers—they're all close to the same amount. The rows with summation numbers match certain trains."

"Ten kilos." Kyle's eyes flashed as he scrolled through the long list, pages long, in fact, of the ship-ments. "If they're adding ten kilos of pure heroin to each of these containers as marked, then it looks like..." He scrolled through the pages of lists. She sat quietly next to him, thinking about whom they could contact at the train depot and the other industry lead-ers for where the tracks ran. "That's a shipment of just over eleven million, street value."

"And that's just one." She couldn't keep from think-ing about Lani and how her OD was just an incon-sequential statistic to ROC, meaningless to the drug runners and dealers, except that it meant one less user to give them money. She felt Kyle's gaze on hers and looked at him. "I lost a high school classmate, someone I kept in touch with up until two or so years ago, to an OD. Her heroin dose had been laced with fentanyl."

"I know—Annie knew her, too, right? Claudia told me. I'm sorry, Portia. I have a former Marine buddy from the war who gave in to it, too." Quiet words of compassion that didn't match his tough-guy demeanor. Another reason to fall so damn hard for Kyle.

"I'm sorry for your loss, too." She sighed. "It's all over the news as an epidemic. It shouldn't be a surprise to anyone how deeply entrenched opioid addiction is in our culture. And yet…"

"And yet it still leaves a hole in your gut?" He looked at her with complete comprehension. "Yeah, I get it, believe me."

"Kyle."

"Hmm?" He was scribbling on a notepad with a tiny pencil as he scrolled through the data.

"I will do whatever I can to help you catch these awful people."

"I appreciate that, but you've already done it. It would have taken me hours to figure out this is a train manifest."

"You can thank Silver Valley High and their research assignments." She smiled at the memory of when she'd first learned how to use a spreadsheet.

The power from the generator flickered, indicated by the warning alarm from the refrigerator that the power had gone out.

"Kyle, I think we should back up all of this to the cloud ASAP, while there's still a working generator to keep the Wi-Fi stable."

"I'm on it." The circling symbol in the middle of the

screen confirmed his claim. As they sat there, Portia realized ROC was waiting it out now, too. No trains were moving anywhere from Virginia up through Maine. For all they knew, the drugs could be offloaded in another town or state, far from the madness that was bound to be Silver Valley while the snowstorm raged.

"This is very specific, Kyle. I'd imagine if you are able to compare these with the bills of loading from the matching corporations and the railroad, you'll figure out the dates of the first deliveries."

"I'll pass what we—what you—figured out to Josh as soon as this backup is done." He looked relieved.

"Could it be this simple?"

His eyes widened slightly. "What's that?"

"That you capture the shipment, prevent the bad guys from getting drugs into the hands of users and in turn apprehend Markova?"

A soft smile etched in his handsome face. "It could be." He didn't say anything more and she didn't press it. It made sense that he'd seen so much that she only could imagine, or read about in a spy novel.

"And that's that." He clicked the spreadsheets back open, the digital backup finished. "I'd be happier with a hard copy, but this will do."

"There's a printer in the home office, and if you have the right cable, we can make it happen. The Wi-Fi's out, so we can't do it wirelessly, but the old-fashioned way works."

"Good idea." Within minutes they'd hauled the printer from the office, plugged it into a working outlet and attached his laptop. Page after page printed, making the dark intent of ROC undeniable.

As the last pages printed, she caught Kyle fighting to keep his eyes open.

"Since we seem to have a bit of a reprieve thanks to the storm, I'd suggest we get some rest. The last reports indicate we'll be stuck here for at least the next two days."

"I can't risk missing something." His frown deepened.

She closed the laptop, plunging them into darkness, save for the gas fireplace, which they'd left on to give the living area some heat since the furnace wasn't keeping up with the cold.

"You stand a better chance of overlooking an important detail because you're exhausted." She stood up and carried the laptop to the coffee table, where she had her portable charger. "I'll plug this in so it's ready to roll in the morning."

"I don't know if I can sleep, Portia. The storm could mask an intruder." He'd walked up to the fireplace, where he stood and leaned against the mantel, looking into the flames.

"It could, but did you see the same weather report I did? The gusts are up to seventy-five miles an hour, and look out the window—visibility is what, a foot or less? The governor's declared a state of emergency for the entire state, as has New Jersey and New York. Anyone who ventures outside is subject to arrest. I know I'm not law enforcement but it seems to me that if I were working for ROC, I'd keep a very low profile. Going out now is too risky. No matter how trained they are."

*There. That should mollify him.* She watched the shadows flick across his face.

"Markova is driven by a need to win. To her, murdering someone in cold blood means nothing if it gets her the prize. Right now her goal is to make sure ROC's plans to distribute heroin through Silver Valley remain intact. She's not going to allow anything to screw it up, including a possible witness. And she won't stop until she knows you're silenced."

Kyle didn't have to tell her how she'd be silenced. By death. Portia knew the woman she was just a little over two weeks ago would have balked at the thought of being targeted by a trained assassin. That woman had changed, though, had faced death twice, survived and also met a once-in-a-lifetime man. A man she couldn't claim, no matter how much she wanted to. They were two different types of people, she and Kyle. He needed to be on the go, constantly in the midst of a mission that somehow involved him saving the world.

All Portia wanted was to make the world more livable. In her library career, she opened worlds to people through books, film, the internet. Her community service work made life a little easier for those who struggled, she hoped.

And she wanted to get back to her life as soon as she could, wanted Kyle and all the involved LEAs to take Markova and any of her pals off the streets. But as she stared at the same flames and Kyle, Portia realized she wasn't afraid. Next to Kyle, she felt invincible, able to tackle anything.

Although the thought of using a gun against any living thing still troubled her, she knew that she'd do what she had to do to stay alive.

"I think it's okay to sleep now. Do another check of the inside perimeter if you want, but I need to get some sleep."

Kyle's gaze sought hers in the dim light and she read weariness, fatigue in the silver depths. "I'll do just that. You haven't considered something else, Portia."

"What now?"

"The house is going to be damned cold once we shut down the fireplace—we can't keep it going all night, if we want the heater to stay decently powered."

She'd seen the thermostat—even with the heater going full blast, the inside temperature of the house was well below a comfortable room setting. "So you want to conserve body heat together? How gallant of you."

He laughed and the warmth that spread through her was all she needed. Nothing delighted her more than to see the serious agent he was 24/7 lighten up.

"It's in my job description."

"Being naked with a civilian?"

He sobered. "No. Not naked. We'll wear our pajamas." His focus on the mission was back full-force.

She scoffed in an effort to help him chill. "Do you even have sleepwear?" She hadn't seen him in anything but his work clothes and naked.

"I have long underwear. It's the only thing that made it bearable to do the long stakeouts I've had to."

Portia felt stupid that she hadn't considered something as simple as long underwear as part of his gear. "I thought you were literally freezing your butt off on the streets, in that awful homeless disguise. By 'awful' I mean it looks really, really authentic."

"Thank you. I appreciate that from you. You'd know right away if someone was a poser in the shelter, I'm sure."

"We've had a few, for sure. One couple dragged their poor kids in with them, said they'd been evicted by an unreasonable landlord."

"And?"

"They'd been evicted, all right, for making meth in the living room. It was a miracle the kids were still healthy enough to walk in with them. The neglect, it—" She broke off, suddenly overcome by tears. "Geez, I'm not usually this emotional."

"You've been under a lot of stress."

"Trust me, there's nothing stressful about this house. And I have all the time I want to work on the gala, so it's been kind of a win-win that way."

"But you're isolated, away from the people and town you thrive on." Kyle rubbed his scruff, shut the fireplace down with one flick of the switch. "Let's do this. We'll use your bed, as it's bigger."

"And has the balcony. So we can escape if we have to. And you can make sure no one climbs onto it. If they do, you'll take care of it then and there. Am I right?"

She couldn't see his face but swore she felt his grin. "You always are." His voice was closer. "Can you follow me back?"

"Yes." She'd follow him anywhere. She'd even looked up the town in California where he'd mentioned he'd grown up. Her job as an information specialist added to her natural curiosity about things in general. Where Kyle was concerned, it could quickly become an obsession. He still hadn't solved the ROC case, Markova remained at large, Portia still had a target on her head, and yet she already felt the pain his departure would leave in its wake.

So much for keeping her defenses up.

* * *

Kyle slid into the bed next to Portia right after he rechecked every single ingress and egress route the large home had to offer. It was a sturdy enough building but even the custom slate roof tiles sounded as though they creaked in the gale-force winds. It was the wind barreling through the eaves, and the way it gusseted the large expanses of lumber and river stone that made up the edifice. He'd been through some dicey weather situations during his military and Trail Hiker time, but this was his first full-fledged blizzard.

He knew it wasn't Markova's. The ROC operative had the advantage of growing up in Russia, where tonight's storm wouldn't have been unfamiliar. Kyle took solace in the fact that Markova was on his turf now, and one thing he knew for sure was that the woman wouldn't be able to just take out Portia DiNapoli. Markova would want to ask Portia how much she knew about him, including whom he worked for. Before she killed Portia.

He wanted Markova to know with zero doubt that he was as dedicated as she. He'd pull a trigger whenever he had to, to stop the threat she brought.

Portia had fallen into a deep slumber—if her light snores were any indication. He watched her sleep for a bit, the soft glow of a night-light his only way to see. True to what he'd promised, he stripped down to his long johns and kept to his side of the bed once in it. Aww, what the hay. He wrapped his arm around her slumbering form and pulled her back up against his front, noting that she, too, was in long-sleeved pajamas with full-length bottoms.

It was impossible to stop the flood of memories at

the nearness of her, the scent of her hair and skin. He inhaled deeply, then forced his eyes shut. The sooner he could drift off, the better for both of them. He had to keep her safe and she was right—this portion of the storm gave them the most protection. The greatest chance to play house would be another perspective, but he reeled his musings back from the danger zone.

He was Portia's protector, and the agent on the case that had the potential to stop ROC in its tracks. Or at least on the train tracks, with the heroin shipment intact and out of the hands of potential users. And victims.

He closed his eyes again, tried to let the constant howl of the wind and the snow battering the house soothe him.

Because if he couldn't sleep, he wasn't sure he'd be able to resist his body's insatiable need for Portia.

# Chapter 15

Portia slept deeply, awaking to a soft sound that didn't match the rhythm of the wind.

*Kyle.*

He snored softly next to her, his body warm and hard against hers. She'd moved to her back and he lay on his side, his arm across her waist, his face snuggled into her shoulder. She slowly stretched, pointing and flexing her toes, allowing reality to sink back in.

Someone wanted to kill her. It made her think about how comfortable her life had been before, how naive she'd been, in many ways, to go about her business and not even consider what others sacrificed so that she could live in a relatively safe town.

Until ROC showed up. But as she thought about it, Silver Valley had faced its demons these past few years. A cult had almost infiltrated the town, its obsessed leader trying to take several innocent children down with him. Fortunately SVPD had stopped them. With a start, she acknowledged that Trail Hikers must have been a part of that, too.

And now she knew TH was actively fighting ROC, and had no doubt played a big role in the recent apprehension of several criminals involved in a human trafficking scheme. Not wanting to wake him, she inched out of Kyle's hold, reaching for the floor with her bare feet. The contrast of the cold air with the warmth she was leaving made her have to force herself to get out of the bed.

"Where you goin'?" His arm tightened around her waist and she hung in limbo, one toe on the throw rug next to the bed frame as her leg dangled.

"I thought I'd make coffee, get another look at the spreadsheets." Since he was awake, she reached for her phone, still charged. Using her cellular connection, she checked the weather reports. And groaned.

"What?" He was propped on his elbow, watching her. She loved the energy he gave off when he did this, making her feel like she was the only woman in the world, and the most beautiful.

"Four feet have fallen already, with up to another foot expected. The below-zero temperatures are going to make for up to ten-foot drifts. And it's going to last for at least another two days."

Two days stuck in the house she'd been basically exiled to didn't seem so bad, not with Kyle next to her.

"Put your phone away, Portia, and get naked." His huge hand playfully batted at hers. As soon as her phone hit the nightstand, he pulled her ass up against his pelvis.

"Oh." His unclothed erection pressed insistently against her cheeks. "You're fully awake, I'd say." She turned onto her back and looked at him. His silver eyes shone through slits and his nostrils flared. "I thought we were trying to keep our distance. To be professional."

"That was before we survived a night in a blizzard together." He leaned in but remained a breath away from her lips, allowing her to make the choice. It was going to hurt like hell when he left town, but her regret would be even deeper if she didn't make the most of the present. With Kyle.

"It's a good idea to maintain a good working relationship, right? Since we're going to be stuck together for at least another forty-eight hours."

"Kiss me, babe."

She pulled his head down and let his mouth work its magic. In the morning light, which was made paler by the storm's blocking of the sun, she reveled in every touch, every caress as he took his time, kissing her until she was breathless, and then moving his mouth to her throat, her breasts, her stomach, making her quiver with want at each juncture. As he gently sucked on the skin inside her thighs, her need rose and she sat up, pushing him onto his back.

"Let me make you feel just as good, Kyle."

"Babe." He actually looked pained, as if going down on her had been all he'd ever wanted to do. Something deep and lasting tugged inside her but she didn't want to take any time or space away from right here, right now.

She pushed on his shoulders, made him lie back and mirrored what he'd done to her, not stopping when she got to the dip of his belly button in his taut, chiseled abs. Her tongue led the way down the hair that led to his erection, hot and hard. For her.

It was so easy to make love to Kyle. As she took him in her mouth, heard his gasp, inhaled his very essence, she'd never been more complete. This was what a true partnership was about. Not waiting for someone to see that you were just as important as their job, not always wondering if you measured up to their last love.

With Kyle, she knew that, in this moment, she was all that mattered to him, and he was all she thought about, all she wanted.

As her tongue licked and circled, her mouth sucked, and her fingers stroked his shaft, the sensitive area between his legs, he grew harder than she thought possible. When she thought his release was near, she prepared to accept it all, but his hands were on her, lifting her atop him.

"Condom," he said between gasps for breath, and his arousal excited her more than she'd ever experienced. With shaky hands, she placed a condom from the night table on him, the mental effort to focus on the task almost too much. Finally, they allowed their instincts to take over.

Kyle's hands grasped her hips and shoved her down on him with no preamble. None was needed, as she was so hot and wet from their leisurely foreplay.

There was nothing leisurely about how they coupled as he thrust up into her again and again, and she matched his every move not only likewise but also writhed her hips over and around him, clenching and unclenching him as she did so, delighting in every gasp she drew out of him. His hands reached for her as he moved, one between her legs, one on her breast, and when he pressed both her nipple and bud at her center, her climax thundered through her. Kyle's cries sounded almost immediately, and even in the throes of the most sensual, lusty sex of her life, she was aware that he'd waited for her to come first.

Kyle always put her first.

Ludmila Markova knew she was in big trouble with Ivanov. The mark hadn't picked up the USB before the storm hit, and now no one but she had access to the spreadsheets. Ivanov told her that she was personally responsible for making sure the shipment arrived in Silver Valley as planned, and that his dealers received what they expected without a hitch.

But the storm was bigger than this spoiled country was used to. Or the trains. Nothing was moving in the town, or in central Pennsylvania. She knew better than to argue with Ivanov. She'd told his number two that she'd make sure everything worked out. And knew she was lucky that they didn't have anyone else to rely on, or they'd have killed her on the spot. ROC suffered fools almost as infrequently as FSB had. Meaning never.

Her rathole trailer shook with the force of the wind. At least in Moscow the concrete edifices that passed for apartments were strong against the elements. The windows might crack but the building would never shake like this.

She sipped the hot tea with lemon and honey, something she only allowed herself in the trailer. It was too Russian, would make her stick out too much in this average American town that seemed to live on coffee.

As she drank the beverage, she fingered the piece of paper she'd taken from the library information desk. Just in case.

It was what the Americans called a "flyer," a public invitation to attend an annual library fund-raising gala, which she surmised was a dance of some sort. There would be charity activities involved somehow. Most important, it was coordinated by none other than Portia DiNapoli, whose name and email were indicated as the RSVP point. The event coincided perfectly with the first of five drops by their suppliers down south. It made her final actions in Silver Valley more complicated, more risky. Ensure the heroin distribution and kill DiNapoli. But challenge was her specialty. She allowed herself to smile. The shipment via rail had been her idea, and despite the storm, which no one could have predicted, it was perfect for what Ivanov wanted. A crushing hand of control over the heroin trade on the East Coast.

She looked out the small, dirty trailer window as the storm intensified, and she made mental preparations for keeping herself warm. Not only in this hovel, but when she went out to explore a bit. To the place she'd followed the man who didn't leave the librarian's side.

Ivanov and ROC still didn't know that she had a potential witness. Two, actually. The librarian, and the man who'd knocked her off the tracks. The same man who'd been in the diner, and while his gaze had lingered a beat too long on her, she was certain he hadn't immediately recognized her in the wig. When his memory put her with the waitress, it'd be too late. She was going to kill him, along with Portia. If Ivanov knew about her probable witnesses, he'd kill her.

There was always someone else to coordinate his heroin trade.

The man always with Portia DiNapoli was a worthy adversary, as he'd demonstrated at the homeless shelter. She assumed it had been him, keeping her from what she'd hoped to be an easy kill. No matter. His devotion to keeping the librarian safe was his Achilles' heel, and she was at her best when stomping on someone's weakest spot.

Her teacup was empty, the lemon slice withered and cold. Time to begin her plan. First she had a couple to put on edge. Let them know they weren't as safe and sound as they thought.

"Smart thinking on the coffee." He sipped the espresso she'd made with an old-fashioned Italian percolator on the gas-burner stovetop. He'd watched her light a match and then the burner, the electric starters rendered useless by the limited power.

"We're lucky the owners had this pot or I'd have had to make pour-over with the grounds."

"That would be fine, too." Anything with her would be fantastic, in fact. He had a killer to catch, a heroin shipment to interdict and ROC to put a dent into. Normally he'd be wired for sound, unable to do anything but focus on the mission until he successfully ripped all of his targets apart.

But now there was Portia.

"The storm's stalled." Portia scrolled through her phone. "They don't know when it'll move out of here. We could be stuck in this house for days!"

He should care, be concerned about the case, the shipment, Markova, ROC.

All he saw was the beautiful woman standing in front of him.

"Portia."

"Hmm?"

"Put down your phone. Let's go back to bed."

# Chapter 16

Sleeping next to a man was a lovely thing. When the man was Kyle King, it was heaven. Portia didn't want to open her eyes, so she snuggled in deeper against him, her body the most relaxed it'd been in months.

She had Kyle's tongue to thank. Unable to remain completely at rest once that thought entered her mind, she carefully rolled onto her back, keeping his arm around her waist. She looked up at his face as he slept. The day's growth of whiskers had been rough against the inside of her thighs, but she'd gladly taken the love injury. And how had he known to use his fingers at the exact right time, to make what his tongue did seem like rookie moves? Desire woke up, deep in her belly, and she smiled, decided to wait as long as it took for him to wake up. She'd watch him until then, get more turned on until he opened his eyes.

A powerful gust of wind rattled the windows, and the French doors that led to the room's balcony shook as if someone was trying to open them.

Portia dragged her gaze from Kyle's gorgeous sleeping face to look through the window. She'd left the blinds up last night, wanting to see the progress of the storm. With the driving snow, there was no chance of anyone seeing inside. Which made it a shock for her to see a person at the window, looking in.

Portia's nails dug into his forearm like a drowning person's death grasp. Kyle opened his eyes, immediately alert, and looked to where her gaze had frozen.

With no preamble, he took them both over the side of the bed furthest from the window, and grabbed one of the pistols he'd positioned on the nightstands—one on each for just such an instance.

Portia scrambled to her knees and crouched as he did behind the bed.

"Did she see us?" Her voice trembled but to her credit she remained at his side, didn't scream or try to run from the room.

"No telling. And we can't be sure it's Markova." Though he'd recognize her shape anywhere. He'd tracked her for months at this point.

*You screwed up in the diner.* He mentally shoved the accusation away. He couldn't change the past but he could keep Portia safe now.

"Well, since she's out to kill me, I think it's a logical conclusion." Portia's wit was something he loved about her, but right now he recognized it for what it was. Nervous chatter.

"Shh." He leveled his weapon at the door, and saw

the intruder try to peer in. "I agree with you. It's Markova." Who else would venture out in this storm and attempt a break-in, knowing Portia wasn't alone? Because if Markova figured out where Portia was, it had to have been via Kyle's movements. He had to review what he'd done, where he'd been, to figure out how she knew. But not now.

Proof of identity came when the climber removed their black balaclava, probably to see the lock she needed to pick better. Her pale blonde hair fell forward. No red wig this time. Son of a bitch—just as he'd suspected, she'd been the waitress in the diner. She must have followed him out here right afterward. He'd been certain he didn't have a trail, but with the visibility so low, it was conceivable she'd followed him with her lights out, using his to guide her.

And then she'd waited until she'd known they were asleep to make her move.

"It's her, Kyle."

"Yes." He took his phone from the dresser, pressed his finger to it to unlock it and then handed it to her. "Here. Call Josh—he's in my recent calls. Tell him what's going on. And once you hang up, take the rifle from underneath the bed and be prepared to use it."

"You put a rifle under the bed I was sleeping on?"

"Of course."

As she called and spoke to Josh, Kyle watched Markova work the lock. The storm raged and yet to her, a native Muscovite, it was business as usual.

"Josh says he can't get anyone out here right now but he's confident you'll take care of her."

"He's right." He didn't take his focus off Markova. "I want you to take the rifle and get out of this room. Go to the storage room on the top floor like we practiced. Lock yourself in and don't come out until I get you."

"No way! You might need backup."

"I can't do this with you right now, Portia. Get. Out. Of. Here." At his last word, the French doors clicked open, followed by huge double *bams* as the wind blew them against the walls.

Portia escaped just in time, and Kyle was pretty sure Markova hadn't seen her. It didn't matter if she did, because he was taking her down, now.

"Freeze." She did, in the catlike pose she'd assumed on the railroad tracks with Portia. It was a prestrike stance, meant to appear defensive but was, in fact, preparation for a lethal move.

"I will shoot you." He didn't reveal he knew who she was, keeping the power balance of information on his side.

"You would have already put the bullet between my eyes if you meant to." She didn't try to hide her accent, unlike at the diner and the times he'd seen her come and go at the library.

"Put your hands over your head and get to your knees." He didn't have cuffs but he had zip ties in the pockets of his cargo pants, next to the bed. They'd do until SVPD arrived.

"Never." She sprang into action, but instead of attempting to take him out as he'd expected, she ran toward the bedroom door that led to the inside hallway and disappeared. Once around the corner, he heard a weapon fire.

*Portia.*

He ran into the hall, his weapon drawn. He expected to face down Markova.

But she was ahead of him, opening the sliding doors to the main living room's outside deck. He ran after her and watched as she slipped through the open door, onto the deck, and disappeared over the edge. Kyle ran to the railing, the assault of wind and driving snow fighting his every movement. Looking down, he saw where she'd dropped and rolled. Of course she was trained to scale any height, but the twenty-foot drop was a bit much. Except that it was shorter by at least four or five feet, thanks to the storm. To his eye, it looked like as much as six or eight feet of snow had drifted up against the back of the house, which overlooked the mountains. Her silhouette was quickly swallowed up by the blinding snow.

It didn't mean she was gone, though. Markova was still on the property. He had two options—jump here and risk injury, or go out the front door and cut her off before she reached the main road again. There was no hope for survival in the woods, not in these conditions.

"That was easy." Portia's shout startled him and he stared at her. It was a full second before he noticed the bloodred stain on her pajama top.

"What the hell are you doing outside the storage room?" Didn't she realize that Markova was no match for her? And right now, challenging his every skill. "She shot you."

Portia shot him a wan smile. "Grazed me, is all. I know, it's probably the adrenaline keeping me from hurting or losing it about now. I was hiding behind the kitchen island and had a clear shot of her, but she saw me and fired first. I know I should have listened to you but I thought you'd need backup. She's not going to let you take her down easily. It's me she wants, Kyle."

Portia was shouting over the wind, her thin pajamas flattened against her body in the gale. A sound lower than the wind reached them and they both turned to see Markova speeding away—on a snowmobile.

Kyle hustled Portia back into the house with him and shut the sliding door behind them, cursing that the bedroom French door didn't have an interior deadbolt as this one and all the ground floor doors and windows did. The one fatal security flaw in the huge home and it had to be on the balcony of the room Portia slept in. He'd overlooked it and failed her. Worse, she could have been shot through the heart if Markova hadn't been in such a hurry to avoid capture.

"Let's get your wound checked."

Portia lifted the fabric from her shoulder, stretched to look at the wound. She'd been correct, it was a graze, but it was starting to sting now that they were back inside. It needed to be cleaned and bandaged.

"Does it hurt?"

"More like a sting. Nothing I can't handle. Don't you think we should double-check the house for any other place Markova tried to break in?"

"Yes—let's do a quick check and then I'm bandaging that for you." As they walked, he called Josh and reported what had happened, what direction he'd seen Markova head in. Josh promised to send an SVPD unit out as soon as it was safe, but warned Kyle that it could take a while, depending on the winds and visibility. And since Kyle was the best protection Portia had, if another incident got called in, it might take priority.

Kyle wasn't feeling like he was the best protector for Portia. Not by a long shot. He looked at her face, checked her pupils. She was okay. It was just a graze, and she'd handled herself well, considering she'd blown off his orders.

"I'm going to check the garage to make sure she didn't steal the snowmobile from us."

"I'll stay here." Portia's expression reflected the contrition he knew she'd never verbalize, so he let it go.

"Not this time." He shot the French door an uneasy look. If Markova made it up the side of the house once, she'd do it again. As much as he felt certain he'd scared her away, he couldn't trust his gut, not after letting his physical need for Portia distract him from keeping vigilance on the house.

"Stay with me."

Portia did as Kyle asked, and stayed with him as they searched the bottom floor of the house first. In the garage, they found the snowmobile and doors intact.

"I'm glad she didn't get in here. We may need the snowmobile," Kyle said as they left the garage and began to inspect the main floor for any evidence of a break-in.

"She was crazy to attempt this, in the storm. You're not thinking of going after her, are you?"

"Of course I am. But I won't." The grim line of his mouth was a far cry from the expression on his generous lips that had brought her to climax less than an hour ago.

"Because you're afraid she'll kill me." Portia stopped at the huge picture windows, stared at the snow blowing sideways. Visibility was still at a minimum. Her shoulder was starting to ache and she knew she'd have to draw attention to taking care of it. To her mistake, the error that could have cost Kyle his life, too, and the entire LEA mission. Shudders hit her and while her brain knew it was a delayed reaction, an accumulation of the hell she'd faced ever since the train tracks, she couldn't stop it.

"Hey." He was next to her in a flash, cupped her face in his hands. "Yes, I'm terrified she could have hurt you more seriously. You saved yourself, you know."

"I'm a librarian, Kyle, an information specialist. Fighting bad guys in person, with a weapon, isn't one of my talents."

"It is now." He kissed her forehead and took a step back. "Let's get the inspection finished so that I can tend to your scrape."

She followed him room by room, covering each window and door, but there were no further signs of a break-in. They found a first aid kit and sat in the master bath on the wide edge of a large garden tub as Kyle began to clean and bandage her shoulder.

Portia fought the urge to put her head on his shoulder, to sink into the strength of his embrace. The sting of antiseptic made her wince. To distract herself from the pain, she focused on the case. "How did she know the master bedroom door was the one that wasn't as secure as the rest of the house?"

Kyle met her eyes briefly before resuming his ministrations to her graze. "She didn't. It was an educated bet, at most. She's been out here, watching the house, seeing which rooms light up and when. Then she saw the balcony at the back part of the house, where the big bathroom windows are, and took a chance. With no stairs attached to the small bedroom deck, she knew there was a good chance that the door might not be as secure."

"You've done a lot of the same, haven't you?"

"Yes, but my motives are different."

"Oh, of course! I know that. I wasn't trying to say that you're at all like Markova, or any of these bad guys."

"I know you weren't. And it's undeniable that we employ a lot of the same skill sets."

"Except you're not corrupt. Or working for the bad guys."

His expression grew thoughtful. "No, no, I'm not."

Kyle's phone rang and he answered it, spoke briefly to the caller before disconnecting. He leveled his silver gaze on her, making her feel at once safe and apprehensive.

"What is it, Kyle?"

"That's Josh. He's going to be here with SVPD and a couple of FBI agents within ten minutes, give or take. The gale and low visibility will make it slower."

"I'll get a quick shower." She knew it might be cold, as the water heater had lost its energy source when they'd lost power. The generator could handle only so much of a load.

"Do more than that, Portia. Pack up your things. You're not safe here any longer." He nodded at her shoulder. "I'll resterilize that and patch it up as soon as you're dry."

She was grateful he left the bathroom immediately. It would be the ultimate humiliation for Kyle to see her tears. Hadn't she already caused enough trouble for him? Adding any kind of emotional burden to his plate wasn't fair. She knew it wasn't her fault that Markova was stalking her, trying to kill her. There wasn't blame to speak of, except that she couldn't expect more from Kyle right now than what he was here to do—bring down Markova and the ROC heroin operation.

The sting of the shower spray against her gunshot wound, no matter how minor the graze was, made her grit her teeth. It was still no match for the pain her heart filled with. She'd known it wasn't going to last, her intimacy with Kyle. But to have it ripped away so abruptly, when the damn storm wasn't even over, made big fat tears roll down her cheeks, mixing with the shower water.

After her shower she used the first aid kit to clean the wound again, and put a big bandage on it. Since it was on the front of her shoulder it was easy to reach, and she didn't think she could keep the tears at bay if Kyle touched her bare skin again right now.

When she walked into the kitchen, Josh and other SVPD officers were already there with Kyle.

Josh didn't consider Portia's request to return to her apartment. She'd wanted to go home to her parents, or at least one of her siblings, but that would put them at risk. If Markova was still after her.

"There's no reason to think she'll stop looking for you, Portia." Josh sat at the kitchen island with her and Kyle as the SVPD and FBI officers took evidence from the back bedroom. "You'll be absolutely safe living with me and Annie. We have plenty of room and this way you can go back to work at the library. Annie can escort you there and back each day, and we have a permanent SVPD officer assigned to protect the library until the case is closed."

"What about the library being used as a way to transfer information by ROC? Are you still going to stake it out?" She knew she sounded like the non-LEA civilian she was, but they'd get her drift.

"That's not your concern, Portia. We're on it. If we need to go in after hours, we will. If your staff asks questions about seeing SVPD or me on the security footage, tell them it's extra precautions due to the heroin epidemic. You don't have to mention ROC to anyone, even though it's been in the media. It's better to not confirm or deny anything related to it. For your sake, as well as Silver Valley's."

"Kyle's correct. I know it doesn't come naturally to you, but play ignorant if anyone asks you about it."

"Will do." Josh knew her, knew she'd follow through on the orders. LEA or not, Portia wanted what was best for all.

And that wasn't what she wanted for herself. Kyle leaned over the counter, engaged in the conversation but his mind drifting. Was he counting the minutes until he'd no longer be responsible for her, be free to go after Markova on his own?

"This won't affect the gala, will it?" It sounded shallow to bring up the charity event now, but her mind needed something to hang on to. Something familiar, solid. It couldn't be Kyle—he had a mission to take down the ROC op.

"It shouldn't." Josh ran his hand over his face. The ROC case was taking a toll on everyone she knew in law enforcement. "Kyle explained that you two figured out what's going on with the trains. Once the storm gets through here, it'll take several days to clear the tracks. Then the shipments will arrive, and we'll be ready to get them before any drug dealers do."

"But what about Markova?"

"As long as she thinks her plan is going smoothly, she'll be busy with that. She's tried to take you out two times for certain, a third if we count the train tracks. Although we couldn't have charged her with anything more than stealing a library laptop at that point."

"Josh is about to say that Markova's figured out that you're too hard of a target to catch. And she's going to be more concerned about getting the heroin unloaded and in the correct hands, so that ROC gets paid. Otherwise she'll have bigger problems than us."

Annie showed up two hours later to take Portia to the home she shared with Josh. Kyle couldn't have picked a better place himself. He trusted both of the TH agents and their training. Portia would be safe. Away from him, mostly. He hated to admit it but he and Portia had gotten too close. Not just for the op, either.

He had no business getting involved with a woman he was supposed to be protecting from the very adversary he was assigned to track and eventually apprehend. Yet he had, because Portia wasn't just any woman, wasn't someone he'd hooked up with out of sheer physical need. He had to have Portia on all levels—emotionally, physically, spiritually. And he couldn't. They didn't fit, on paper or elsewhere.

"I'm ready." Portia walked back into the kitchen, where he waited with Josh and Annie. She looked at each of them, her gaze resting the longest on him.

"Let's talk before you go." He looked at Annie and Josh.

"Excuse us."

Portia stilled and he thought she was going to refuse to talk to him. He wouldn't blame her—he hadn't softened any of this. The forensics team was still in the house, and what had been their prison and paradise was gone, another crime scene among the thousands he'd witnessed.

"Sure. Whatever you need." He walked past her and motioned for her to follow him to the back bedroom neither of them had used. It would be too hard to say goodbye in the very room they'd so recently made love in.

If only he'd been able to leave it at sex with her.

Impossible with Portia.

Once in the room, he closed the door behind them. The single large window overlooked the front part of the house and the snowfall continued, although the wind had begun to die down.

Portia's form was in a defensive posture, with her arms crossed over her chest. Meeting her eyes was the hardest mission he'd ever completed.

"What do you want to say, Kyle?" Ah, this was the Portia he knew.

"You never back down from a challenge, do you?" His hands twitched to cup her face, run his thumb along her soft skin.

"By 'challenge,' you mean accepting that there's nothing between us. Don't worry, Kyle. I'm sure you have a string of women behind you. I'm not one of them—I knew what I was getting into when we got together the first time."

As she spoke, it occurred to him that he'd lived a lifetime with her in just a couple of weeks. From the first time he'd seen her, to holding her in his arms after knocking her off the tracks, to their first hot kiss, to the way they'd devoured one another in many parts of this house, including the hot tub.

"Did you, Portia? Because I sure as hell didn't. I had no idea that we'd end up here, having to end something that shouldn't have started in the first place. And I sure as heck didn't know it was going to be this difficult."

She raised her chin and he waited to see a trembling lip, a tear positioned to fall on her lids. But she was tough, his Portia.

"You always have made it clear you're a short-timer here, Kyle. You've made a commitment to move to California. And let's face it, it's for the best, right? If you were going to stay here longer, you wouldn't want a relationship cluttering up your work with Trail Hikers. Silver Valley's not for you, Kyle. It's okay. We got each other through a tough time, with everything going on. Don't worry about me. Josh and Annie are going to keep me safe."

He'd planned to keep this cool, easy. But Portia made everything complicated.

And all he wanted to do was stop all of this, stop time by kissing her.

So he did.

Portia knew she should remain detached, tell Kyle that a kiss wasn't part of a professional send-off. Yet as much as they'd shared by working and solving part of the ROC case together, the bulk of what had passed between them had been incredibly personal.

Like this kiss. When his lips touched hers, Portia grabbed his face and held him there, afraid he'd pull away before she allowed herself this one last long drink of Kyle.

His tongue plunged into her mouth, circled hers, and she sucked on it, wanting to remind him—no, make sure he never forgot—that what they'd shared hadn't been a fling or sexual release. She wasn't the only woman who'd shared his bed. No doubt he'd had women who'd been more worldly and sophisticated than her, for sure. But none had seen into Kyle's soul the way she did. She was positive about this because Kyle had seen the depths of her soul, too. And still cared about her, enough to protect her and make love to her like she was the most beautiful woman on earth.

Had she made him feel the same? She pulled back from the kiss, looked at his closed eyes, heard the ragged intake of breath.

"Kyle. Look at me." Only when his silver gaze focused on her did she continue. "Did you feel it, feel this when we were together? Did you feel like I appreciated you?"

He stared at her and she thought he might let go of her right there and then, refuse to answer. He blinked. One side of his mouth curved up. "Babe, you were the best."

His words cut through the sexual haze he always wove around her and pierced her temporary reprieve from reality. She and Kyle were saying goodbye. He knew it, too, because his smile was gone, his eyes back to the steely hue she'd witnessed so many times over the last weeks.

"I've…I've got to go. To—"

"To Josh's. I know. Listen, I'm not going to be able to text you for the next several days, most likely."

"I understand." She'd never want to distract him in the middle of a life-or-death situation.

He gave her a quick kiss on her forehead, as if she were a platonic friend. "Be safe, listen to whatever they tell you that you need to do. And good luck with your gala."

He turned and opened the door, motioned for her to go first.

Portia left and didn't look back as she returned to the kitchen, grabbed her bags and nodded at Annie. "Let's go."

The advantage of having a best friend like Annie, who'd known her for so long and knew her every expression and mood, was that there were no explanations needed. Annie gave Josh a quick kiss goodbye and left with Portia.

# Chapter 17

Portia leaned her head against the passenger headrest in Annie's four-wheel-drive crossover vehicle. Annie expertly drove them to her and Josh's place in the rugged car, the safest bet as the storm still held on for its last gasps. It was supposed to end by nightfall.

They were headed to the home Josh had grown up in and where he had raised his younger sister, Becky, until recently. Becky had mental and emotional disabilities that required constant monitoring, which Josh had done until recently. His sister had moved into an adult community living situation a few months ago, which left a lot of room in the sprawling house.

"How's Becky doing?"

Annie's face lit up. "She's fantastic. Josh couldn't have picked a better place to take her, and she's made so many friends."

"I know you were so worried about her." Portia bit her lip. She wasn't the only one who'd struggled to find the perfect partner. Except unlike Annie, while Portia might have found him, he wasn't going to stay in Silver Valley.

"I was. I'm more concerned about you right now, though. It seems to me that your last few minutes with Kyle weren't great."

They were too great—at least that kiss had been. Nothing she was ready to share with Annie, though. "I'm good. We both knew what we were doing, Annie. It's been an emotional roller coaster, yes. We're also both adults."

Annie opened her mouth to say something, then closed it. They shared several moments of silence, a reprieve Portia was thankful for. She needed space and time between her and Kyle, and some alone time to deal with the burning hole in her heart.

"On another topic, Markova's a wicked person—she has caused a lot of trouble for SVPD and the community, not just you." Annie didn't look at her as she spoke, her attention on the road.

"Besides the library theft and surveillance?"

Annie nodded as she gripped the steering wheel, inching forward slowly to stay within the safety parameters of the visibility. "Hmm. I'm not sure how much Kyle has told you, but I do know you spoke to Claudia."

Portia perked up. "Yes, I have spoken to her. Which of course makes me wonder how you know her."

Annie shot her a sly grin without taking her gaze off the road. "Let's just say that some of my SVPD work spills over into aiding other LEAs with the tougher cases." She didn't have to say that ROC was a harder case than most. Portia knew it, firsthand.

"It's certainly not like the movies. I would have expected Kyle to stop Markova in her tracks once she broke into the house, but he gave her room to be able to take off. I know I'm not cut out for law enforcement because I would have shot first and answered any questions later."

"That's easy, and in this instance, in the master bedroom, fair to say. But it's a perfect example of why someone like Kyle is such an invaluable asset to have on our side. Not just with this case, which affects us locally, but with the bigger, more globally concerning issues. His measure of self-control is unheard of. Trust me, most other agents would have apprehended Markova on the spot, or at least fired their weapon at her. But he kept his head, waited to see what she'd say or do."

"I didn't ask him what she said in the bedroom. I heard her say something." She'd been out of earshot, close enough to know Markova had entered the room but too far to distinguish the individual words.

"We can talk about ROC and Markova for hours on end, Portia. But you're not telling me what I really care about."

Was Annie working another case? "What?"

"You. And Kyle. Josh says you might be more than friendly."

Portia squirmed in the heated leather passenger seat, and it wasn't from the gusts of wind that rocked the vehicle as they left the shelter of the mountain forest and hit the flat road that led into Silver Valley. "We may be. But it doesn't matter. He's leaving as soon as this case is solved. It's been his plan for a lot longer than he's been here."

"You mean, since he's met you."

"Yeah, well, even that is a bit questionable. It turns out he was staking out the library for weeks before I met him. As well as the homeless shelter, can you believe it?" She shot a glance at her friend, who remained intensely focused on the road. "Of course you believe it—you've probably been working this, too, haven't you? Is this why I haven't been able to get you out for our girls' meet-ups quite so often?" She'd thought it had been because Annie and Josh were spending every waking minute together. And sleeping.

The rueful twist of Annie's mouth said it all. "Yes. I wasn't free to tell you why I was working so many hours at SVPD, not when the case was still completely confidential. Of course the details still are, but we couldn't keep the horror of ROC out of the media."

"I'm sure SVPD didn't want to—the citizens who are most at risk from ROC deserve to know what you're fighting. What we're all fighting."

"Yes." Annie's reply was loud in its quietness. "I worked with cops—when I was still on staff at NYPD—who had burned out from trying to crack various ROC factions, stop their crimes before they happened. ROC is merciless, and innocent civilians aren't its only victims. The very people they attract and promise to take care of more often than not also become victims."

"There's nothing good about ROC."

They sat in their very familiar, loving silence. She and Annie had been best friends for so long that they understood one another without question. Annie knew that Portia wasn't blaming the criminals for the ill that befell them from ROC, and she knew that Annie wasn't defending the criminals. They were simply laying out the facts.

She grew so comfortable in the passenger seat that she almost missed the flash of black, followed by two tiny red taillights, in the white haze of the storm. Her eyes fully opened and she gripped the dash.

"Annie, did you—"

"What do you have, Annie?" Josh's voice filled the car. Annie had used her hands-free to phone him.

"Probable Markova sighting, route one-one-four, heading back into town. Dressed in dark clothing, riding a snowmobile going at least sixty. I'm going thirty and she flashed by us."

"Okay, what's your crossroad?"

Portia caught the green sign to her right, through the slanting snowfall. "Hilltop Drive."

"That you, Portia? Thanks." Josh sounded happy to have the information. "I'll turn this around ASAP. You two stay safe and hunker down when you get to our place."

"Will do." Annie answered as she drove.

"Love you." Josh's reply was so casually genuine that Portia blinked at the tears his deep love for Annie prompted.

"Love you, too, babe." Annie disconnected and cast Portia a bemused glance. "He's super affectionate."

"So I hear." They both laughed, and Portia welcomed the release after the constant stress of being on the lookout for Markova. She sobered. "She didn't know we were in this car, did she?"

"Nope. My guess is that she's been taking the back

snowmobile routes down the mountain, and crossed onto the main highway just as we did. If she knew it was us, we'd be fighting her right now."

"You mean if she knew it was me, I'd already be shot."

"Yes."

"She's going to figure out I'm at your place. It's inevitable."

"Not really. I've had some training since I quit NYPD, here with SVPD. Between Josh and me, we'll keep you safe. Just don't go outside the routine we'll establish."

"I'd think routine would be anathema to me staying alive."

"What I mean is our tactical routine. We're going to shake up when you go to the library, your start and stop times, and you'll never be alone. I'll be taking you to and from work, and there will be an SVPD officer with you at all times in the library."

"But cops don't do personal security." Neither did undercover agents, yet Kyle had protected her. The loss of proximity to him was already affecting her and it'd only been thirty minutes. She felt something akin to panic but it wasn't as frightening.

"The entire town is at risk, which includes a public building like the library. Keeping you out of harm's way is an added benefit." Annie gently pressed on the brakes as they came to a four-way stop at the entrance of Josh's subdivision.

Correction, Annie and Josh's neighborhood. A pang of a different kind hit her in the solar plexus and Portia had to sit still and accept that for the first time in her life, she was jealous of her best friend. She wished that she could at least fantasize about having a place of her own with a man like Kyle. Okay, not a man like him, but him. Kyle, the person she'd shared more with in the past week and a half than anyone else in her life.

"We're here." Annie put the car in park and slid out of the driver's seat. Portia saw her friend's slim shape bow against the brunt of the wind, which was still strong, even as the storm was reportedly beginning its departure. She paused before opening her door, and sent up a hope that this would be a new start for her, so quickly after her entire life had changed. But from now on she had to let go of any permanent-type thoughts of Kyle. Their time together had been great while it lasted.

She had a gala to organize.

Kyle had said goodbye to other women he'd dated, accepted a fling for what it was. But as he'd watched Portia shove her things into her backpack, he'd felt like anything but experienced at bidding a woman farewell. Worse, he'd had to fight every fiber of his being that told him not to let her go.

It wasn't ever going to last. There were no guarantees it'd be easy. He'd known it the first time he'd set sight on Portia in the library. She was the woman who'd stay with him years after this. When ROC and Ludmila Markova were distant black-and-white memories, what he'd shared with Portia would be as fresh as the several feet of snow now blanketing Silver Valley.

*You could change your mind. Stay here.*

He shook off the damning accusation. His involvement with Portia had almost cost her everything. If he'd been more alert instead of sleeping off their most recent round of lovemaking, he'd have Markova in custody instead of still out there, targeting Portia.

"You okay, man?" Josh's hand hit his back in a friendly wake-up. They were alone in the kitchen area as the SVPD forensic team finished up their work.

"I could have gotten her killed, Josh." The confession came out unbidden, and didn't do anything to ease the razor blades of recrimination stabbing his soul.

"Oh, no, you don't. Absolutely do *not* go there. It's a quick path to insanity. Trust me on this—I was there last year with Annie, when she got involved in our human trafficking case."

"You were?" Since Kyle had only been in Silver Valley for the last couple of months, he'd never known Josh before he'd been connected to Annie. "I can't picture you as the overwrought type."

"When it comes to keeping an innocent bystander safe, we're all vulnerable. The fact that I had feelings for Annie made it harder to stay detached enough to get the job done. And I faced what you just did—wondering where I went wrong, seeing only the fact that Annie could have been hurt or worse, because I'd turned my head a split second too late or never picked up on a clue because I was otherwise engaged."

The noose of guilt loosened its hold on him, a tiny notch. "I had no idea."

"None of us do, until we're in the thick of it." Josh put his phone down for a minute. "It's never easy, what we do, but it's a hell of lot simpler when there's not someone special who's at risk and their life rests in our hands. And even tougher for me was accepting that I wanted to come home to Annie every night, which meant I had to face my fears over leaving her widowed. It's part of our job description."

"Yeah, it is." He wasn't about to divulge all of his thoughts to Josh. Especially when he knew he still had sorting to do. It all had to wait, though, until ROC's heroin shipment was seized, and Markova was behind bars.

"We'll get Markova, Kyle. It might not be here in central Pennsylvania—she's the slippery type. But she'll meet hers. TH is all over the globe, and FBI has had her on their wanted list for a couple of years. Her future's not going to be pretty."

"I know that. I'd like to take down as many of the ROC thugs as we can."

"Me, too, but our priority is to stop the drugs from hitting the street. On that note, you should probably find a different place to stay other than your apartment. You've been made, and Markova knows you're with Portia."

"I'll take one of the TH safe houses." Trail Hikers maintained a half dozen or so apartments that were completely secure, on the outskirts of town. They looked like farmhouses from the road, and unless he was followed directly there, it'd be very difficult to know anyone but a farmer was in residence.

"I was going to suggest that. We can get Portia out to see you, Annie or I. Just let me know."

"That's not on the table." He had to keep Portia alive, and being with him wasn't to her advantage. His stomach rolled into a sickening lead ball and he refused to look at why. If he did, he might hop on the snowmobile in the garage and go after Portia right now.

"Well, if you change your mind." Josh was looking at his phone again, which lit up with a text at the same moment Kyle's vibrated with the same message, from Claudia.

Train's on the move again, from Texas, following back of storm by two days. Expect shipment to arrive SV within the week.

They looked at one another.

"Looks like we're closer than we thought." Josh spoke.

"This is all thanks to Portia's work. She pieced it all together, the shipments and amounts in each."

Josh gathered his laptop and put on his coat. "I'll make the slow drive back to town and see that we have all we need at the station to apprehend whoever Markova brings with her to give the packages to."

Kyle nodded. "I can do the briefing if you'd like." Things were looking up. If they captured this, the largest amount of heroin ever shipped through any East Coast distribution area, they'd send a big message to ROC. Along with arresting their dealers and Markova, it would cripple ROC drug ops for at least a month, maybe six weeks.

And it would keep Portia alive, allow her to return to her regular life sooner than he'd expected. A mental image of her in the library, working with a patron, seared through him as keenly as one of his many sexual memories of her.

But it didn't matter how much, how deeply, Portia DiNapoli was under his skin. As soon as they had Markova, he was headed for California.

# Chapter 18

Portia reluctantly set up shop at Josh and Annie's. They'd given her a back bedroom and she had the guest bathroom to herself, so she didn't feel she was in their way. The storm was dwindling and she heard the loud purr of the snowplows on each of the first two nights she slept there, indicating that Silver Valley would soon be back to full operation.

"You're looking forward to going into the library tomorrow, aren't you?" Annie smiled at her over Chinese takeout, a nice treat after the power had been restored to town. Josh was out late, as he'd been the night before.

"Of course." She moved her orange chicken around with her chopsticks. Hunger hadn't been top on her list since she'd left the country house.

"Okay, let's talk." Annie put her napkin down. "You've been moping around since you left Kyle. Have you talked to him?"

"No, of course not. We're not a couple—you know that."

"Except that you've done everything a couple does, Portia. I know it's on an accelerated timeline. Kyle's not a man who has the time to give you the full-blown dating deal. But it doesn't mean he's not more sincere than anyone else you've ever been with."

"I was never with anyone else before. Sure, I thought I was, but Kyle makes all of those men, those relationships, seem adolescent. Even Rob—he looked all adult and fancy in his nice suits and smooth talk. He's a consummate politician. And even if he hadn't been such a dog, I'd still have broken up with him. He didn't hold up the end of a conversation like Kyle does." And no other man's touch aroused her, made her willing to let go and enjoy the moment—no man except Kyle.

"Have you told Kyle this?" Annie asked. Her eyes expressed her concern, her compassion for Portia's pain. It was more than Annie's counseling skills, too. This was what Portia valued about their friendship the most.

"You get me, Annie. I don't know what I'd do if I didn't have you to talk to about all of this."

Annie reached over the island and squeezed her hand. "It goes both ways, sweetie." She pulled back and picked up her chopsticks. "I do think that it'd be worth speaking to Kyle one more time. What do you have to lose, Portia? If he blows you off, then there, you have an answer. But it could work out into something you never expected. Something wonderful."

Portia made a show of rolling her eyes and got the desired laugh out of Annie. "Look, just because you're glowing like the nuclear station at Three Mile Island could have forty years ago, don't think my relationship with Kyle is anything like yours with Josh. First, you knew Josh your entire life until you left Silver Valley. I've only known Kyle for what, two weeks?" She shook her head. "It's not possible to have anything long term between us. Real commitment takes time and that's one thing we don't have. He's going back to California, where he grew up, as soon as the case is over."

"Like I said already, it's not about the timeline, Portia. You know as well as I do that while we have a shared history that cements our friendship, if we met today, we'd still hit it off and be friends. We click, we operate on the same frequency. As, it appears to me, do you and Kyle."

"'Frequency' is a good way to put it." She chewed on her dinner thoughtfully, swallowed and had a swig of the jasmine tea Annie had brewed. "And I do agree—the length of time just isn't a factor. Kyle's the real deal." But it didn't mean they'd make it as a couple.

"Then the next question you need to look at is if you're interested in checking out California."

Portia sputtered. "Wait a minute—that's too far. Kyle hasn't said anything about wanting more than what we've had here so far." And he'd never mentioned nor asked her if she'd want to visit, much less live, there. Would she?

It was too risky to her heart to contemplate anything more with Kyle than what they'd shared here, in Silver Valley. The elation at just the thought of having more time with Kyle scared her in its intensity. Was Annie's question about California reasonable? Sure. And yes, she'd consider going there. But Kyle had never asked her for anything past now. She was pretty certain he'd have already suggested that she at least visit California to see him after he moved back there. Which meant the inevitable ending—the nonending, as far as she could see—was going to be excruciating.

She looked at her friend. Annie was happily in love with the man of her dreams, and that was great. Sure, Annie had left New York City to come back to her hometown, said she was going to, regardless of what happened between her and Josh. But Portia knew her friend. Annie would have been heartbroken, inconsolable, if things with Josh hadn't worked out. She got that, totally.

Of course she did. She was already in the inconsolable phase over Kyle.

Kyle buried himself in the ROC op for the next several days. Without Portia by his side, it was the only remedy for the way his conscience gnawed at him. Finding Markova and tracking her every move had been almost too easy, but he figured it was because the shipment was imminent. Even Markova answered to higher-ups, and if she didn't come through with the coordinated distribution of drugs to preselected dealers, and get the cash from the sales, she'd be out of a job. Except ROC didn't fire people in a conventional way. They killed them.

Claudia had called another meeting, this time at TH headquarters, to go over what they had so far. He sat in the secured office space next to Josh, opposite Claudia and Chief Colt Todd.

"I take it you decided to leave Portia out of this briefing, Kyle?" Claudia never minced words.

"I did. She's done immeasurable good work for us,

helping me figure out what was on the USB stick. My desire is to keep her safe and as far away from Markova as possible."

"The good news is that Markova seems to have switched her focus back to the drug shipment." Colt nodded at Claudia. "We've compared what you've reported from following these last days to the intel we've received from other sources about the shipment and what the East Coast ROC is focused on at the moment." She looked at Josh, indicating he should continue.

Josh cleared his throat. "The train is moving again, after the long wait from the storm. And you already know that Markova is busy making sure every dealer's on the hook for the shipment. We've also gotten reports that this is only the first of as many as six shipments planned this year. We're hoping that by stamping this one out, we'll let ROC know they won't get away with it. But we have to be prepared as a town and community to face repercussions from them."

"Like you haven't already dealt with?" Kyle hadn't been here for it but SVPD and TH had dealt with several different local human trafficking rings, all led by ROC.

"We've only touched the tip of their iceberg." Claudia's proclamation cut through the discussion. "TH is deployed globally, fighting against criminals and despots 24/7. Over the last five years, US LEAs have had to dedicate up to 20 percent more resources in the fight against ROC."

"Why did they pick Silver Valley, Claudia? It doesn't make sense to me. Sure, from logistical and geographical standpoints, but Silver Valley isn't New York or

Miami. While a stranger or new transplant might not stand out as quickly as they would in a small town, Silver Valley isn't big enough for ROC to hide very many of their operatives."

"I don't have the answer to that, Kyle. We're working on it, because there's no such thing as coincidence in the ROC world." Claudia hated admitting she didn't know something, so Kyle knew this had to cut deep.

"The bigger picture isn't what I'm worried about," Colt broke in. "Right now we can make a difference for hundreds, thousands of Silver Valley residents by keeping the drugs from becoming available."

"Not to mention the entire Harrisburg area." Josh added his take on it. "ROC has operated on both sides of the river since they showed up in the area." The Susquehanna River separated the state capitol from many suburbs, including Silver Valley. SVPD was the largest police force on the west shore, though, and often worked closely with the Harrisburg PD.

"Right." Colt looked at Kyle. "We wouldn't have gotten this far without your contribution."

Kyle wished Colt would save the appreciation for after they wrapped up the case. He wouldn't be satisfied until they locked up Markova and every last one of the drug dealers whose hands itched to distribute products that would make them big bucks and keep addicts using, too many becoming OD victims.

He shifted in his seat and focused on what his teammates were saying, but always, always knew he'd be more comfortable if Portia were here. As his partner analyzing ROC data, as his confidante, as his lover.

Good thing he'd learned early in life that you don't always get what you want most.

* * *

On the morning of the gala, Portia made her coffee and grabbed a yogurt from Josh and Annie's refrigerator. The lack of Josh's presence the last couple of days was telling. And it raised her concerns over Kyle, who hadn't contacted her, by mutual agreement, when she'd left the safe house. He had to focus on his job. Still, a text would have been nice.

She heard Annie's footsteps and looked up to see her friend drag herself into the kitchen, circles under her eyes.

"Good morning. I'm guessing your exhaustion isn't from a long night of knitting?" Portia was pretty certain Annie only helped at her grandmother's yarn shop on an as-needed basis, on the weekends or evenings. And she wouldn't be working there while the ROC case was ongoing.

Annie offered a smile. "And you would be correct. I was at the station most of the night, helping Josh and Kyle put together a tactical team."

Portia's concern ratcheted to alarm. Her lungs struggled to grab a breath and her heart felt as though it needed every ounce of energy she had to beat. "Kyle— is he okay? Are they safe, Annie?"

Annie helped herself to a cup of coffee. "They're fine, but the train is due in tonight. Anytime between 7:00 and 9:00 p.m. It made good time after it resumed its trip north, once the storm here cleared."

"Okay, so by the end of tonight, this will all be over?"

Annie slung into a kitchen chair at a large family table. Josh hadn't completely revamped his childhood home, saving sentimental pieces like his parents' kitchen table. He'd lost them both tragically in an auto accident and had singlehandedly raised his sister.

"That's the tough thing, Portia. This case isn't going to be over until the ringleader, the head of the East Coast ROC operations, is caught. And hopefully he'll turn, give us the information we need to eradicate the entire network of criminals."

"Ivanov." She'd read about the man, the swath of crime and murderous devastation he'd cut across the Eastern Seaboard, and now he was digging his claws in deeper, heading toward the Midwest.

"Yes. Did Kyle tell you?"

"Not that much, actually. I've read up on ROC since I saw the news about their connection to the heroin trade. Right after Lani died."

Annie grimaced. Lani had been Annie's classmate, too. "That hit home, didn't it? Have you heard how her family is doing?"

"I spoke with them before the storm, before I met, got involved with, oh, what's the use? Before Kyle."

"And? How were they doing?" Annie wasn't going to put up with Portia's self-pity and she loved her friend all the more for understanding her and not giving her less attractive character traits any time.

"As well as can be expected. As you know from your line of work, better than I, it'll take time. They've thrown themselves into legislative activism, hoping to get the laws changed."

"Just when we think we've handled it from every angle, the opioid epidemic slams us back down." Annie peeled a banana. "There's so much to it. But if LEA does its job, it'll help a lot. Keep the drugs off the streets."

"I've thanked you before, Annie, but I can't tell you

enough how much I appreciate your, and Josh's, service. It has to be stressful on you both when you're working a case like this."

"As the TH and SVPD police psychologist, my job is mostly taking care of the agents and officers, making sure they're getting the practical support they require from their agency. It's a measure of how big this ROC case is that I'm doing as much as I am with the actual tactical operations. I never worked on ops like this when I was with NYPD."

"Was it a hugely hard decision to move back here? I know you loved New York."

"Not at all. I was in the process of figuring out I wanted out of the city, and then Josh came along. Yes, I love New York but I love Josh more. And what's not to like about Silver Valley? We're only fifteen minutes from the Harrisburg Amtrak, three hours from the city. Two from Philly. And two hours to DC, driving. We live in an ideal place."

"We do."

"And that's why we're going to stomp ROC right out of here."

"I'll be at the gala all night, but can you keep me informed?" There were two sets of SVPD patrols assigned to monitor the gala, along with a private security firm, but Portia didn't expect them to be in on all the details of the case.

"Of course I will. I'll be at the gala, too. There won't be anything for me to do during the actual takedown. Claudia and Colt don't allow me near active ops for either TH or SVPD if they can help it. I need to be available afterward, fully functioning to help whomever needs it."

* * *

Kyle stood off from the group of SVPD, FBI and Trail Hiker colleagues who were spread out inconspicuously over a two-mile length of train track that ran straight through the heart of Silver Valley. Their intention was to stop the train at the juncture where the rail curved off and into the part of town where he'd saved Portia from being hit.

"You ready, Kyle?" Claudia's voice reached him on his wireless headset.

"Standing by."

"Train is one mile out." Another TH agent, this one working communications, sounded in his ear. Months of investigation and intelligence analysis, countless frozen nights of surveillance, and more than one hand-to-hand altercation with Markova had led to this. He'd have preferred it was during broad daylight, but the train had been delayed by the storm and they had to work with what was, not wish for a better situation.

As a former Marine and present Trail Hiker, he had every confidence in his ability to complete his mission.

If only he had that with Portia.

He'd stopped trying to fight the visions of her that taunted him day and night. He missed her—not just the sex, and yes, he missed that beyond measure. Portia understood him, accepted him for the man he was. She'd made love to him knowing he couldn't offer her any promise beyond their short time together. And she'd fought alongside him as needed, readily took instruction in weapons and how to avoid getting killed by Markova.

He looked at his watch. Eight fifteen in the evening and it was pitch dark, in the middle of winter. Portia was at the gala she'd so carefully planned. It was the one thing he was grateful for, that she'd be safe and Markova's focus was on the incoming shipment. Still, he hadn't stopped himself from putting on his oversize tuxedo over his body armor, under his plainclothes, also a size too big. He'd used the tux as an undercover agent in various situations, including embassy receptions all over the globe. But tonight, if by some act of God the mission went down more quickly than they'd planned, he'd show up at that gala and…

This is where he was stuck. What would he do? Ask Portia for one last night together before he went out west? Or would he ask for one dance, say goodbye that way?

"Lights." He looked down the track and saw the tiny pinpoint of the engine's headlight. Inhaling the frozen air, he silently practiced his role. The engineer had been replaced by an undercover agent, who would stop the train along this stretch of track to allow for the various LEA officers to board and inspect. Once they found the heroin and any other unknown contraband, they'd replace it with artificial, harmless substances. Then they'd move quickly to be in place where they suspected Markova waited. Where he knew she waited—he'd verified she was in the area just fifteen minutes ago, before he'd driven down here. He wondered if she thought she'd lost him as her tail.

"A quarter mile to go, folks. Stand by."

Kyle waited, wanting the night to be over without incident more than ever before, and knowing in the deepest part of his being that his best course of action was to complete the mission and get out of Silver Valley. Before he risked hurting Portia more than he knew he already had.

\* \* \*

Portia entered the catering barn she'd rented on behalf of the gala committee a year ago and actually had a moment of feeling like a princess. Her sparkling ruby-red halter gown was a far cry from the more practical wardrobe she relied on working in the library, and at the homeless shelter many evenings. She'd splurged on dangling rhinestone earrings and a matching bracelet.

The historical barn had been converted into a remarkable venue, complete with a parquet dance floor, which was large enough for most of the several hundred guests in attendance. It was early yet; the main rush of attendees would begin in forty-five minutes or so.

Satisfaction curled in her belly as she eyed the dozens of round dinner tables, set with the signature Silver Valley colors of forest green, representing the Appalachian Mountains, and a deep agate blue that mirrored the blue shadows of the range from downtown. Gold candles floated in cylindrical vases, imbuing the room with a sense of rich anticipation. Swaths of pale blue muslin reached from the high ceiling and half dozen chandeliers, draping around wrought-iron frames to the floor below.

"What do you think?" Coral Stauffer, the woman who'd bought the barn a few years ago after returning to her hometown after a disastrous divorce from another Silver Valley native she'd happened to meet in California, stood next to her.

"It's spectacular, Coral! I can't thank you enough."

"Aw, honey, you did the hard work. My team put it together like we do for all the other events. Although this is the biggest of the year for us." Coral's bright sapphire-blue eyes reflected deeper emotion than expected for a charity event, but Portia didn't push her school friend. Like Annie, they'd known one another for years and she knew not to push Coral for details on the life she'd had in Southern California before returning to Silver Valley.

"You have been so patient with me."

"You're the expert, Portia. Everyone raves about how nice these evenings are."

"And this will be the biggest and best yet." She held up her hand, fingers crossed.

"No luck needed. Your hard work has paid off." Coral rubbed her bare shoulders. She too was in an evening gown, but one that was much more sedate than Portia's, as it was black and had a simple yet elegant high crew neck. "The storm's gone in time, thank goodness, but I'm going to turn the heat up until the room fills up."

"Do you miss it? The warmer weather in California?" The question came out of her without bidding and she wanted to bite her tongue. And not just from the obvious discomfort she'd brought to Coral, who bit her lower lip. Why was she torturing herself with her obsession over going to California with Kyle? He'd never indicated he wanted her to go with him there.

"I miss some of my friends that I made. I was there for almost ten years, as you know. College and after. But it was the right decision to come back to Silver Valley. Speaking of which, I read in the paper today that you've been through quite a bit lately, with some person stealing laptops from the library, and then you almost got hit on the train tracks? You never mentioned it, even with all the work we've done together."

Portia knew when to play it lightly. "I happened to

be in the wrong place at some of the right times for a criminal to show up. That's all." Her stomach tightened as fierce, protective instincts for the TH and SVPD ops against ROC roared. Who was she kidding, though? It was the only way she could be a part of Kyle's world now. Maintain the confidentiality of the takedown op. Which according to Josh, would have already happened, about an hour ago. She hadn't heard the contrary from Annie and she'd know in about two hours, depending on whether or not they showed up to the gala.

"I have a sneaking suspicion you're playing it far too cool, but we don't have time to talk now. I'm going to turn the heat up and then head for the kitchens. Is there anything you need from me now?"

"No, thanks, Coral. I'll do a quick look-over of the silent auction items." She walked in the opposite direction of Coral, across the dance floor, conscious of her very high strappy silver heels. When was the last time she'd taken such care with her appearance? And why hadn't she ever thought to get made-up for Kyle?

Because they'd been too busy running from a lethal threat or making love.

There, she'd admitted it. It had been making love with Kyle, all of it. She blinked back tears, grateful she'd picked her tube of waterproof mascara. But this was the gala, not a funeral. Lifting her chin and throwing her very chilly shoulders back, she kept going. As she looked at her hands, a huge cocktail ring winked from her right, while her left hand was bare. And would remain so, and that was okay.

It was ridiculous to even think she'd been that close to something big with Kyle. And even after Annie's prompting, she'd decided to be brave and…let Kyle go. She'd pursued Rob and thought she'd successfully landed a good partner, only to be proved wrong, ruefully so. What she'd shared with Kyle had been powerful and she wasn't going to demean it by trying to make it into something it wasn't: permanent.

But as she checked out the tables laden with item after item for the silent auction, in the room off the main dance and dinner area, her heart's whispers haunted her.

# Chapter 19

"That was fast, even for TH," said the agent, Benjamin Michaels, who was sitting next to Kyle, whom he was shadowing.

"Don't count on it. The next part is going to be the trickiest. Ready?" Kyle motioned for Ben to follow him and they got to Kyle's vehicle in minutes. Within five more minutes, they were parked in the diner lot, which ran right up to the train tracks. Intel indicated the meeting of the ROC dealers would be in this spot. SVPD would handle the apprehensions, of which they expected at least a dozen. One for every car that they'd found the heroin stashed in.

"Do you think it's all heroin, or is some of it fentanyl?"

"Both the SVPD and FBI substance experts called it half-and-half on the spot."

"Which means it would have for sure been a death sentence. For how many?"

"Too many." Kyle's resolve strengthened. It was good to have a partner to talk to, in the moment. Not that it kept all thoughts of Portia out of his mind, but it did help him keep his A-game going during such a long day and night.

"Look, on the other side of the tracks." As Ben pointed out the five people, all dressed for the weather and with ski masks, Claudia's voice sounded in their headsets.

"We've got affirmative sighting of fifteen possible ROC."

Fifteen? He scanned the other side but the train pulled into view, and even though it moved very slowly, unlike the day he'd had to shove Portia off the track, it wasn't slow enough. Their view of the probable ROC operatives was blocked by the cargo containers.

They waited for the train to stop, as it often did to allow for the track to be switched to allow the cars to continue to the myriad distribution centers on the other side of town.

"We've got to get to other side of the tracks." Kyle was used to a case coming together at the very end, and knew that they were racing against Markova's clock. "Markova won't be here—she'll hang out where more civilians are. It's how she's blended in and disappeared from so many crimes before."

"I'm with you, Kyle." Ben's complete trust in his deduction gave Kyle pause. Another first. Usually he accepted professional respect as another part of the job, just as he gave it to his colleagues. But he'd discovered a new meaning to the word, since meeting Portia.

She'd trusted him to keep her alive.

"Let's go." He drove the vehicle out of the diner lot and headed for the closest cross street behind the train.

"You've done such a lovely job here, Portia." The mayor of Silver Valley shook her hand and she smiled at her.

"Thank you so much! It wouldn't have happened without the support of your office and the Rotary Club." She held her hand out to the woman standing with the mayor, her wife, and thanked her, too. "The community's really come together for this. Did you have a chance to look at all of the silent auction items?"

"Yes, and I'm afraid we may have bid on too many." The mayor cast a mock disparaging look at her spouse. "Why, exactly, did we bid on a fishing trip?"

"It's a perfect gift for your father." The mayor's wife responded with a smile and Portia thanked them for their support. If everyone present had bid as much as these two, they were bound to make a record amount tonight. Good for the library, wonderful for the homeless shelter.

"Enjoy the night. The dancing is about to start." She left the couple and continued to work the room, making sure to thank everyone who'd helped her put the event together. It was really almost everyone in the room.

As she walked from group to group, table to table, couple to couple, she received many compliments for the event, the silent auction items, even her dress. She knew it was pure immaturity that her disappointment was like that of a spoiled child's. But she couldn't help it. She'd hoped Kyle would be here, see her as the woman he'd helped her become. There were transition points in life, clear markers where she'd gone from her comfort zone to who she was meant to be. Kyle had been alongside her for this most recent, most important one. Portia had transitioned from someone content with her status quo, pouring her energy into what her town and its library patrons needed, to a woman who wanted what was best for herself.

Her big problem now was that Kyle didn't think what she wanted was viable. She wanted him.

Kyle looked at his watch for the hundredth time that night. Nine thirty-three. Portia would be announcing the last time allowed for the silent auction bids. He knew because he'd read her paperwork, proofed the program for her, at her request. She'd been all doe-eyed and hopeful when she'd approached him to help her out with the planning. But he knew better. She'd seen that he was bored, once they'd figured out ROC's shipping plans. It had helped the time pass more quickly, as had their lovemaking.

Actions that could have led to her death. He knew he'd never forgive himself for letting Markova get that close to Portia, but he could make a difference now by apprehending Markova the minute she showed up to coordinate the offload.

Kyle and Ben observed from the parking lot of the train station as the train pulled to a stop a full half mile before it was supposed to. It was extremely unusual for a cargo train to pull in at the local, or any, passenger terminal. But not for a shipment that had ROC's backing. Claudia's briefing before they'd prepared to come down here tonight put all the pieces together. ROC had spent almost a million dollars bribing the train conductors along the route from the southern border, where the original shipment of heroin had occurred, to each waypoint where yet another container was loaded with whatever the shipment was, en route to central Pennsylvania.

She reported that Ivanov had been alarmed when the storm hit and shut down all transportation, overreacting a bit by the trains being stuck for so many days. It was record breaking and risky—the shipping companies and receiving customers could have opted to move their goods via other means, like eighteen-wheel trucks. But a storm the size of the one they'd just experienced had shut down all possibilities. A stroke of good fortune for ROC, as far as Ivanov was concerned.

Better luck for SVPD, TH and all the other LEAs working to confiscate the illegal drugs. It meant they'd be able to proceed with the plan of attack they'd practiced for the past several weeks.

"Is that her?" Ben asked and nodded toward a beat-up sedan that had sputtered to a stop in the lot, at the very edge of the plowed pavement, next to a twelve-foot mound of snow.

"Sure looks like it." But before he raised his binoculars to his eyes, gunshots rang through the night air, their pitch higher than the squeal of the train's brakes.

"Go, go, go!" He shot out the order as much to himself as Ben and they exited their vehicle, low on the ground, weapons drawn. Using their doors as shields, they looked around to see the source of the gunfire.

It was two men, from their size, at the engine's door. By the time Kyle ascertained the scenario, one of the shooters was down flat on the ground, and he watched the second drop as the "engineer' dismounted from the engine.

"Two shooters down," a female voice sounded in his headset. So the FBI had used a female agent. And she'd done her job as well as Kyle knew he could have. Probably better tonight, as he was fighting like heck to keep thoughts of Portia from distracting him.

"Copy that. Remove their weapons from the scene and—" Claudia's orders were cut off as more gunfire sounded. The undercover FBI train engineer ducked back, but she needn't have, because the bullets pinged off Kyle and Ben's vehicle.

"Kyle and Ben are under fire, repeat, we are under fire." Kyle issued the report as he stayed low, avoiding the bullets that strafed their car. The initial shots had turned into rapid fire, indicating either a second gunman or weapon. Only an automatic weapon could fire so relentlessly.

"Sounds like AR-15 fire to me," he spoke into his headset but for Ben's benefit. "Trademark Markova. She's happiest with a Kalashnikov, though."

"Stay down and hold your fire. We have the shooter in target range," said Claudia. Her voice revealed nothing but her orders, yet Kyle suspected she wasn't amused by their musings over Markova's weapon of choice.

Another sign that he was tired and had allowed his feelings for Portia to affect him. He was avoiding the reality that he could be killed and never speak to Portia again. It was one thing when he made that choice, decided to go off to California for good. Being killed by his ROC target was a whole other matter, though.

Kyle felt helpless as he and Ben witnessed the takedown of fifteen ROC drug dealers who'd showed up to get their share of the shipment. He wanted to find Markova, be the one to cuff her.

After what seemed like hours, the all-clear came.

"Do we have Markova?" He held his breath, waiting for an affirmative from one of his colleagues.

"Agent Girardi has a female suspect in custody who was driving Markova's vehicle," Claudia informed him, but her statement wasn't good enough.

"Are we sure it's her?"

"You're free to go see for yourself, Kyle."

Kyle didn't spare Ben a glance. "Follow me."

"With you."

They had to walk around several clusters of LEAs, who were taking potential drug dealers into custody. Their statements would be recorded at SVPD, then analyzed to see what new ROC information could be gleaned.

Kyle didn't care about anything but being able to look Markova in the eyes and let her know he'd been on to her all along.

He approached the group of LEAs, three women and two men, who surrounded the petite woman. Anticipation built, but he refused to allow himself the pleasure of thinking about how soon he could see Portia, tell her she was completely safe.

"Excuse me," he said.

The officers parted to let him into the process and he looked for Markova's signature glacial blue gaze. The mark of her sociopathic personality.

Instead he looked into two very wide, very shocked eyes.

"Who the hell are you?"

The woman didn't speak, just trembled as tears rained down her cheeks. He saw the blonde wig on the dirty snow, recognized Markova's clothing on the woman. She spoke in broken English with a good smattering of Russian.

"She says Markova made her do this," one of the FBI agents informed him, while tapping into a tablet. He looked up. "And left you a message." He then read from his notes, "Portia DiNapoli and the man protecting her will enjoy fireworks at the end of the Library Fund-raising Gala. On me."

Among Markova's many criminal skills was a talent for explosives. She'd taken out an entire SWAT team in New York City two years ago. ROC had claimed it but intelligence pointed to Markova as the actual culprit.

Markova was going to blow up the gala venue. With Portia in it.

Kyle leaned past the FBI agent to grab the woman, to find out where Markova had gone, but Ben stopped him. "Easy, Kyle. She's not your target."

He turned toward him, and Ben visibly braced himself. *He thinks I'm going to hit him.* Kyle realized he was tensed as if for the fight of his life.

But it wasn't his life he was concerned about; it was Portia's. And possibly everyone else's at the gala.

He began to run back to his car, with Ben on his heels.

"Where are we going?"

"Gala. At the Weddings and More Barn."

He heard Ben relay the information to Claudia over the wireless headsets but it was in his peripheral awareness. Kyle had no room to focus on anything but getting to Portia.

Before Markova did.

* * *

Markova grinned as she took the best seat in the house at the top of the silo, with a throwaway phone at hand to call in to SVPD when the bomb's timer was at the ten-minute mark. Her rifle was in top shape and ready to go. She'd even splurged on a laser tracer after watching an American war movie. It had inspired her to use their own tactics against them.

She might be working for ROC for another twenty minutes, but she couldn't help her FSB background. It came to the forefront as she faced down what she'd learned was American arrogance. Did Portia DiNapoli and the man she'd seen her with, who she knew had to be an undercover cop or FBI, think they'd survive against the best training Russia offered its agents? Ludmila's training, combined with ROC money and backing, made her invincible.

Almost. What really pushed her abilities into the unstoppable range was her desire to be free of all of this. She had a disguise waiting in the brand-new SUV she'd just stolen and placed fake license plates on. They'd never find her. No one. Not ROC, which would want retribution, nor FSB, which was still sore she'd left after only a couple of tours of duty. And the American law enforcement agencies? Amateurs, all of them.

She looked at her watch, and then called in to the Silver Valley Police Department. It was 9-1-1 that she dialed, but she knew who'd get the message.

"9-1-1. What's your emergency?"

"I don't have an emergency, but your police department does. There's a bomb in place at the Weddings and More Barn on highway two-twenty-two outside Silver Valley. It's going to blow in ten minutes." She loved that she'd perfected her American accent while still in the FSB. It made tasks like this so easy.

"Who are you, ma'am?"

She disconnected and picked up her other cell phone. With a sense of purpose she'd never felt before, because this was not only the end of her duties for ROC, the end of the annoying investigators and agents who'd tried to stymie her efforts, it also was her beginning.

She touched the button and started the bomb timer. A laugh escaped her at her generosity. She'd given the stupid Americans an extra thirty seconds.

# Chapter 20

Portia's jaw began to ache from constantly smiling. In truth, it was because as happy as she was that the gala was going well and had raised twice as much as last year, allowing for funding for the homeless shelter, it wasn't completely what she'd envisioned.

Since he'd come into her life, she'd dreamed of Kyle being at the event with her. What good was success if she didn't have someone to share it with?

And she'd shared in Kyle's accomplishment by working on the spreadsheets with him and discovering how ROC was trafficking heroin via rail transport. By now, he'd finished his mission. Markova would be behind bars, and hopefully so would many other ROC operatives.

She couldn't wait to find out that her town was safe again.

"Portia!" Annie appeared from the midst of the

swaying crowd, with at least half of the attendees on the dance floor following the instructions of the dee-jay to flap like a chicken. Annie wasn't laughing along with the dance, though, her face tight with concern. Portia's stomach flipped. *Kyle.*

"What's going on?"

"I need you to follow me, quickly."

"Can it wait? I've got to announce the silent auction winners in five minutes."

Annie's expression chilled Portia to the marrow. She stepped closer and whispered in Portia's ear. "Josh texted me. They've stopped the shipment, arrested all the players except one. Markova. Kyle thinks she's on her way here."

The silent auction items could wait.

"Where do you want me to go?"

"For starters, follow me out to my car. We're get-ting you out of here."

"I'm right behind you." She followed Annie through the crowd, danced her way through several overzeal-ous groups of liquored-up guests. They'd each paid for their tickets, which included an open bar, and Portia would have made a mental note about reexamining that policy for next year's gala. Except she was being targeted by an assassin.

"Hey, Portia! Come dance with us." Gary, one of the volunteers at the homeless shelter, circled her waist with his beefy arm and pulled her off course. In the center of a dance circle, she lost sight of Annie. Gary was a friendly guy, and did a lot of the heavy lifting at the shelter, from repair work to stocking the pantry. She was no match for his brute strength. What Gary didn't know, and what she couldn't tell him, was that his jubilation could very well be what got her killed. Worse, she was putting all of the guests at risk the longer she remained in the barn. She looked around for Annie, knowing her friend would circle back the second she discovered Portia had been waylaid.

But Annie was still making a beeline for the back of the hall, toward the kitchen.

"Annie!" Portia yelled as loudly as she could, but to no avail. Her competition from the partygoers and booming music was too great. She'd have to get out of here on her own.

Forcing a bright smile, she yanked Gary down far enough that she could shout in his ear. "I've got to pee! I'll be right back."

"You'd better!" Gary said, and then guffawed as he made an opening for her, and she wished she'd thought to use the excuse as soon as he'd drawn her in.

Finally she was free, making good headway through the rest of the dancers. Until she slammed into a large man blocking her path. She saw the white tuxedo shirt, the shiny black studs, and looked up to excuse herself as the man's arms encircled her, his hands on her forearms.

"Excu—" She looked up into the only eyes that made her head spin and her heart flip. Silver eyes.

"Portia." Kyle's face was a mask of taut tension and she froze. He was here because of Markova. Of course.

"I know, Kyle. I'm getting out of here, like Annie said to." She looked over his shoulder, searching for her friend. Why hadn't Annie returned to get her?

"Annie's busy taking care of things," he shouted, but then leaned toward her ear, just as Gary had moments before. But instead of sweat and fermenting alcohol, she smelled Kyle's too-familiar musk, mingled with the scent of the bar soap he favored. She fought to stay focused, keep her mind on getting out of the barn, but the assault on her senses threw her. She blinked, and his voice gave her the anchor she needed.

"Listen to me, Portia. Markova's rigged this barn to blow up in six minutes. Five by now. I need you to go to the mic and tell the deejay you have an announcement. Then tell your guests to use the four exits and leave as quietly and as quickly as possible. Stay calm, keep them from panicking. Then you go with them."

She looked into his eyes for a full heartbeat, absorbing all he'd said, knowing from the steady intensity in his gaze that he was telling the truth. They might all die right now.

"Do it, Portia." He gave her a slight shake, a squeeze to her forearms, where he'd gripped her since she'd slammed into him. And then he kissed her, hard, his lips a seal of his promise to keep her safe but more, a show of his confidence in her ability to carry through.

Portia whirled around and made her way to the soundstage, elbowing anyone in her way. Acutely conscious of the ticking clock, which in this case was really a bomb, she got to the deejay.

"Cut the music! We have an emergency!" she shouted in his ear. To his credit he complied, handing her the mic. Before the guests' groans of disappointment turned into a chorus, she held up her hand.

"We have an emergency, folks. Please stay calm. I need you to pick one of the four exit doors around you and leave the building now." She pointed to each door, saw that the guests were paying attention, their heads moving and their bodies following. "We believe there's a minor gas leak in the kitchen but we have to make sure it's nothing serious. Please exit and make your way to the ice sculpture display, in the field directly behind the second barn."

To her great relief, the guests followed her directions. There were whiners, a few people who didn't want to go out into the cold without their coats, but fortunately the more sober and levelheaded attendees prevailed. As she watched the last ones leave, she put the mic down and headed for the nearest exit. Kyle was gone, but this wasn't the time to wish she'd said something to him, told him how she really felt. She had to get out of the building, too.

She stepped onto the exit door threshold, only to notice an odd red line across her arms, which turned into a dot on her chest. Her reaction was automatic as she ducked back behind the doorframe and hit the floor. Shots hit the building on either side of the door and she scrambled to get on the other side of the sound-stage, placing the foot-high structure between her and the open exit.

Kyle and Annie cleared out the few remaining workers in the kitchen area, who might have not been able to hear Portia's announcement. Satisfied that the building was empty, he ignored his mental ticking clock as he worked with Annie to find the explosive. His Marine Corps training had included a rudimentary EOD, Explosive Ordnance Disposal, course but it'd be enough to identify the device and its location for the bomb squad, which was due here imminently.

"What am I looking for, exactly, besides something

with a clock and wires on it?" Annie asked as she searched under cabinets.

"It won't be obvious, out here in plain sight. It's probably close to an energy source." As he spoke, he realized he needed to find where the pipes that brought in the natural gas were. Gas was the primary source of heat and energy in Pennsylvania, second only to electricity. He hadn't seen propane tanks outside, so there had to be a shut-off valve inside the barn, as well as a main switch somewhere on the property.

He stopped to put his hands on Annie's shoulders. "Stop. I need you to get out of here, clear the area surrounding the building."

"You should come with me, Kyle. We don't have more than three minutes left."

"I'm right behind you, Annie. Get out." He didn't look up but heard the sound of her feet hitting the tiles as she reached the ground on the other side of the propped-open door.

The silence that descended made him insane with the need to find the device. It was then that he smelled the telltale scent of natural gas, at the same moment he heard a gunshot. And then several following.

"Kyle, get out behind Annie. Now." Claudia's voice in his ear, he ran to the sound of the shots.

"Gunshots, out by the dance floor."

"It doesn't matter, Kyle. You're down to ninety seconds. *Get out.*"

He ripped the earpiece out and ran into the main room, searching for the source of the shots. He immediately spotted Portia lying up against the soundstage, saw the laser target against the doorjamb as shots continued to hit the building. At least he didn't smell the gas here, or the building would already be gone.

With Portia still in it.

Kyle didn't take time to process or reason things out, or even to figure out the best point of egress. He acted on pure instinct and ran for Portia, not stopping until he slid in next to her.

Portia felt the body slam up against hers and closed her eyes tight. Was this it? Had the building exploded and was she dead, unable to feel any pain?

Familiar hands, arms around her. "Portia. Are you with me?"

She turned and faced Kyle. This had to be heaven. Except he didn't look blissed out but incredibly stressed, an almost animal-like countenance to his expression.

"I'm fine. I'm hiding from the shooter."

"We have to get out of here, now. It's going to blow in less than a minute. Stay behind me, whatever you do." He stood up amid the barrage of more bullets and hauled her up, placing her behind him. They ran for the door, opposite the side where the bullets sprayed plywood from the wall, the doorframe a mess of bullet holes. At the very edge of the exit, hidden from the shooter, he turned and looked at her as if he'd never see her again.

"We are going to run outside, crouched low, zigzagging. We'll make it to the pile of snow and then lie flat." His eyes blazed and Portia wanted to ask him why they were doing this, why they had to leave here right now, in the face of a shooter she'd bet was Markova. Their choices were lethal. And then she smelled it. Natural gas.

"Kyle!" She screamed but he didn't wait, turned with her hand in his and they plunged into the dark night. Into the path of certain death.

Portia thought the air should feel cold against her bared skin, her evening gown no match for the Pennsylvania winter.

Kyle still held her hand, pulling her along, his arm behind his back, blocking her from the shots that rained down on them like errant, lethal snowflakes. The snowbank was so close but Kyle changed direction and she thought she felt a bullet hit him, as he jumped at the moment of impact. Yet he remained on his feet, taking them past the original place he'd set and kept going. Out into the farm field, where a plowed path from the barn parking lot to a silo allowed them traction.

They ran through the night, past the edge of the sculptures, and she had a fleeting thought about the gala guests but they were on the other side of the sculptures, farther from the barn.

"No, no!" she screamed as more bullets hit the snow on either side of them. When Kyle stumbled, her heart seemed to stop. No, no, no—not Kyle.

*You should have told him you love him.*

Portia opened her mouth to yell at him, to tell him, before they were both blasted into oblivion. But the inevitable explosion happened, rolling across the ground under her feet.

She felt like she was floating, that time was standing still. As she began to fly through the air, all she was conscious of was Kyle's grip on her hand. He'd never let go, never stopped protecting her from the gunfire. His actions resulted in her experiencing every bit of the detonation.

Somewhere in her mind, she registered that the gunfire had stopped.

A sharp flash of light, followed by the loudest sound she'd ever heard, mixed with the hot air that buoyed their flight. A second explosion!

And still they were flying, moving through the air, across the barn's field, as if they were hawks swooping for groundhogs. After they hit the ground, she rolled on the hard packed snow, until coming to a stop atop the frosty white coating.

She looked up to see the barn completely gone, engulfed by flames. Plywood smacked down next to her, narrowly missing her head. And her hands were bloody, but from what? Her hands...

"Kyle!" She screamed but only a croak emerged from her throat. Or was her hearing messed up? Belatedly she discovered that she could hear nothing but a dull roar. She looked around her, saw him lying in the snow no more than a foot from her. Portia tried to move, strained to reach him. His still form shocked her more than any explosion could. He lay on his side, facing her, only a small part of his face visible. Tears and holes in his tuxedo jacket and shirt revealed he'd been hit by bullets. A trickle of blood ran from his nostril to the visible part of his cheek. Shock began to roll through her. Her teeth shattered, her body shook and her heart broke for the love of her life.

Searing pain kept her present, and she looked at its source, the heeled boot painfully crushing her hand.

Raising her gaze up the calf boot to the pants, the jacket, the face of Ludmila Markova.

The woman had a rifle almost as long as her petite torso strapped across her back and a handgun in her grip. But the deadly weapons weren't what frightened Portia. It was the evil smile Markova gave her in the flickering light, the darkness only broken by the burning building behind them. No siren lights, no SVPD units surrounded them.

It was Portia, Markova and an either very injured, or more likely, dead Kyle. Despair that she'd never previously experienced threatened to swallow her as it invited her to a hell she'd only ever imagined.

"Don't look so sad, Portia DiNapoli. They say it's very peaceful after the bullet." Markova kept her pistol pointed at Portia as she kicked Kyle's still body, to no reaction from Kyle. Portia couldn't stop the gagging, the bile that rose as she realized the love of her life was gone, and she was soon going to join him.

This was so not how she'd planned getting back together with Kyle. Her mind flashed to how good she'd felt in his arms, how safe, how protected. How he'd challenged her to face down her choice to settle for her quiet, albeit full, life in Silver Valley. Kyle had invited her to take a chance on having the time of her life with him.

"Your guardian angel has lost his wings, Portia. Time for you to join him."

Portia refused to look at Markova. She kept her gaze on Kyle, knowing that he was the last thing she wanted to see before she died. But the ROC operative denied her that, crouching next to her and placing her face next to Portia's. She must think Portia was injured more than she was.

"You stupid fool. You thought you'd get away from me. Now look at both of you." The cold barrel of the gun felt like ice on Portia's temple and she closed her eyes, acting dead. Before Markova could get a shot off, Portia summoned all the strength she had left and grabbed the hand holding the gun, forcing it away from them. She head-butted Markova, ignoring the smattering of stars across her field of vision. Before Markova regained her wits, Portia rolled her to her back and held the woman's arms over her head, working to get the weapon out of her hand.

But Markova was better trained, more experienced. She flipped Portia off her as if she were no more than a tiny kitten, shoved her heeled boot into Portia's solar plexus. Portia landed hard on her back, the wind out of her sails. She might not have finished the job against Markova but she'd die trying.

Markova loomed over her, furious and prepared to kill her. This time Portia knew she'd reached her limit. She closed her eyes and thought of the one man who'd ever loved her for who she was.

*Kyle.*

Kyle came to on his right side, in the field, with his face shoved into several inches of snow. He couldn't open his left eye, and from how much it hurt, he figured it was swollen shut. Looking for Portia, his right eye found her, lying just inches from him. She was on her stomach, lifting her head, looking around. Portia had made it.

*Thank God.*

He focused on trying to assess his injuries, to figure out what he was capable of doing. He could only see Portia, and there was no sign of backup. Not yet.

Markova couldn't be discounted, explosion or not. Years of undercover work and countless situations just like this one had his mind moving automatically into recovery mode. He knew the barn was gone, and that the scene around it would be in chaos until SVPD and TH got everyone taken care of. He sent up another silent prayer that Portia had convinced the guests to leave, that Claudia and he had found out about the explosive soon enough.

His breathing deepened and he winced. His bulletproof vest had done its job; he was alive. But getting hit with automatic weapon ammo still hurt.

He sensed her before he saw her walk into his field of vision. Markova, an AR-47 strapped on her back, a .45 in her hands. She said something to Portia but he wasn't listening. He was watching her actions, preparing to take her out. She turned toward him and he lay still, feigning unconsciousness. The kick wasn't unexpected but still rocked him, and more than anything he had to fight his instinctual reaction to grab Markova's ankle, yank her off balance and hold her down until Josh or someone else arrived.

Her attention was back on Portia and he surreptitiously tested the fingers of his right hand, underneath him. He closed his grip around his weapon, which had landed right in front of his stomach. His left arm had hidden it from Markova.

Before he had a chance to move, Markova's backside was in front of him, and within two seconds, Portia had pulled the woman down—and wait, had Portia just head-butted Markova?

As much as he'd love to see anyone take out Markova, he wasn't risking Portia's life for it. He drew his weapon, took aim and fired.

Markova's form fell, her handgun dropping to the ground, unused. Portia's scream reached his ears, dimly, as the roar of the explosions had made his tinnitus flare. Her scream was enough to tell him all he needed to know. Portia was still alive.

# *Chapter 21*

"You've got several abrasions from flying debris, with your hands being the most severely injured. But they'll heal quickly. Just keep the ointment on them, and replace the bandages after each shower. You're lucky you didn't need any stitches."

Portia paid attention to the ER doctor as much as she could, with her ears still ringing and her head spinning from the night's events. It'd only been twenty minutes since they'd arrived at the ER, an hour tops since the explosion. Since she'd been next to Kyle. But she couldn't stop looking at the door, willing him to walk through it.

"Thank you, Doctor," Annie responded, standing near the exam table. "I'll make sure she waits to sign out."

"Thanks. Best to both of you, and thank you for your service." He nodded at Annie on his way out. She wore her SVPD ID around her neck. While dirty and dusty from all she'd done, Annie looked like a fresh spring daisy next to Portia.

"All I want is my coat and a warm bed." And Kyle.

"I'm afraid your coat, and anything else you had at the gala, is gone."

"Including all the silent auction items."

Annie smiled ruefully. "But you got the pledges. No one will take back their donations, trust me. They're all happy to be alive."

"Mmm." She looked at the door the doctor had just exited. Still no Kyle.

"He's being examined, too. They took him to Harrisburg, in case he needed surgery."

"Surgery?"

"He had several gunshot hits, you know. But his vest caught them all. Josh texted that he's fine and moving around."

But he wasn't here. "Can I go see him?"

Annie looked uncomfortable.

"What, Annie? Tell me."

"Kyle asked that you don't try to find him. He's got a lot of work to do, to wrap up his part of this case, and—"

"No, stop, I don't need to know any more. That's okay." It wasn't okay, though, not really. She ached for him, for the comfort only he brought her. He'd given it so freely, always had her back, kept her alive. She owed him everything, for saving her life twice and more. For showing her what true love really was. Kyle didn't owe her anything, though. And as she'd told him herself, she'd known the deal when she'd been with him. The gaping hole in her heart was something she'd known was inevitable. Kyle was still California-bound, then back to his undercover world, the way he liked it best. With no strings.

"Come on, let's get you home. We'll ask the check-out desk to hurry it up."

"Don't I have to file a report with SVPD?"

"Yes, but your statement will wait until tomorrow. They have their hands full, helping the FBI with Markova's interview."

"So that's it, it's all over?"

Annie shook her head. "Unfortunately, no, as this was just the first wave of several planned shipments. But we made a big dent in their profits, for sure. And Markova, once she recovers from the bullet to her gut, will never see the outside of a prison for the rest of her life, with the charges filed. She singlehandedly orchestrated the shipment of millions of dollars of heroin, including a package of fentanyl that could have killed as many as ten thousand. And she put several hundred lives at risk by blowing up the barn when she knew the gala was there. Not to mention shooting at you and Kyle."

"And breaking into the house." The memories of the days she'd spent snowbound with Kyle overwhelmed her and she let the tears fall. "I'm fine, don't worry. This is probably shock."

Annie's arm was around her shoulders. "More like seeing the person you love take a hit for you."

She sniffed, nodded. No use hiding her feelings from Annie, who saw through her.

"What's this?" Claudia asked as she walked into the room, dressed in casual clothes, her hair messier than its normal smooth bob. It'd been a tough night for the director. "Portia, you have gone above and beyond tonight and this past month. Please accept my thank-you on behalf of my entire agency."

Portia wiped her eyes. "It's been my privilege. Was anyone seriously hurt tonight?"

"Other than ROC's attempt to infiltrate Silver Valley and make it its epicenter of East Coast crime?" Claudia smiled, then shook her head. "No. And a lot of the credit goes to you for staying calm and clearing the barn as quickly as you did."

"Annie helped, in the kitchen, from what she's told me. And I couldn't have done it without Kyle telling me what to do."

"You did it. And you fought Markova—you know, if you ever want to give a job with my group a try, I'd be willing to vouch for you."

Portia managed a weak laugh. "No, thank you. I'll stick to information resources, and the service work I've already signed up for. Finding a new venue for next year's gala is going to be a full-time job!"

Claudia nodded. "Nevertheless, the offer stands. You're adept at intelligence analysis."

"Thank you, Claudia."

"You're getting her home?" Claudia addressed Annie, who nodded. "I'll check in on you next week, Portia. Go home and get some rest."

Claudia left and Annie turned to her. "You're coming home with me, for now. Your apartment is safe, you can go back there, but you shouldn't be alone right now. You've had several major shocks."

Portia didn't argue as she accepted her friend's help. She'd be alone again soon enough.

* * *

Kyle spent the next two weeks wrapping up the case, including several interviews with Markova. True to form, she refused to turn, doing nothing to help any of the law enforcement agencies defeat ROC. After he signed the last reporting document on the case, he loaded his car with his possessions, ended his monthly lease and drove west.

He had to fight from calling Portia, from showing up at her doorstep each minute of every day. But he couldn't go to her until he had his life in order. Until he knew he could be the man Portia deserved.

# Chapter 22

*One month later*

"You'll find a personal hygiene kit, towels and an extra blanket on the end of your bed." Portia gave the newest patron of the homeless shelter a bag of nonperishable food items.

"There's always hot coffee and water, along with fresh muffins, in the dining room. They'll be serving dinner until 10:00 p.m."

"Thanks." The woman met her eyes before she headed for the stairs, which Portia considered a minor victory. It was hard to admit you needed help at any time, but she'd witnessed countless homeless persons struggle the hardest. The cold drove them in from the street, the only place they felt totally independent.

"You're almost done tonight, Portia. Got a hot date?"

Gary joked from the front door, where he added an additional helping hand to the security guard. They'd had a minor altercation earlier in the week with a group of apparent heroin addicts looking for a score. They'd heard a dealer was spending the night in the shelter and wanted to "come in for a quick few minutes." The guard and Gary had chased them off and called SVPD.

"Nope, not tonight, but I'm meeting my best friend for coffee after." She hadn't had any dates or even the dream of one in the last month. How could she, when her heart belonged to a man she'd never have?

*Kyle.* He'd been in California for a full month, yesterday. Not that she was counting. She'd left Josh and Annie's a few nights after the gala, and without constant contact with Josh, she lost her inside track to Kyle's life. Not that Josh gave away much—he claimed he knew nothing, but Portia knew better. Both men worked with TH and she knew that Kyle was setting up the West Coast TH office. Kyle would have to report back to Claudia on that basis alone, which in turn meant the rest of the agents understandably knew at least a few details of the project.

Portia didn't give a groundhog's butt about the TH project or anything else work-related, including her own job. All she cared was that Kyle was safe and happy.

At least one of them should find joy after what they'd shared.

"You need to go home now, Portia, before the storm hits." Gary treated her like a little sister but she didn't mind. He wasn't patronizing, just caring.

She bundled up in her parka, wrapped the scarf Annie had knit her "just because" and headed into the cold night. Another storm was coming in, accounting for the uptick in shelter patrons. As she walked the few short blocks to her apartment, her cheeks were hit with fat flakes. The last time she'd been snowbound, it'd been in a beautiful home and not her tiny apartment over a coffee shop.

The shop still had its neon OPEN sign lit, and the warm inside light spilled onto the street, where snow quickly accumulated. Annie had sent her a quick text earlier, saying she wasn't sure they'd be able to meet for their girls' night tomorrow, with the storm predicted to bring things to a stop for at least two days. So she'd suggested they meet at the shop next to Portia's apartment.

Portia sighed as she pulled open the heavy door of the former prison, marveling again at how clever the coffee shop owner had been to pick the historical building to begin a new business in Silver Valley. It was a way to preserve the past but infuse it with the promise of tomorrow, and definitely in a more positive way. She preferred it as a café over the local prison it had once been. Scents of coffee and chocolate hit her and she saw a giggling group of teens near the fireplace, their hands holding mugs with the shop's logo. No sign of Annie yet, so she went up to the counter to order a small pot of chamomile tea. She wanted nothing to keep her awake past her usual bedtime. That led to thoughts of Kyle, which led to a sleepless night.

"What can I get you?" The usual college student barista had been replaced since last night. This barista had the same voice as the man she'd dreamed about, been unable to keep her mind and heart off, since she'd met him. Portia's heart swelled, but her fear of having lost her mind tempered her joy.

"Kyle?"

Kyle's silver gaze was lit with a fire she'd only dreamed of, his tall form startling against the backdrop of the espresso machine and pastry case. He didn't speak, as he appeared as hungry as she was, and not for the sweets on the shelf.

"What are you doing here?"

"I'm afraid that's not on our menu, ma'am." His grin was so full of happiness, she wasn't sure if she wanted to jump the counter and kiss him, or turn and run. It was scary, facing her life's dream like this. Her heart's desire.

"I thought you were in California."

His gaze never left hers, but she saw him take her in, really look at her. A worry line appeared on his brow. "You're not eating enough."

"Need some help, Kyle?" The lanky barista she was familiar with appeared next to Kyle, who nodded.

"Thanks, Ryan. I'll be back next week for my shift." Portia watched Kyle as he walked around the counter and put his arms around her. "We're going to be in the front room for a bit, Ryan. A private function," Kyle said to the barista but his eyes never left hers.

"What's this about, Kyle? I'm meeting Annie…" She trailed off as he ushered her into the front room, where she'd often spent long hours reading or going over gala details. Annie had not planned to meet her, after all. It'd been a setup. Portia hoped it meant more than Annie employing her matchmaking tendencies. And what if Kyle only wanted to talk, to have some kind of stupid closure before saying they'd never see one another again?

Although he'd been working behind the counter.

She shrugged away from Kyle, took her coat off and sat in the chair he held out for her. Kyle closed the door, and the room immediately felt smaller, cozier.

Safer.

Kyle sat in the chair opposite her, leaning forward, their knees touching. He reached for her hands and she gave them with no argument. "You'd better have a damned good explanation for disappearing for a month." She'd meant to sound stern but her voice shook and she barely kept from bursting into tears.

"That's for you to decide." He reached up and moved a stray strand of her curly hair behind her ear. The tips of his fingers touched her earlobe and she closed her eyes against the assault of emotions.

"Kyle."

"I need your eyes open for this, babe. When they're closed like that, all I want to do is get to the kissing and I've got some talking to do first."

She opened her eyes, ready to listen. "Shoot."

Kyle's eyes glistened. No way. Was her secret undercover agent tearing up?

"I had to go back to California to take care of some business. The least important was what you know, to set up the office Claudia wants out there. But the other part…" He squeezed her hands and she squeezed back. It was automatic to support him in whatever he had to say.

"Go on."

"I bought a piece of land years ago, to give myself an anchor. A place I'd have to go back to, whether between missions, on leave or for a permanent residence. I went back there—it's next to an almond farm—and I took time for myself. The last several years have been one op after another. That worked for me for a long time, but no longer." He looked away as if gathering his thoughts. When he met her gaze again, she swore she saw down to his soul. And knew he saw the same in her eyes.

"The thing is, Portia, none of it's the same anymore. Since I first laid eyes on you, I knew you were special. I'm not one for woo-woo stuff, but I swear my soul recognized you. And then when we were together— there's no one else for me, Portia."

"Kyle, I feel the same."

"I was hoping you'd say that, but here's the deal. I'm not going to push you on this. You take as long as you want. But I'm putting my roots down here, in Silver Valley. I'll still work for TH, of course, and I'll work in this coffee shop. Maybe pick up some other part-time jobs, too. They're all good cover for when I'm not out on an op."

She couldn't keep the grin from stretching across her face if she wanted to. Portia took her hands from his and cupped his face, leaning in close. "I never thought of you as a barista, but I kind of like it. Imagine what we could do with frothed milk."

He sucked in a breath and his pupils dilated in the brightly lit room. She'd missed turning him on so much.

"Hold on, babe." His hands were on her waist, his fingers digging in just enough to make her go hot all over. He'd better say whatever else he wanted to quickly, because she was about to jump him.

"I'm not doing this to see how it works out, or worse, if it'll work out. We're going to do whatever it takes to make this work, Portia, because what we have is big time. The kind of thing that lasts a lifetime."

"'Kind of thing,' Kyle?" She wanted to hear him say it.

"Love, Portia. I love you and I will until my last dying breath."

"I love you, too." She leaned in then but he was already there, kissing her with as much love and abandon as she had.

"Um, I think we'd better get upstairs to my apartment." She didn't want to have her first time with Kyle since he'd returned be on top of the coffee shop table. Although…

"Well, since you've mentioned it, there's a storm coming. And I happen to have the keys to a place with a hot tub. We could get stuck there for several days…"

She kissed him. "Quick then, let's go. Let's hurry up and start the rest of our lives together."

"Oh, we've already begun that, babe. The day I first laid eyes on you."

\* \* \* \* \*

# COMING SOON!

We really hope you enjoyed reading this book. If you're looking for more romance, be sure to head to the shops when new books are available on

# Thursday 10th January

To see which titles are coming soon, please visit

**millsandboon.co.uk/nextmonth**

# LET'S TALK
## Romance

For exclusive extracts, competitions
and special offers, find us online: